She had no place to run.

She never had. She was who she was. A woman who cared deeply. Who was loyal to death. Who'd been in love with a man for more than ten years and had never let herself admit it.

The thought of Liam actually going to jail was almost more than she could bear. Living without his kisses was something she could endure. But a world without Liam at all?

Her reaction to the reality that had hit her at the FBI office the day before had finally opened her eyes to the truth.

She couldn't stop herself from being in love with Liam Connelly.

Dear Reader,

Welcome to The Historic Arapahoe! And to my first original title in Harlequin's Heartwarming series! I am very happy to be joining the Heartwarming family and look forward to many more stories of the heart to come.

And I'm still ttq all the way. Bringing you stories that are emotionally intense, psychological looks at life. An editor once said, a long time ago, that when you read ttq books, you live the life. My hope is that when you read my books, you get something to take with you in your life. Even if it's just a smile. A renewed memory. The hope of happily-ever-after in the real world.

On the surface, *Once Upon a Friendship* was kind of ordinary when I started writing. Three friends who buy an old apartment building together to keep the senior citizens who live there from being kicked out onto the street. But in the first chapter a Ponzi scheme appeared. And one of the friends could be involved. His father is arrested. I wanted to stop it all from happening. After all, this was my sweet apartment-building book. But as I've come to accept over the years, the book wasn't really mine. The story belongs to Liam and Gabi and Marie. And the things that happened to them are not mine to change.

They belong to you now.

All the best,

Tara Taylor

HEARTWARMING

Once Upon a Friendship

———

USA TODAY Bestselling Author

Tara Taylor Quinn

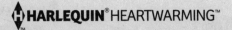

Recycling programs
for this product may
not exist in your area.

ISBN-13: 978-0-373-36734-4

Once Upon a Friendship

Copyright © 2015 by Tara Taylor Quinn

Printed in U.S.A.

The author of more than seventy novels, **Tara Taylor Quinn** is a *USA TODAY* bestselling author with over seven million copies sold. She is known for delivering emotional and psychologically astute novels of suspense and romance. Tara is the past president of Romance Writers of America and served eight years on that board of directors. She has appeared on national and local TV across the country, including CBS *Sunday Morning*, and is a frequent guest speaker. In her spare time Tara likes to travel and enjoys crafting and in-line skating. She is a supporter of the National Domestic Violence Hotline. If you or someone you know might be a victim of domestic violence in the United States, please contact 1-800-799-7233.

Books by Tara Taylor Quinn

Harlequin Superromance

Where Secrets are Safe

Wife by Design
Once a Family
Husband by Choice
Child by Chance
Mother by Fate
The Good Father

Shelter Valley Stories

Sophie's Secret
Full Contact
It's Never Too Late
Second Time's the Charm
The Moment of Truth

It Happened in Comfort Cove

A Son's Tale
A Daughter's Story
The Truth About Comfort Cove

MIRA Books

Where the Road Ends
Street Smart
Hidden
In Plain Sight
Behind Closed Doors
At Close Range
The Second Lie
The Third Secret
The Fourth Victim
The Friendship Pact

Visit the Author Profile page at Harlequin.com for more titles.

For Rachel, whose life introduced me
to Boulder, Colorado. I thought of you,
of walking with you on campus,
as I wrote this book.

PROLOGUE

Nine years ago
Junior year, University of Colorado, Boulder

WITH A WAD OF money in his pocket and a couple of beers in his system, business and journalism major Liam Connelly had to thank the old man for having taken away his every mode of personal transportation back in freshman year. While the deprivation had only lasted nine months—and had been lifted two years ago—he'd never have discovered the beauty of a long walk at night if he hadn't been without a car. Walking took longer, but the cool Colorado spring air cleared his head.

Yeah, the old man had done him a huge favor back then when he'd come storming up to his dorm room, pissed because Liam had moved into the dorm instead of the upscale apartment, complete with doorman, that his father had chosen for him off campus. As Liam had suspected, he'd later had confirmation that his father had prepaid the doorman to keep an eye on Liam's comings and goings and submit weekly written reports.

The brutal match of wills that had taken place two years before hadn't been pretty. The old man had demanded—not kindly or softly, either—that Liam leave with him immediately. That night had been the first time Liam had openly stood his ground with his father. Face-to-face, instead of in the quietly rebellious ways he'd managed prior to that—such as deliberately answering questions wrong on his college entrance exams so that he didn't score high enough to be shipped off to Harvard.

But that night in his dorm, he'd called the old man's bluff. He'd lost motor vehicle privileges, including his BMW 3 Series sports car, all three boats and the Jet Skis, but the price had been a small one to pay.

But humiliating, when he'd found out that the two girls who lived in the room next door had heard every word of the ugly altercation.

That was the night he'd met Gabrielle Miller and Marie Bustamante.

Detouring from his path to the plush apartment he'd moved into at the beginning of his sophomore year—in a bargain with his father to get his car back—he headed toward an upperclassman dorm on the Boulder campus. This dorm was different from the one two years ago.

The girls had moved twice since freshman year: at the beginning of sophomore year, and again at the beginning of their junior year. They'd been talking about getting an apartment for senior year. Gabrielle was leery of the extra cost. Marie, who was majoring in food and nutrition, wanted a place closer to the coffee shop where she'd been promoted to senior barista.

Didn't matter to him one way or another as long as he knew where to find them.

He might be the only guy who visited a confessional before he slept off his sins, but he'd found that he woke up better that way. Besides, if more guys had a two-girl confessor instead of a priest, there'd probably be a whole lot more confessing.

He knocked. And waited. Past midnight on Saturday, they might be asleep. But they'd get up for him. Just as he'd done for them the time Gabrielle's car had broken down when they'd gone to Denver for some Wednesday night charity thing to raise money for one of the kitchens or something she was always volunteering at.

And the time Marie'd been invited to a frat party and had had two guys trying to force her to spend the night there.

He'd called his father for the first issue. The old man had sent a tow truck for the car and a cab to take the girls to Gabrielle's mother's house. Liam had personally paid to have the car fixed so the girls could drive it back to Boulder.

The second one, the frat party that had gotten out of hand, he'd handled himself. With a fist, because the guys were too drunk to reason with, and then the next day, when they'd sobered, he'd issued threats. Neither Marie nor Gabrielle had been bothered by the frat boys since.

He knocked again, glanced at his watch and then tried to discern if light was coming from beneath the door. The sweep prevented such a tell. They could both be out. Marie had been dating a guy she'd met at the coffee shop. Some older dude in med school. And Gabrielle— she'd talked about going home to Denver for the weekend. One of her younger brothers played baseball for his high school team and had a tournament game. He'd thought she was leaving the next day. Saturday. Gabi didn't really like spending the night at her mother's place.

Not that Liam blamed her. The place had seen better days. And better neighbors. His BMW wasn't safe parked out front...

Just as he was turning to leave, the door opened. Both girls stood there in flannel pants and baggy, thigh-length T-shirts, staring at him. Gabrielle's short black hair was sticking up randomly—pillow hair, she called it. Marie's hair was pulled back into her usual ponytail.

"You guys in bed already? It's Saturday night." Liam sauntered into the barely lit room, dropping down to the beanbag chair he'd left in their room freshman year when it had become obvious to him that they were going to be his keepers.

His conscience.

Hell, he might as well admit it—because he'd had two beers—they were his best friends.

The room wasn't much different from the others the girls had shared throughout college— two beds, two built-in desks, wall cabinets for dressers, a closet and a small private bathroom. At least this john they didn't have to share with suite mates who took exception to a guy using it.

"It's one o'clock in the morning." Gabrielle yawned, not bothering to turn on any more than the small lamp between the girl's beds, which she'd probably switched on when he'd knocked. "What's up?"

"Let me guess, hot girl of the week passed out on you?" Marie's sarcasm was out of character, making him hesitate in his plan to spill all, as she plopped her perfectly shaped, not quite five-foot-two body cross-legged on her unmade bed.

Gabrielle curled her long legs on her desk chair, arms hooked on the back of it, resting her chin on top of her hands.

Guys he hung with ribbed him. Insinuating

that something was wrong with him for not going for one or both of the girls. Everyone said the way they let him come and go made it pretty obvious that he could take things further with either one of them anytime. But he couldn't. They were like...sisters to him. Ever since that first night in the dorm when they'd overheard his father coming at him so hard and had come to see if he was okay. He'd been annoyed at first. Knowing that they'd heard. And then secretly thankful to have them there.

He'd never had siblings. Never had anyone close enough to have his back where his father's mental and emotional abuse were concerned— and had only begun to realize in the past few years that the old man was, in his own way, abusive. In a weak moment he'd bared his soul to the girls.

And then hadn't been able to quit.

So...yeah...they had way too much on him.

And were about to have more.

"No one passed out on me," he said now, in a hurry to get this done and get out, not discounting that there might have been a hot girl of the week.

He couldn't help it that girls sought him out.

"I played cards tonight..."

"Liiiaammm." That one drawn-out word was all Gabrielle said out loud. Her expression said the rest. Those silver-blue eyes of hers could be like pinpricks when she wanted them to be. He'd disappointed her.

The soft lamplight was not unkind to the gray-and-white commercial tile on their dorm room floor. Marie's purple rugs still helped, though.

"You're going to get yourself in trouble." Marie was always the more vocal one. And the more fearful. "How much did you lose?" the blonde asked.

He swallowed. Thinking about beer. Wishing, for a brief second, that he was still on the stupid drinking binge he'd ridden freshman year. And hadn't boarded since.

"You won, didn't you?" Gabrielle's tone was soft. He didn't have to look in her direction to know that those coal-black eyebrows of hers would be drawn. And her lips would be pursed, too.

"Yeah."

"How much?"

He thought about his answer. About what she'd think. She waited. They both stared at him.

Another flash of memory from that night two years before came to him. Gabrielle telling him that she'd been ready to write him off when, through the thin wall separating them, she'd heard him ask his father how he was going to get to work without a car. She'd thought he was buckling. Finding justification for doing so. A guy had to have a car to get to work.

The old man had told him to take the bus. All the way to Denver, though she hadn't yet known that part.

"So I still have a job?" he'd asked. Not daunted by the more than an hour-long public commute each way.

According to Gabrielle, when he'd asked that question, instead of fighting about having to take the bus, he'd won her admiration and friendship.

"You're my son. You will work in the family business and earn your keep."

"Fine."

His father had slammed out of his room, and five minutes later Gabrielle and Marie had knocked on his door. When he'd answered, they'd both just looked at him, as though they could see right into him.

Just like they were doing now.

"I won two thousand dollars," he said. Which told them he hadn't been playing with the college boys.

Marie's hissed intake of breath, the worry shining in her eyes, were his penance. The reason he'd come to them…

He'd remember their disapproval the next time he was tempted to rebel against his father and do something stupid.

Gabrielle didn't lift her chin from her hands as she asked, "You going to report it to the IRS?"

He hadn't thought that far. "Yeah." He played by the books.

"You know you're going to get yourself in trouble if you keep this up." Gabrielle again.

He did. Which was why he was in their dorm room instead of home in bed. Why, every time, in his quest for freedom from manipulation over the past three years, he'd run his antics by them first before carrying anything out. But not this time.

"You're winning now, but it won't last," Marie added. They knew his life story. Knew where and how to turn the screws. If he'd played cards that night just because he'd wanted a game of chance, then so be it. But he hadn't. He'd played because he'd been looking for a way to slap the old man in the face. His son gambling would do it.

The heir to his fortune, caught up in the excitement of the win…

An excitement that had almost cost Walter everything. Liam had heard the story from his mother. And had repeated it to the girls on the anniversary of her death. Walter had earned his first million, married and had Liam. His whole life had been filled with the excitement of getting the carrot dangling in front of him. And suddenly, he'd been content. He had all he'd needed or ever wanted.

That's when his father-in-law had invited him to sit in on a game of cards. A game that had taken him to Atlantic City and then to Las Vegas, where he'd squandered away his own million and had started dipping into his wife's money.

The second chance she'd given him had been enough, though. Connelly Investments was healthy and Walter made back all he'd lost plus an extra billion or so. He never touched a card again. And had ordered his son never to do so.

"You've been drinking." Gabrielle, the practical one of the two, broke into his reverie. She didn't ask. She told. Annoying thing was, she was usually right.

"Yeah."

She didn't react. "What did he do this time?"

"I was dropping off a folder to the legal department today." Liam's current position in Connelly Investments was as liaison between upper management and the lower echelons. A fancy way of saying he was an interoffice mail boy. So, his father had justified, he could have a presence in every department. See how they all worked. Get to know everyone.

It was a step up from sorting the incoming mail, which was what he'd been doing the previous year. His first year of college, after thwarting his father's living arrangement plan, he'd been employed as a night janitor.

Marie pulled her knees up to her ample chest, wrapping her arms around herself. "And?"

"I overheard the head counsel, my father's second in command, making overly optimistic return promises to a potential investor on land that we don't own."

The facts sounded even worse out loud than they had rambling through his mind all night.

Gabrielle, a prelaw student who lived life in black-and-white, sat up. "That's illegal."

He shouldn't have said anything. Shouldn't have betrayed his father. He'd let his fear get the better of him.

Something a boy would do.

"It's not illegal unless he actually took money, which he didn't," he quickly assured his friend. "The agreement is only verbal at this point. Thing is, it's land that my father has wanted to develop into a mountain resort for as long as I can remember. Buying the land isn't such a big deal. But he never did because it would have to be rezoned before he could do anything with it. And because it borders Indian land, there would have to be an agreement between him and the tribe to develop it, and the Indians refuse to even consider the idea. Which is why Dad's never purchased the land. So why is this guy even talking to investors about it?"

"Did you ask your dad?" Marie scooted to the end of her bed, both hands on the edge of the mattress.

"Yeah." That was when he'd have taken a big gulp of beer if he'd had one in front of him. He'd had two already that night. The first in months. He wasn't going back down that road again.

"And?"

He turned as Gabrielle asked the question. Her brow was raised in concern now. Because it was late and he was tired, he allowed himself to wallow a moment in that look. And then said, "He told me that George Costas, lead attorney and top executive at Connelly, knows his business better than anyone. That he trusted George with his life—and mine. And that there was talk regarding the land, though he didn't say who was talking, and they had to have investors lined up and ready because if the time came to move, the window of opportunity to do so would be very small."

"Sounds legit."

"Yeah."

"So what's the problem?"

Right. He was probably overreacting. "Problem is, the only way he's going to get that land rezoned anytime soon—and there's still no development agreement with the tribe, I checked—would be to back a politician who we both know takes bribes."

"A particular politician?" Marie asked now, poking at his beanbag seat with the tip of her toe.

"Yeah. A state senator who's up for reelection in the fall."

"Let me guess, your dad's a new campaign contributor." Gabrielle's dry response washed over him.

Liam shrugged.

"You didn't ask?" Gabrielle again. Sounding more than a little surprised.

"I asked. He told me to mind my own business," Liam relayed. But he left out exactly how his father reacted to him daring to question the old man or implying that George was not trustworthy, in light of Liam's own lack of support.

"He can't contribute through the corporation." Gabrielle joined Marie on the end of her bed. "It's against Colorado law. He'd have to do it as an individual. And the candidate is required to report it, including name and employment, within a specified period of time depending on the office being sought, but it's usually within a month."

"I'm not worried about the legalities of the contribution," Liam said. "Not with George watching over everything with his eagle eye. But the one thing I really admired about my dad was his integrity. He might not be around when you need him, or care about what you need as opposed to what he wants from you, but you can count on him to speak the truth and stand by his convictions. It is, I hope, the one way I take after him. This senator is a snake. I can't believe my father would ever get into bed with him. Yeah, money rules him, but it's always only gained legally, and he's always drawn the line at bigotry. Which is how he made it from pauper to millionaire in ten years. People know they can trust him."

"He made it from pauper to *billionaire* because he made savvy investments at a time when real estate was booming. And then invested with uncanny cleverness." Gabrielle's expression was droll.

She was repeating his words back to him. Words spoken in previous late-night sessions. Usually after he'd come back to Boulder from time in Denver with his father.

"And he built his reputation on integrity," he added, though why he was defending the man, he wasn't sure. "He was faithful to my mother until the day she died."

His junior year in high school. Of heart disease. Something they'd discovered she had when she was pregnant with him. Which was why he was an only child.

"Are you afraid he's changed?" Marie's question brought him back to the present. Where Gabrielle focused on the practical, Marie always homed in on the emotional aspect of things. They made a great team for him.

And for each other.

He wanted to tell Marie he wasn't afraid. But these were his best friends. The one place he was completely honest with himself. "Maybe."

"So playing cards tonight…that was to get back at him for it?" Gabrielle's derogatory opinion was clear.

"I don't know. Maybe."

"Don't throw your life away because of him." Marie spoke next. "Don't throw your life away for anyone." Her tone took on a bitter note that had him studying her more closely. And then he remembered something. She never went to bed with her hair still in a ponytail. He'd woken them up enough times to know that. The three of them had probably had a late-night conversation somewhere along the way about getting ready for bed, too. They'd talked about everything else in the world over the past three years.

"You guys weren't asleep, were you?"

"No."

He sat forward, studying the two of them as he jetted himself out of the self-pitying fog he'd allowed himself to sink into.

"What's going on? What happened?" he asked, ready to get up and go find whoever had upset them.

At one in the morning.

Gabrielle looked at Marie, as though waiting for her to tell him. As if it was Marie's story to tell. Which meant...

"It's the med student, isn't it? What'd he do?"

Marie's lower lip started to quiver.

"He has some big presentation coming up Monday and was going to be studying tonight, so Marie agreed to cover for a coworker who wanted the night off," Gabrielle said. "As it turns out they were slow and Marie got off early. She made jerk face's favorite coffee drink and took it over to his place to surprise him."

"He was...with the girl I was covering for at work."

Now he understood the edge Marie was carrying. It hadn't been about the hour of his visit, or him at all. "They knew you wouldn't find out because they made sure you were busy," Liam summarized, watching Marie fight with heartache, wondering what on earth he was supposed to say to her.

This was why he could never even think about getting involved with either one of them. He'd rather die than be the cause of that look on Marie's face.

And then it occurred to him. "You know this isn't about you, right?"

Marie and Gabrielle exchanged a glance. One of *those* glances. The ones that left him out in the cold.

"You're gorgeous, Marie. That blond hair and brown eyes…"

"I'm too short."

She was shorter than Gabrielle, who was long and leggy, but— "You are definitely not too short."

"It's not about her looks," Gabrielle interrupted, with a sound resembling a snort. She was gorgeous, too. Not an obvious showstopper like Marie. But more in line with the kind of girl he went for. He was more of a leg man.

"What is it with men?" Marie's derisive tone wasn't directed at him, but he sure felt as if it was. And took the brunt of her watery brown-eyed glare for all men. "Why can't they be trustworthy?"

"They can be." Of that he was sure. Which

was why his father's actions earlier that day had upset him so much.

"I sure didn't see that tonight. Nor a good part of the time I was growing up…"

Her father, who'd been unfaithful to her mother in the past and who'd only a few years earlier been brought back into the family fold, had been with another woman at their cabin in northern Arizona that summer. The girls had been the ones to discover him there. From what Gabrielle had told him, Marie had taken it pretty hard.

"And Brad, freshman year." A guy Gabi had dated who'd broken up with her when she wouldn't sleep with him.

"Jimmy Jones." A cowboy the girls had met when they'd gone to a rodeo the year before. He'd played one for the other and gotten caught in the middle. For a day or two there, Liam had sweated that the jerk might break up a friendship he'd considered unbreakable. But the girls had surprised him—seeing through Jimmy and giving him a taste of his own medicine. Poor guy hadn't seen what was coming…

"Don't forget Mark," Marie said. She'd dated him the beginning of sophomore year. Until she'd found out that he had a fiancée at home in Phoenix.

"All right, already," Liam said, holding up a hand in surrender.

"It's like guys' drive for sex is stronger than their hearts. Or their morals," Marie added.

"It's a driving force," Liam allowed, feeling only a little uncomfortable in his beanbag seat beneath the girls. They were family. Talked about anything. Everything. "The desire to have sex with women is always there," he continued, knowing that the one thing he could give his friends was an honesty they probably wouldn't get anywhere else. "It doesn't matter how much you're in love with a girl—you can't help reacting when you see a beautiful woman. You're right about that. But being attracted and acting on that feeling are two entirely different things."

"So when you were going with Karen last year, you were still attracted to other women?"

"Of course!" His honesty was going to help Marie see that this had nothing to do with her. Needing to do what he could to erase the hurt from her eyes, he continued. "Karen had this woman who groomed her dog. I don't know what it was about her, but she did it to me every time. I just had to see someone that reminded me of her and…"

"Did you ever come on to her?"

"No." It would have been indecent and, having grown up in a superficial world, Liam put his highest value on authenticity. As his father had taught him by example. And that wasn't what this conversation was about. He was trying to save Marie from self-flagellation. "But that didn't mean I didn't want to. Or that I didn't think about it. Or try to find her when Karen and I broke up. She'd moved." And he'd moved on.

Marie's med student was a schmuck. But since there was no chance that they would still have a relationship, there was no reason to belabor that point.

"Did Karen know?" Gabi's question was softly spoken.

"Of course not." He was authentic—not stupid. "I didn't tell her when I thought the dress she had on made her look heavier than she was, either," he said, to prove his point. "Nor did I admit it when she asked me if I saw the cellulite on her thigh." He'd grabbed her up in a hug instead, telling her that she was beautiful and she needed to quit worrying so much. He'd distracted her with a kiss.

And he'd noticed that cellulite every time he saw her after that. But only because she'd made such a big deal about it. Not because it changed—in any way—how he felt about her.

"So, like I said, guys are jerks," Marie said.

But she was kind of smiling and didn't look as though she was going to break any minute.

"I wouldn't go that far." Liam had to defend his sex. "Some take longer to mature than others." He was grinning, too. And then sobered. "I think there are men who, for whatever reason, just like women. In the plural," he told her with complete honesty.

"Like you."

"Maybe. And maybe I'm just immature. But whichever, at least I'm accountable enough to know not to promise forever. And if I'm in a monogamous relationship, it stays that way until I'm out."

"You don't think you'll ever marry?"

"Not unless something changes inside of me. Right now…" He shrugged. "I figure I'm just not the marrying kind."

They'd passed through the bullet hole, on to the other side. Again.

The three of them chatted for another half hour. Gabrielle cajoled Marie and Liam into volunteering with her that next weekend, bagging donated food to hand out to homeless people. They talked about meeting up for pizza on Sunday. And then, with a shudder at the thought of graduating from college and the three of them going off their separate ways, Liam reminded himself not to borrow trouble and went home to bed.

CHAPTER ONE

Present day

IT WAS REALLY going to happen.

Standing at the window of the bank, her back to the seats where Liam and Marie were sipping cheap coffee from takeout cups, public lawyer Gabrielle Miller gazed out at the snow-covered Denver sidewalks and focused on breathing. Not too deep. She didn't want to hyperventilate. But passing out from lack of oxygen wouldn't serve her well, either.

You'd think with five years of professional practice under her belt, and having personally vetted the contract they were all about to sign, she would be calm about the day's events. It wasn't as if they were buying a home that they were going to be moving into. No, they were simply transferring into their names the ownership of the historic Arapahoe—the old apartment building she and Marie had been living in and that Liam had been visiting as regularly as he'd visited their dorm rooms in college eight years ago. She and Marie were still going to be sharing the roomy three-bedroom unit that comprised part of the second floor of the eight-floor building in historic Denver. Marie's coffee shop, a thriving business, was still going to encompass the entire bottom floor.

Liam would now be an official part of them, part of the family, instead of just an honorary member.

Gabi's portion of the down payment hadn't been a problem. She'd worked nearly full-time all four years of college in preparation for the law school loans that would eventually come due in her future. She'd continued to add to that account by working for Marie when she could during three years of law school, and when her loans had been paid off by the state as part of her employment agreement, she'd been able to slowly grow her savings.

Three-quarters of it was going into this deal.

But all but two of the thirty-eight apartments were rented on long-term leases that were transferring to them as the new owners, the majority of them held by residents who'd been in the building fifty years or more. They had guaranteed rent money coming. Most of them government checks.

Until the friends had made an offer on the place, most of the elderly residents had been trying desperately to find new homes. A few already had. The current owner's rent increase, coming in a matter of weeks, would have put most of the elderly occupants out on the streets or into government-subsidized nursing homes. Fixed incomes could only be stretched so far.

Those who could afford to move had done so.

Most of those left had been in tears when Threefold had held a meeting with the residents to officially announce that they would soon be making rent checks out to them instead. In the same amount they'd been paying—not the new increased price.

Threefold. The name she and Liam and Marie had chosen for the LLC they'd formed to purchase the somewhat decrepit building and manage it, too.

Marie had come up with the name.

Neither she nor Liam had argued.

Gabrielle felt someone come up beside her, but she didn't turn to look. Marie generally didn't let anyone sulk for long.

"You having second thoughts?" Liam's voice surprised her. He'd been over for dinner the night before—at least a biweekly ritual for the past nine years. When he was in town. And not in a relationship. Not that he didn't come when he was in one. Just not as frequently.

The night before, the three of them had gone over all of the paperwork together. One more time.

"No. You?"

His tone was too distant. Impersonal. Something was wrong. She'd known the second he'd come toward them in the bank parking lot.

Maybe that was when she'd started to panic.

And now he was seeking her out alone. That only happened when he was in need of analytical thinking without the emotional twist.

Liam might prefer to be a freelance journalist rather than a financier, and he might even be better at it if the current success rate of his stories was anything to go by, but business was in his blood. And first on his college degree, too, with journalism as a minor. Business, working for his father at Connelly Investments, provided his substantial paycheck.

"No second thoughts at all." Amazed at the instant calm that came over her at the words, she turned to look at him.

"You sure? Because I can't afford to make a mistake here, Liam. If our figures are out of line, if you think there's real risk here, I just can't afford to take it. I mean, we're looking at almost a solid year with no real income from rent. The elevator fix alone is going to eat up the first two months and…"

His smile made her smile. And she heard what she was doing.

"We're going to be fine." He reminded her of the extra money that was being rolled into their loan to keep in an account for unforeseen maintenance. Of the monies she and Marie would be saving in rent that would offset the building's common utility costs. Of the down payment monies they'd all three contributed, which were keeping her third of the Arapahoe's monthly mortgage payments within her means...

He was right about all of it.

And... "Something's bothering you." Were his suit and tie for the benefit of the real estate closing they were all about to attend? Or had he been at Connelly Investments that day? As his father's patsy, he had a nice office on the top floor of the corporate office building. And put in a minimum of forty hours a week. But a lot of that time was spent at dinners and functions that bored him. Or at his personal computer on the desk in his home office in the fancy high-rise condominium that was his as part of his employee benefits. He analyzed. He reported. He made innocuous decisions. His father wouldn't let him make any of the major ones.

"My father found out about the deal," he said now.

"I thought you told him." They'd specifically

discussed the matter—he and she and Marie. They'd stressed to Liam the importance of keeping his father informed. The old man had the power to make Liam's life miserable if he chose to do so.

And, in retrospect, theirs, too.

Taking Liam on as a partner meant taking on the unhealthy and rocky relationship he had with his old man.

Rocking back and forth in his expensive leather shoes, Liam shoved his hands into the pockets of his gray pants and looked down. "I intended to. Right after the papers were signed."

She wanted to ask who'd spilled the beans to the elder Connelly, but the who didn't matter. Nor, really, did the why. When you lived in circles where money was the most important factor, people stabbed friends and family if it meant they had a chance to climb even half a step.

Which was part of the reason, she knew, that Liam had adopted her and Marie as his family all those years ago. Because they weren't part of that circle.

And didn't want to be.

"So what'd he say?"

Liam's shrug didn't tell her enough.

"He didn't forbid it?" Which was what she and Marie had expected.

"He can't." Liam's jaw was firm, his gaze hard as he looked straight at her. "I'm using money earned from my writing, you know that."

Only for the down payment.

"You're living off your Connelly salary and living in a Connelly building."

Best that the deal fall through now. Before any of them were financially ruined.

But…not really.

Because if they didn't sign those papers today, more than fifty elderly people were going to be booted from their homes. Many of them had raised their families in that building and still had penciled lines on the walls in the kitchens marking the growth of their offspring through the years.

Matilda Schwann had color-coded hers…

"If your father doesn't support you on this, you won't have the money to pay your third of the mortgage."

They weren't college kids anymore. He couldn't sign this deal and then capitulate.

Not that Liam would choose to leave elderly folks homeless. He'd give them the shirt off his back.

But Liam had never lived in the real world. His life, while not easy, had certainly been privileged.

"I have trust money that has been set up

legally to pay my portion of the mortgage. I wanted to make certain that you both were covered if something ever happened to me..."

And she knew...

"That's how he found out, isn't it? Someone told him when you accessed your trust." But the money was his to do with as he pleased.

"I can only assume that George told him, though he swore to me that he wouldn't."

"Did you pay him, as your attorney, to handle the transaction for you?"

She was an attorney. And while she chose to work at a local legal services organization, making a pittance compared to what she could be making in average attorney fees in the private sector, Liam had always seemed to trust her abilities as much as he did those of the millionaire lawyer who'd worked for his family most of his life.

But she'd consider it a conflict of interest to represent him on this deal, as she was one of the involved parties.

"Of course I paid him. Separately and apart from Connelly Investments."

"Then legally and ethically he's in violation if he said anything."

And a pertinent piece of paper could have fallen on the floor at Liam's father's feet when the elder Connelly was in the office of his head legal counsel. She knew how the world worked.

"You should have hired someone outside the Connelly circle," she said now, though she knew the words didn't help anything. She was trying to think. To determine their next move.

Did they sign the papers? Or not?

"I trust George with my life. Or I did until today."

Hadn't he once said something similar about his father's feelings for George? Liam couldn't be blamed for believing the man would uphold his word. And maybe he had. They were only assuming George had been the leak. So often when something was amiss the obvious culprit was not at fault. At least in her experience. None of which was helping the current situation.

"So what did your father say? Is he going to be difficult?" The building was not going to be a money-maker. It was more in line of a community project that was hopefully not going to cost them anything out of pocket in the long run. And, best-case scenario, it would make them a few dollars apiece a year or two down the road.

It was also doubling as a home for Marie and Gabrielle. Marie's coffee shop would be paying them rent under the contract they were assuming from the current owner. Its success had provided her portion of the Arapahoe down payment.

"No, he's not going to be difficult." Liam stared out the window and Gabrielle thought about the cup of coffee she'd turned down when the three of them had arrived. She didn't need the caffeine. But now she wanted the warmth.

"I have his word that he will not, in any way, interfere with, hamper or attempt to destroy Threefold or its holdings."

She stared at him. Then this was good, right? So why that mixed expression of lost boy and grim defender on his face?

Until he caught her looking. Then he smiled. Gave her a soft fist to the shoulder of her blue suit jacket and said, "Let's go buy a building, partner."

Wishing, inanely, that she could hold his hand, Gabrielle followed Liam back to Marie.

They were her family. More so than the mother and two college-dropout brothers who'd moved down south a couple of years before and depended on her for financial help more months than not. Help she could give them, even on her salary, because she was good at what she did. She had already made enough of a name for herself to be able to pick up extra work, privately, when she had to. And her own living expenses were small since she still lived with Marie in the apartment they'd rented straight out of college.

But her financial obligation was about to change.

She was going to be a business owner.

She, the girl who'd had to wear thrift-store clothes and shoes for the first eighteen years of her life, was about to become partners with one of the richest bachelors in Denver.

Funny how life had a way of sounding like so much more than it was.

CHAPTER TWO

LIAM MADE IT through the signing of the papers. He paid attention. Read and reread the forms he'd already vetted. After Gabrielle had vetted them. The deal was sound.

He'd planned to take his new partners out to lunch at the Capitol Grille—a place in historic Latimer Square where Denver's elite and powerful movers and shakers were known to dine—but knew he wouldn't be able to maintain the calm facade long enough for lunch to be served.

Instead, he gave them both a big hug. Thanked them for taking him on. Promised that their future together would be even better than their past, and told them he'd see them at the Arapahoe in an hour or so.

Gabi was working from home that afternoon, and Marie would be returning to the coffee shop.

What they didn't know was that with some help, he'd arranged a surprise party to celebrate this milestone that was the biggest in each of their lives, if maybe for different reasons. He wasn't going to miss it.

But first, he had to get back to Connelly Investments. To find out what in the hell was going on and to take on the fight of his life with his old man. Walter Connelly had been ruling Liam by threats for as long as he could remember. Today was the day it stopped.

Today was the day he'd called his father's bluff in the real world.

And now it was time to guide himself and the old man into the new regime. He'd have liked to feel better prepared.

He'd planned to schedule a meeting with his father after the Threefold papers had been signed. Walter would have been displeased, to say the least, but there would have been no opportunity for him to issue threats that he'd then have to follow through on. At least in part.

He'd planned to prevent the threat stage and talk like rational adults.

To have more solid plans, a clearer vision as to exactly what the new world would look like. He was going to be writing more. He knew that much. Covering stories that had some meat in them, not just being a glorified society-page freelancer while on Connelly-financed vacations. Writing about the world's biggest catch didn't interest him nearly as much at thirty as it had a few years ago.

Skating in behind another car that was entering the bar-coded private garage, so that he didn't have to wait for the bar to lower and the scanner to read his windshield, Liam waved to the woman in front of him—someone from accounting—who turned in the direction opposite of the front spaces reserved for top-floor personnel.

Liam's gut clenched when he pulled into his prime parking spot under Connelly Investments corporate offices. His nameplate—the one his father had gifted him for his college graduation—was no longer hanging on the wall. In its stead were two ditches in the cement, marking the nails that had just been pulled, and a rectangle of paint that was brighter than the rest of the wall.

Eight years. Had it been that long since he'd officially become a man? Taken up a life of full-time work? He wasn't proud of that. It was a wonder Gabi and Marie wanted to go into business with him at all.

Slamming the door of his Lexus, he strode toward the top floor's private, secured entry, listening for the horn to emit its half honk, letting him know that the car locked itself as the key fob in his pocket reached the required distance away from the vehicle.

That part of the garage was devoid of other human presence at four o'clock, leaving him too aware of the sound of his own leather soles stepping across the cold cement. So good old Dad had wasted no time in having his name stripped from his parking spot. The old man was trying to scare him. Just as he'd done freshman year.

Walter Connelly was, in his own twisted way, still making a man out of his son. And he was doing it one threat at a time.

So now what? He'd have him parking in a public lot that would require him to pay a monthly stipend and walk across the street to get to work? Putting him in his place, like when he'd had to ride the bus from Boulder to Denver to get to work?

Liam swiped his card with a bit more force than necessary to get into the building. But when he pulled on the door and it refused to open, he swiped it again calmly. Technology didn't respond to brute force. And as of today, neither did he.

The click that sounded when his card gained him entrance…didn't sound.

Liam tried half a dozen times before he finally realized that his father had had his key card stripped of its clearance.

Instead of worrying him into capitulation, the action only angered him more. And maybe it was meant to do so, if Walter was making him into a man.

Returning to his car, he backed up and sped out of the garage, around the corner, and pulled to a quick stop at a meter a block away from the front of the Connelly building. A walk in the frigid Denver air would do him good.

Clear his head.

He might have to replace the shoes on his feet if the snow and salt had a chance to sit on the leather and ruin it. It would be a small price to pay for his freedom from tyranny.

All he'd wanted to do was use his own funds to buy a lousy apartment building. He'd made a deal on his own, daring to rely on his own acumen without consulting the father first. For eight years he'd subjugated his own adult interests out of respect for the man. Out of admiration. His father was hard, yes, but hardworking, too. Successful. And honest.

Still, buying an apartment building with his own funds and his desire to write some news pieces about things that were notable to him while traveling were hardly deserving of stripping him of his parking space and easy access key.

He was still hot, in spite of the cold, by the time he pulled open the heavy bullet-proof glass front door on the Connelly building. If

James, the doorman, tried to stop him, he was going to...

"Afternoon, Mr. Connelly," the guard said, as though Liam entering the building through the public entrance was a regular occurrence.

"James." Liam nodded his head. Hoped he appeared more civil than he felt, and avoided eye contact with any other employees as he made a beeline for the elevator.

Half expecting his elevator card to be defunct as well, he was considering taking the stairs to the top floor, when he stepped into the arriving car to find a top-floor aide—Amy something or other—standing there. "Thirty-six, Mr. Connelly?" she asked, naming their destination like an elevator attendant.

"Yes, please." He didn't have to fake the smile he bestowed upon her. Amy was...nice on the eyes.

And his split from Jenna had happened over a week ago. Not that that made any difference. Liam didn't hit on employees.

Or date them.

That was bad for business. Fodder for lawsuits. And made life far more complicated than it needed to be.

Just like he'd never, ever look at Marie or Gabrielle in that way. Not because he feared a lawsuit. No, something far worse. He feared losing them.

It was the worst thing he could imagine. Worse even than catching a deadly disease and being told he only had months to live.

Okay, that was a little dramatic, he allowed silently, as he watched the lit floor numbers climb slowly upward. When the button for floor thirty-six was pressed, the elevator didn't stop on its way up or down.

Firmly in check, he thought about the imminent showdown with his old man. Pretty Amy was completely forgotten when the door opened, giving Liam access to the sacred top floor. His office was to the right. Though he was curious now to see if the old man had ordered his things to be packed, Liam didn't bother to check.

Walter might take a hard line and make harsh threats, but Liam wasn't a kid anymore. And his father wasn't getting any younger.

The old man needed him.

They'd work through this.

His father's office door was closed. Meaning nothing. It was always closed.

He didn't kid himself. The hours, weeks, months ahead were not going to be easy. His father would do anything he could to make him pay for his obstinacy.

But in the end, he'd also acknowledge that

Liam had done the right thing. Walter wouldn't respect a man who didn't know how to be strong in the face of adversity.

He didn't knock. And didn't listen as Gloria, his father's personal assistant, tried to object to Liam's occupancy in the private sanctum without an appointment. He wasn't the least bit intimidated by the woman who was known to many in the company as the battle-ax. She'd been around since Liam was too young to know what battle-ax meant. She liked him.

He liked her, too.

Bursting into his father's office, Liam was ready for battle.

Or he would have been if the door had opened. Turning the handle a second time, his sweaty palm slipped against the locked hardware.

"What's going on?" He turned to Gloria. "Where's my father?"

"He took the rest of the day off."

Liam glanced back at the closed door. "He doesn't ever take the day off." Not even on Christmas—though he did tend to work at home more often than not on holidays.

Gloria shuffled a pile of papers, shrugged and said, "Well, he did." She was glancing between her computer screen and the file folder she was sliding the newly aligned papers into.

He could try to charm information out of her, but he didn't. His issues were with his father.

Besides, he knew now where the old man would be. Turning, he left the office without another word and went straight to his own. Where his father would have expected him to go first.

Just as he'd suspected, Walter was there. Sitting in Liam's chair. Surrounded by…not a lot. Other than the mahogany desk and matching chair Liam had picked out for himself when he'd been promoted to the thirty-sixth floor five years before, the room was stripped bare.

"You work fast." He leaned against the door he'd just closed. The thirty-sixth floor offices were soundproofed and what he had to say to his father had to stay between the two of them.

"You signed the papers. I told you what would happen if you did."

"You had a spy at the bank?" Why the thought hadn't occurred to him before then, he didn't know. Walter was ruthless.

And Liam felt stupid. Thinking he was going to walk right in and announce to his father that he'd refused to give in to his threat. And then deliver the speech he'd been rehashing for years. The one where he told his father how much he respected and admired him, told him that he'd continue to serve him, but that he also had to have a life, a mind, of his own.

Building up to the part where he told him that while he still planned to give forty-plus hours a week to Connelly Investments, he was also going to more seriously pursue a career in journalism. Pointing out the benefits to the firm if he continued to rise to success in a world of internet information delivery.

"A spy, Liam? You think we're playing some kind of game here? Grow up, man."

He listened for the disappointment hiding in the derision in his father's voice. The seemingly imperceptible note of fear.

And missed them both.

"I want to know about the conversation I overheard in George's office this morning." Liam stuck to his plan to fight aggression with aggression if he had to. If reason didn't work. "Why would our head counsel promise someone an impossible investment return? Even at its best, the holding he mentioned didn't promise those kinds of returns."

Liam had overheard just a small bit of the conversation, but enough to know that something didn't add up. He gave his father the particulars.

George had been on the phone and hadn't heard Liam wander in. It had been before seven, before office staff started to arrive. Just before Walter had called Liam into his private sanctum to issue yet another threat—the one where he'd be cut off if he went through with the Arapahoe deal.

Otherwise Liam would have asked the question earlier that morning.

"That investment will not be impossible to meet." Walter's words were quiet. Deadening. "And you are no longer welcome here."

Steel could not have been stronger. Or more cold.

"I heard what George said. I know that account. There's no way it's going to make that kind of return. I deserve to know what's going on."

"How dare you practice duplicity and then stand here and demand answers?"

Liam checked himself against the accusation of duplicity. The pause allowed his father to move in for the kill.

"I thought you'd learned your lesson freshman year, Liam. Today you have proven that you did not. We cannot be a team, you and I. I can no longer trust you. If you will go behind my back, keeping pertinent information from me because your two harlots call your name, there is no end to the possibilities of other ways you could betray me."

"Buying that building had nothing to do with you, or with Connelly Investments. It wasn't a lucrative purchase. Or a building you'd have any interest in. And they are not my, or anyone else's, harlots. As I've told you before, they are family to me."

More family to him than Walter was.

"You moved trust monies behind my back."

"My trust money. I'm a man, Dad. I have to be able to do some things on my own."

"But not behind my back. That trust money was yours, but it was family money."

"From my mother's family." Walter had met Margaret, Liam's mother, after he'd scratched and clawed his way to his first million. She'd been born into the privileged life.

"It was our money, your mother's and mine, when we opened that trust for you."

Technically. It had been given to them at his maternal grandfather's death, with the express wish that if they didn't need it to secure their own futures it be put in trust for Liam.

"If I'd told you about the building, you'd have done everything in your power to block that sale."

"It's a stupid purchase. Those old folks are paying far below average rent. You'll never be able to turn a decent profit."

"They're paying all they can afford on fixed incomes." Liam stated the more pertinent truth. "And we aren't going to lose money on the deal.

We didn't go into it with an eye to support ourselves. Marie has her coffee shop. Gabrielle's a lawyer. I told you that."

"And you, Liam? While you're so busy exerting your manhood, you still expect me to support you?"

"I earn every dime you pay me."

"You say you're a man, but you didn't tell me about that old apartment building because you were afraid."

The little bit of truth that lurked in the ugly words spurred Liam onward in a battle he didn't want to fight.

"I'm standing up to you now."

Going into business with Gabrielle and Marie…it had been his way to solidify his place in their future. To make the three of them, their little family, a brother and his sisters, legal. He'd done what he had to do.

"You are standing only because you don't have a chair to sit on."

The old man was sitting in the only chair left in the office. "What's going on, Dad? What deal did I stumble on this morning that you don't want me to know about? Because that's what this is about, isn't it? This has nothing to do with a loser apartment building I sunk my own pittance into."

"You stumbled onto nothing more than a joke,

Liam. A *joke*." Spittle sprayed on Liam's desk as his father repeated the word. "George was on the phone with Bob Sternan. They were mocking Senator Billingsley and his promises regarding the Indian land he recently purchased."

Land that his father had purchased, with a signed agreement from the tribe, and developed several years before. A development that he'd since sold and which was for sale again. A development currently owned by Senator Ronald Billingsley—the immoral man whose campaign Liam had once thought his father had supported. He'd later found that neither his father nor anyone closely associated with Connelly Investments had been listed as campaign contributors.

And his father had told him to his face, looking him in the eye, that he'd never support the crooked politician.

Mock him, though, yes.

George had been on the line with Bob Sternan. A senator who'd proven himself trustworthy again and again. A family man who chose to serve his state without lining his own pockets.

Jenna's dad.

Another man he respected whom he'd disappointed. Jenna had broken up with him. But Liam had agreed to take the blame so she didn't have to face her father's lectures. They hadn't been in love. Nor had they relished the idea of a match made for business or the sake of the public good. They hadn't wanted to marry just to bring together an appearance of money and morals that would instill public trust in their families.

Liam had asked her to marry him because he was thirty years old and the old man had been ragging on him constantly about his duties to provide a Connelly heir.

And Jenna had agreed because she hadn't had the gumption to stand up to her father.

But when the wedding date started to get closer and neither one of them had been able to see themselves married to the other…

Liam had told himself he'd go through with it out of duty. He'd given his word. And because the idea of a kid of his own someday was kind of growing on him.

He'd have been faithful to Jenna.

He just wouldn't have been happy with her.

So when she'd begged him to dump her, he had.

Liam was batting a thousand here at striking out.

"I'm sorry," he said. Because it was the right thing to do. "I should have told you about the deal. I am grateful for all that you've done for me. I just need to be my own man, Dad. Surely you can understand that."

His father's steely blue gaze didn't warm a bit. "I understand only that I can no longer trust you."

"Of course you can. You know me."

"That's where you're wrong, son. I would have bet this building, my entire empire, on the fact that you would never be duplicitous with me."

He'd needed to make the deal on his own. He needed Marie and Gabrielle solidly in his life. To have something, someone, to call his own. Someone he could trust with his inside self.

"It's a worthless apartment building." By Connelly standards.

"Then you're stupider than I thought, trading your future for a worthless piece of real estate."

The old man was testing him. There was a way to turn this around. He had to know his father well enough to find it.

"Get out."

He wanted to speak, to come up with the right words.

"Dad…"

"Get out, Liam. I've had George remove you from my will. You are no longer my son."

He was bluffing. It wasn't the first time Walter had said such a thing. And he'd done worse.

Walter had once likened Liam to a terminal disease. He'd called him a fool. Told him time and time and time again that he'd never make it in the world.

And then he'd buy him a new car. Give him a promotion…

"Anything personal you had in this room has been relocated to your apartment. You have twenty-four hours to get that cleared out. Anything left there at this time tomorrow will be disposed of when the locks are changed. You can keep the car."

"Dad…"

"Get out."

The man sitting calmly in Liam's chair didn't blink. His hands weren't trembling. His mouth didn't twitch.

Liam looked at him and saw a stranger.

"You are no longer welcome here, Liam," Walter said as though he was ordering a glass of water with the coffee he'd just been served. "Either you go quietly or I will call security."

Liam didn't remember getting back to his car. He knew he'd done so on his own. Without escort. He climbed behind the wheel, starting the car with a calm he'd probably feel if he felt anything at all.

What did you do when you realized that what

you'd counted on to never change didn't even exist?

All these years he'd put up with the man's abuse because he'd thought he understood him. Thought that, ultimately, he and his father would be a team.

The old man was really capable of disowning him? What honorable man did that? Threaten, yes. Make life hell, maybe, if he thought his son needed toughening up.

But denounce him completely, as though he didn't exist?

He had someplace to be. So he drove.

He turned away from the showpiece building that housed Connelly Investments, heading toward historic downtown, and then found a moving and storage company with his satellite phone service. Placed an order for the following morning.

And only faltered once—when the friendly female voice on the other end of the line asked him the final delivery address for his packed-up life.

He told them he'd have to get back to them.

CHAPTER THREE

MARIE AND GABRIELLE took each other out to a quick lunch at their favorite salad shop—not the fine dining Liam would have preferred. The building's purchase was a big deal—more for Gabrielle than any of them, as no one in her immediate family had ever owned anything more than a car.

"I might not be able to eat out again for a while." Gabrielle chuckled as she slid her arm through her friend's, hugging Marie's elbow to her side as they left the self-serve restaurant and headed toward her car. "I'll just have to take scraps from our business tenant's kitchen."

"I have a feeling our new business tenant, the owner of that famous coffee shop downstairs, will give both of us anything we want," Marie said laconically. They were heading back to the coffee shop. Marie had good, dependable employees, a few of whom were qualified to run the shop in her absence. She just didn't enjoy being absent.

"Yeah, and if history serves, the owner will

work us both to the bone for it, too." Gabrielle had been with Marie from the very beginning, traipsing around Denver looking for just the right space to lease. Spending eighteen-hour days cleaning the place. Choosing a logo. Ordering. And working until they dropped when business picked up before Marie had had a chance, or enough profit, to hire employees.

"Can you believe it?" Marie skipped as she glanced at Gabrielle, yanking a bit on her arm. "We actually did it. We own an entire historic apartment building!"

Gabrielle smiled. And worried, too. About Liam. The future. The mammoth undertaking they'd agreed to. The fifty or more senior citizens who were counting on them to keep a roof over their heads.

The empty apartments they had yet to rent. Hopefully to a young family or two. Starting a new generation of traditions.

She wanted to tell Marie about Liam's despondency regarding his father that morning. But why put a damper on her friend's joy? Especially since the only evidence she had that anything was wrong was her own sense of foreboding...

Still, she couldn't help but ponder the practical ramifications of their new responsibility while she drove the two of them home. Parking in her reserved spot in the small lot behind the building—parking was going to be a problem if, in the future, they rented to too many young, two-car families—she put a smile on her face as she followed Marie out of the car.

"Let's go in the front door," Marie said, her grin bubbling over as Gabrielle pulled out her key and turned toward the private back entrance off the parking lot. "Let's be like landlords checking up on our business tenant…"

Even at thirty, Marie had a playful, girly streak. It was one of the things Gabrielle loved about her. "You *are* the business tenant," she reminded her on a laugh.

They were in partnership, she and Marie and Liam. A legally binding arrangement that kept the three of them together. Solidifying their odd little family into the future. More than the building, the investment, the asset, it was that fact that put the smile on Gabrielle's face.

"WHAT'S TAKING THEM so long?"

"They're coming around the front."

"Janice, watch your mother, she's at it again."

Standing behind the counter of Marie's quickly decorated coffee shop, Liam turned when he heard Grace speaking to Janice in the cacophony of voices around him.

Janice's mother Clara, a ninety-five-year-old woman who lived with her seventy-three-year-old daughter in apartment 491, was picking up the chocolate Hershey's Kisses that Grace had had a couple of women spreading around the tables. Clara was stashing them away in the covered compartment beneath the seat of her walker. The old woman was known for her stealing. Most often involving chocolate.

Marie was known for buying chocolate and purposely leaving it lying around just to watch the elderly woman's joy as she found it. Grace, an eighty-year-old resident who baked every morning for Marie and was the organizer of all functions among the residents of the building, was still tying balloons to chairs. Knowing everyone well from his years of visiting the girls, Liam had known just whom to seek out in planning the homecoming that was to have been in lieu of dessert after the fancy lunch that was supposed to have happened that day.

The lunch, of course, hadn't happened. And the party would have gone on, with or without him, too. That's how it usually was with him and the girls. He came and went at his pleasure. If he was there, great. If not, no big deal. Was that why it worked so well?

The realization, on this day of standing up as a man, didn't sit well with him. At all. He loved Marie and Gabrielle more than anyone else on earth. They were his sisters in his heart. He looked out for them. Felt protective of them.

And, he supposed, he used them, too. Like a brother used sisters.

To whine to.

To have them always be there.

And to know they'd always be happy to see him when he bothered to show up.

Like now, as he stood there, hands in his pockets, watching as the residents got ready for the big moment. He'd paid for the party.

And here he was thinking it was a bonus that he'd been able to show up.

Liam didn't like the man he was seeing.

At all.

Was the old man right then? Was he worthless?

"Shh, quiet, everyone, they're rounding the corner! They're coming in the front!" Susan Gruber, wife to Dale, said, with a sideways smile to her husband. Liam had never seen one without the other.

The front door opened. He pasted a huge smile on his face, glad that he'd made it back in time.

"Surprise!" More than fifty voices chorused at once. His was among them. And the shocked happiness on both of the girls' faces was worth the effort it was costing him to hang around, to pretend that all was well. That he was going to be fine.

He was a good man. Maybe he'd taken advantage of the girls all these years. Maybe he hadn't seen that. And maybe, now that he did see it, it was up to him to do what he could to rectify the situation. Maybe, very soon, he'd be in a position to be around more, to tend to them for a change.

Because he was decent. His father be damned.

He'd remembered every birthday. Always took them out. Brought gifts that he'd picked out himself and that they'd loved. Whenever they needed a favor, he did what he had to do to grant it.

He should have noticed that they didn't call much.

And maybe he should call them more often, instead of just stopping in for his weekly home-cooked meals when he didn't have anything else to do. Or dropping by after an evening function when he needed to whine.

He watched as their gazes scanned the crowd gathering around them—residents and many of Marie's regular coffee customers, all with cards and good wishes. Both of his partners were grinning from ear to ear. Gabi noticed him first, elbowed Marie and nodded in his direction. Their shock at his presence was obvious.

Their gazes met with his. Nothing was said. They didn't know he'd just lost the only life he'd ever known. They'd just been glad to find him there.

And he was glad he'd come.

PEOPLE STAYED FOR over an hour. Eating cake. Drinking coffee. Conversation flurried. As some of the older residents drifted upstairs to their homes, more customers came in with cards and congratulatory messages. Police officers. A couple of board members from a downtown historical society. The district state representative.

They might not be expecting to turn much of a profit, but the building they'd purchased was valuable to the community. At least in a historical sense.

And Liam had written the guest list. Gabrielle had just learned that from Grace. But she knew that he'd wanted people to know that a good thing was happening at the Arapahoe. He thought if people knew, they'd be more apt to support Marie's shop.

He'd wanted that for her.

He'd always wanted what was best for them.

Gabrielle couldn't remember feeling so utterly...almost content. They'd done a good thing, her and Marie and Liam. *Threefold.* A goofy name for their business, but it fit them.

Her partners, who were both more social than she was, were working the room now, moving from group to group while Gabi made certain that everyone had enough to drink. Liam had stood back until she and Marie finally noticed him there. But he was making up for his reticence. And seemed to be just fine. So, good. Her concern that morning had been unwarranted.

Grace was keeping the coffee flowing. The shop was still open to the public and business went on even in the midst of celebration. Sam, one of Marie's full-time employees, was taking orders and serving organic sandwiches as well as coffee.

Gabi had to get back to work, too. While she'd kept her afternoon clear of appointments, she had a hearing in the morning regarding an estate dispute between siblings and had notes to prepare. She'd brought everything with her to work from home where she wouldn't be interrupted.

She was surprised Liam hadn't left.

Glancing his way as she carried a coffeepot around the room, refilling the cups of those who were just drinking it straight and black, she tried to catch his eye. He'd been managing to avoid her.

Because they were crowded with well-wishers?

Or because he had something to hide? Maybe her relief had been premature.

"Have you had a chance to talk to Liam?" she leaned in to ask in Marie's ear as she passed her friend standing with a couple who ran a print shop down the street.

"Not a word," Marie told her, and then said, "Put that pot down, Gabi. This is your party, too."

Nodding, Gabi continued on through the room, filling cups and accepting well-wishes as she made her way back to the counter to dispose of the pot. Two hours and fifteen minutes had passed since her lunch hour. She needed to get upstairs and could probably say a quick word to Marie and slip out without many noticing…

"I need to talk to you before you leave." Liam was suddenly there, standing beside her, a smile on his face for the room to see, but a seriousness in his gaze. Her being shifted, accepting the weight that settled upon her shoulders at his words.

Nodding, she stepped toward the hallway leading to the back of the store.

Liam grabbed her arm, letting go as soon as she stopped. "To both of you."

His tone didn't sound ominous. Fear filled her heart anyway. But before she could question him any further, he'd rejoined the throng. She was going to have to wait.

"I'D LIKE TO RENT 321 and 324 and knock out the wall in between them," Liam said as soon as Marie walked into the small office in the back of the coffee shop and shut the door. Gabi, who'd been sitting at Marie's desk for close to an hour, working from the briefcase she'd brought in from her car, watched him, as though waiting for him to say more.

He'd given her all he had. A carefully re-hearsed all-he-had. He wasn't going to worry them.

Bottom line: no worry for them.

Or from them.

Whatever. No worry in the girl department. He was going to be fine.

"It's your building, too," Marie said. She was standing next to him. Closest to him. So why was it Gabi's stare that he felt cutting into him? "We've got the biggest apartment in the place. You're certainly entitled to two smaller ones," she added.

"What's up?" Gabrielle's question tacked on to the end of Marie's comment.

"You want to use it as an office for your writing?" Marie asked.

Made sense. Or would have, if he'd still been

the person he'd been when they'd purchased the building that morning.

"Since your dad's so anal about you not spending any time writing in your real office, and the desk in your condo isn't going to hold many more of those research files."

He could say yes. Leave it at that. For now. Until he gave his dad time to cool down. To come to his senses...

"No." Liam hadn't realized he'd spoken aloud until he heard his voice crack out into the room. "No," he said again. "I want to live here."

Other than the nine months he'd spent in the dorm his freshman year of college, he'd never even lived in a building without a doorman.

"Live here?" Both women spoke at once.

"With association fees, my living expenses at the condo are more than rent and utilities will be here." He'd studied the spreadsheets.

"Especially since, as owners, we aren't paying rent," Gabi said dryly. Her frown bothered him far more than the words. She was always on to him first.

"I cannot spend the rest of my life living under my father's thumb in a building he owns and relying only on him for my livelihood." They'd heard the part about the livelihood before. More than once. "If I'm going to be the man I claim to be, I have to do more than just talk."

After sharing a long look with Gabrielle, Marie caught up. "What's going on?"

"He kicked you out, didn't he? For buying this place. He took away your condo." Elbows on the desk, Gabrielle didn't move. He felt as though she'd punched him.

"He thinks he can take away your home, like he took away your car freshman year? Who does that?" Marie asked, a horrified expression on her face. "That's ludicrous."

Her horror made his stomach crawl. As though he was far worse off than he'd allowed himself to believe. And they didn't even know the half of it.

"Liam?" Gabrielle had him with just one word. But he couldn't lean on her. Not this time. He didn't have to prove to himself that he was a man. He knew the hell he'd been through with his father, how hard it had been to bite his tongue and offer the old man the respect he'd deserved. He knew of the responsibilities he'd carried at Connelly Investments—all with successful results.

But seeing himself in Gabi's eyes and then in Marie's, right then, homeless and disowned, he saw what they'd seen, what he was afraid they still saw: that eighteen-year-old kid whose father had stripped him of his keys...

"My father has agreed to leave me completely alone," he said. "I am choosing to move here. I am tired of having people look at me as the two of you are looking at me right now. Like my existence depends upon my father. Like ultimately my decisions rest with him."

There was no moral obligation to tell them he'd been disinherited. Their investment, backed by the trust which his father couldn't touch, was completely safe. If he was truly going to stand up and take control of his life, he had to do this on his own. A part of Liam eased at the thought. Leaning on no one meant that no one could yank the rug out from under his feet. The loss of a job, of a fancy home, were worth that freedom.

He was going to be someone people leaned on. Starting with Gabi and Marie.

"I'll pay for the renovations," he told them. For instance, he wasn't going to need two kitchens. The idea was growing on him. He'd make one kitchen an office. Or maybe one of the four bedrooms should be used for that purpose. Truth was, he had no idea what he was going to do with the space. He just knew he wanted it.

More and more with every minute that passed. He didn't feel quite as desperate anymore.

"And another thing," he added, nodding as he looked first at one and then the other. "I've decided to give myself one year to make it as a writer. I'm going to devote myself to full-time writing. And if, at the end of the year, I'm not self-supporting, I'll go back into finance."

"Your father agreed to that?" Marie's shock was evident. Liam looked at Gabrielle. Expecting—he didn't know what. Doubt, maybe? Concern, certainly. She always saw the risks.

And saw through him, too.

She was staring at him, and for once he couldn't tell at all what she was thinking.

"You don't think I can do it." Why he said the words, he didn't know. Didn't much matter what she thought. His life was unfolding before him, one wilted petal at a time.

"When are you moving in?" she asked.

"Tomorrow."

She nodded. And he figured she knew his father had disowned him.

"If you need any help unpacking, I'll be home after four."

Chin jutting, hands in his pockets, he nodded.

"Tomorrow? Before the renovations?" Marie asked.

"We signed the papers today because it's the end of the month and that worked out best financially," Gabrielle said before Liam could think of a believable explanation. "Liam's expenses run month to month as well, I'm sure."

"That's right," he said. "Not that I paid rent, of course, but the association fee will come due tomorrow..." The twelve hundred a month he paid for his share of the doorman and upkeep of the communal facilities.

Marie looked at them for a minute. And then she nodded, too. Something was going on. They all knew it. And somehow had just agreed to leave it alone.

They talked a couple more minutes. Marie offered to make dinner for the three of them the next night, since Liam would be busy getting settled. And then she was called out to help with a rush up front and was gone.

"Are you okay?" Gabi didn't move from her seat at the desk. So why did he feel as though she'd hugged him—and like the feeling? Was he really that pathetic? That he needed a hug because his daddy was mad at him?

"I am okay." Surprisingly, he was. "It's past time, my doing this."

She studied him a long minute longer. "Okay, then," she said, glancing back down at her papers. Not dismissing him. Just going on with life as though everything was normal.

So he turned to go. Because it was what he

would have done the day before. The week before. The year before.

"Liam?"

Hearing his name, he turned back. Looked at her.

"Good to have you in the partnership," she said. Her gaze, her voice, was completely calm. Serious. And filled with something else, too. Something new. Something he needed. And something they were never going to talk about.

"Good to be here."

He smiled. So did she.

And his new life had begun.

CHAPTER FOUR

GABRIELLE HOPED THAT Liam would talk to her about his father. After so many years of being half of his sounding board, she was concerned about his silence on a move so bold. Which was why she'd left work early the day after Threefold's big purchase to help him move in. And why she'd decided to stay and help him unpack after Marie left to take the dinner left-overs to Alice in 409, who'd had knee replacement surgery.

He didn't mention his father at all.

She found reasons to run into him every day that first week of his residency in their building— an easy enough feat, considering that they'd just gone into business partnership and there were a lot of decisions to make, regarding the order of tasks the old building needed them to complete.

All three of them agreed that the elevator was priority one. They wanted its historical value preserved but needed it to be dependable and safe. Liam knew which historic renovation company to hire and even obtained a quote at 40 percent off the going rate.

A day passed, then six, and still he hadn't mentioned his father.

He'd written a couple of human interest stories, though. One regarding an incident that had happened that week outside a yoga studio close to their building, a near abduction. He'd heard the call on a new scanner he'd purchased, had been on the scene and had sold his story all within a matter of hours.

"I made a whole fifty dollars," he'd told Gabi when she stopped up to see him after work the Monday following his move. He was brimming with something she'd never seen in him before.

Pride, maybe? Not that he'd ever been lacking in that department. But...this was different.

He wasn't the same old Liam he'd always been. She loved the old Liam. He was family to her.

And yet, the difference was... Well, she didn't know.

"I've been watching the site," she told him, standing there in the arch between his kitchen and dining table, leaning on the wall. "Marie sent me the link. Your article's the headliner."

"Yeah, it's had thousands of hits. But when it's a hundred thousand I'll get excited," he told her. His grin was different, too. It made her stomach jump.

Shaking her head, Gabi asked him about the editor of the independent news site who'd published him, June Fryburg—a local woman he'd sold travel stories to in the past. She wasn't making millions, but she was making a living. And she believed that if Liam turned his focus to human interest, with his ability to see inside the story to the honest emotions that made everything come alive, he could be the one who took her to the big leagues.

Gabrielle wanted to ask what was going on with his father. But she didn't.

And he didn't say. He'd never not said before.

Maybe that was why she didn't just ask. She'd been awake in the middle of the night two nights that week—concerned about Liam. And glad that he was living upstairs.

It wasn't until that Wednesday, when Marie called her at the office to tell her that someone from the FBI had just been in the coffee shop and asked to see Liam, that Gabrielle's reticence ended. Finishing up with her last client—a divorced woman with three children who needed help with child custody enforcement—Gabi packed up for the day, slung her bulging softsided briefcase over her shoulder and locked her office door.

She didn't stop to say goodbye to anyone and sped home as fast as Denver traffic allowed. She wanted to get to Liam before the agents left. To invoke his right to counsel, just in case. Liam tended to think that everything was going to be fine. He didn't always take things as seriously as Gabrielle knew he should.

And…he was hers. Hers and Marie's. They looked out for him whenever he was around. And now that they had him full-time again—for the first time in more than a decade—she felt… extra responsible. At least until he settled in.

Clearly his father hadn't been pleased by the Arapahoe deal. That, mixed with Liam suddenly moving and not talking about the old man for the first time ever…

Once home, she opted not to wait for the as yet unfixed and very slow elevator in their building and took the stairs to Liam's.

She knew she'd done the right thing—barging in on him uninvited like this—when Liam opened the door to her knock. He was white with shock and let her in without saying a word—not even asking how she'd known to be there. Heart thudding, she followed him to the living room, where a man and a woman, both dressed in dark pants with matching suit coats, sat on opposite ends of the sofa.

Liam introduced her by name. She added, "I'm an attorney."

The female agent, introducing herself as Gwen Menard, and her associate as Mark Howard, showed her badge and looked at Liam. "You called your attorney?"

"No, he didn't call me," Gabrielle said before Liam could respond. "A…friend of ours…let me know you were here."

The agents looked at each other. Shared a frown. And she realized, too late, that her sudden invasion made Liam look guilty.

"Gabi's a friend of mine from college," Liam said. "She and Marie—the woman you met in the coffee shop—live in the building. They've appointed themselves my guardian angels." He shrugged, looking handsome, all male and as though having unsolicited attention from pretty women was all in a day's living for him.

He stood with his back to the window, the sunlight behind him casting shadows on his face. A face other women fell for. In droves.

He had his hands in his pockets.

Something she'd long ago noticed he did when he was unsure of himself.

"So what's going on?" She stepped forward and took a seat in the armchair opposite the agents, inviting herself into their gathering whether they wanted her there or not.

They looked at Liam. He looked back.

"You want her to stay, Mr. Connelly?"

She held her breath.

"Of course."

She didn't know whether to be relieved or not. Did he want her there because he knew something she didn't and thought he might need her? Professionally?

Or was this just him sharing his private business with her again?

Years before, Liam had made some stupid, rebellious mistakes, but nothing even close to breaking the law. He was a man of integrity.

Gwen Menard had Gabrielle's full attention when she started to speak.

"What can you tell us, Mr. Connelly, about the Grayson deal?"

"Nothing."

"What do you know about it?" Agent Mark Howard addressed Liam with narrowed eyes.

"Nothing."

"Is Liam in trouble?" Gabrielle had to ask.

"No," Agent Menard said, directing a serious look at Gabrielle before returning her attention to Liam. "At least at this point we have no reason to believe he is."

"Obstruction of justice is a crime," Howard said, his gaze never leaving Liam. Probably watching for a reaction to his not so veiled threat. Gabrielle could have told him he was wasting his time, not only because she believed Liam wouldn't have committed a crime, but because she'd never met anyone with as much skill at hiding his reaction to threats.

Liam had had a lifetime of practice. "He's right, Liam," she said, just in case he didn't know that this threat was not empty. "If you know something about this Grayson deal, and it turns out to be illegal, and you didn't say anything, you could be brought up on charges."

He nodded, pulling his hands out of his pockets to cross his arms. Not in self-protection, but in a way that showed a confidence that was all Liam. "The Grayson deal is the Indian land," he told her.

"I thought that sold to Senator Billingsley."

"It did."

Menard and Howard were looking at them intently.

Liam had been out of college by the time his father had gotten all of the agreements and changes he'd needed and actually purchased the land that bordered the Indian reservation. He'd been on the top floor when his father sold the completed development.

A sale that had never made sense to her. The elder Connelly had wanted that land, to develop it, seemingly forever. He'd finally gotten the tribe to sign an agreement allowing the development, created the successful upscale shopping, eating and housing community he'd envisioned, and then had promptly sold it.

"Did you have anything to do with the sale?"

"Are you kidding?" Liam asked. "Grayson was my father's dream. No way would he entrust that to me."

Walter Connelly was not only a controlling jerk, in Gabrielle's opinion, but he was also plain stupid where his only offspring was concerned. Liam might appreciate beautiful women a bit too much for Gabrielle's taste, and was prone to wanting expensive things, but he was 100 percent trustworthy. She'd bet her life on that fact. He also had a good business head on his shoulders.

"What about in your Connelly files?" Menard asked.

"I am not in possession of a single file that is the property of Connelly Investments."

Gabrielle practically gave herself whiplash as her gaze shot to Liam. What? No files? That didn't make sense.

"Access to them, then," Howard said.

When Liam turned, giving her only a side view of him, as though he was shutting her out, Gabrielle's stomach clenched.

"I already told you," Liam was telling the

agents, "I no longer have access to anything pertaining to Connelly Investments. My father took my key card, emptied my office and wrote me out of his will."

The air was cold on her face.

His father had completely cut him off? She'd known something was wrong, that Walter Connelly was acting out another threat of some kind, but surely even in the worst case scenario, the man wouldn't cut Liam out of his will.

She'd always believed, as Liam had said, that deep down his father not only loved him but needed him. Other than Liam, the old man was alone in the world.

"Just before Ms. Miller interrupted, you were about to tell us why your father just happened to disown you a week before the FBI served his office with a search warrant."

Oh. No. This was bad.

"I think I can tell you why," Gabrielle blurted, afraid that they'd twist whatever Liam might say. "Walter Connelly has been controlling Liam for his entire life. He gives him the world so that he can then take it away if he does anything he doesn't like..."

Menard's gaze softened as she looked at Liam. "Is this true?"

He shrugged. Grinned. "Pretty much." And

then he added, "Last week I really pissed him off."

"I have been privy to the private details of Liam's dealings with his father for more than a decade," Gabrielle said, needing these two powerful people to understand that Liam was not one of their suspects. "He insisted that Liam work in the family business and then kept him doing menial jobs. He promoted him to the top floor so that he had the status to appear at social functions as a Connelly, but paid him less than middle department managers. Liam has degrees in journalism and finance, and wanted to seriously pursue his writing. Mr. Connelly sent a piece Liam had done to a friend of his in the business and gave it back completely slashed up. He told Liam that it was time he faced the truth and grew up. That's when he moved him to the top floor."

"It's okay, Gabi." Liam's smile was turned on her. And she was so shocked she fell silent. He must have meant that look for Gwen Menard. Liam never, ever gave her or Marie *that* look. He smiled at them, of course. Laughed at them, or with them, mostly. But that warm look, the way-a-man-looks-at-a-woman look—never. "I didn't take the editor's criticisms to heart. I knew he'd probably paid the guy to fill my article with red ink. And I didn't stop writing."

He turned to the agents. "I have a couple of mother hens who look out for me."

"He took away Liam's car our freshman year of college just because Liam wanted to live in a dorm, forcing him to take a bus from Boulder to Denver five nights a week to work, and then demoted him from mail room clerk to night janitor." Gabrielle wanted these people to know that Liam's father was over-the-top mean.

To the point of abusive.

"One Christmas, when Liam wanted to have dinner here with Marie and me, Walter forbade it. He gave Liam ten thousand dollars' worth of gifts that year, and then when Liam came to dinner anyway, he took every one of them back. He was also the only Connelly employee that year who didn't receive a bonus."

"It was an expensive dinner," Liam said with a smile. "But worth every bite."

Liam might not want others to know about his father's tactics. She understood that he was embarrassed, even humiliated. But these were federal officials. They hadn't just come around to chat. "Anyway, Liam went into partnership with Marie and me—you can check us out, Threefold, we formed an LLC—to buy this building. We closed last week. Liam didn't tell his father about the deal, but Mr. Connelly found out just before we closed. He confronted Liam. Liam closed on the deal anyway…"

She might not have Liam's testimony or proof of the exact facts, but the truth was clear to anyone who'd been Liam Connelly's friend during the twelve years he'd been on the road to being his own man while still tending to familial responsibility.

Menard turned to Liam, her big brown eyes softening even more. "So you're saying that your father disowned you for purchasing this building?"

"I believe his exact words were, 'We cannot be a team, you and I. I can no longer trust you.'"

Gabrielle's breath caught in her throat.

"He can no longer trust you?" Agent Howard's investigative manner wasn't softening at all. "For buying an old building?"

"For using money he and my late mother put in a trust for me without telling him. He claims that I was duplicitous in that I deliberately hid from him an investment of 'family' money."

"This guy sounds like a real…" Gwen Menard stopped herself.

But the agents had a few pieces of information to impart before they left.

The FBI was seeking charges against Walter Connelly, for running a Ponzi scheme and money laundering. They were accusing him of defrauding clients out of millions of dollars. He'd taken their money, telling them he was investing it in the Grayson Communities, after he'd already sold the development. He'd used a small portion of that new money to purchase land that he'd billed as phase two of Grayson but that had, in fact, been swampland. He'd continued to take investments and then used the newer monies gained to pay dividends to earlier investors. The rest of the money had been deposited into legitimate businesses but then spent to buy things that did not exist anywhere except on paper. In reality the money had been given back to Walter, who could spend it at will without any way for it to be traced.

Any Connelly assets that were part of the investigation had been frozen.

Walter Connelly was under arrest.

CHAPTER FIVE

LIAM WASN'T GOING to panic.

"If I'm somehow going to be implicated, I'm going to cooperate fully," he said to Gabi, who was sitting in the passenger seat of his BMW an hour and a half after she'd burst into his apartment. They were on their way to FBI headquarters, where his father was being held for questioning before being booked into a city holding cell.

If Agents Menard and Howard had thought they were going to get a reaction out of him by informing him that he no longer had access to any of his father's assets—as if his reaction to the news was somehow going to trap him in his supposed lies—they must have been disappointed.

They were a week late on that blow. He'd already lost everything. Knowing that some of Connelly's assets were frozen didn't change his day a bit.

"Did you call George?" Gabi's question kept him focused—unlike the horror on Marie's face when they'd let her know what was going on. He'd felt a stab of fear then.

But he was a man, in spite of his father treating him like the stupid kid he might once have been. He'd handle this.

"I called him," he said. "While you were out front getting Marie." They'd told her the news in the coffee shop's back office. "He wasn't in his office and didn't answer his cell. I left messages both places."

"Chances are he's with your father."

He agreed. Which made him more eager than ever to get where they were going. Ten miles had never seemed so far.

"Did your father really cut you out of his will?"

Did he detect a note of hurt in her voice? Liam glanced in her direction. Gabi was watching the traffic. Of course. She was always on the lookout for the dangers ahead.

"Yes."

"Last week?"

"Yes."

"Oh." The bite in her tone bothered him. He'd hurt her. As usual, he'd been thinking about his own life.

"It had nothing to do with you or Marie, so my not telling you—"

"It's okay."

"No, it's not. And I should have known that. I'm... I didn't like the way I saw myself in your eyes." They were stopped at a light and he glanced over at her. "Like I'm some kid whose daddy abuses him and he just keeps going back for more." It was humiliating. And worse.

Her gaze softened. "You might have wanted to check your vision against ours," she said. The small smile on her lips had him looking back at the road. Staring at it.

He'd...felt...something. From Gabi. His Gabi. The feeling hadn't been sister-like.

And that was not only humiliating. It was horrible.

"You're way stronger than you know, Liam," she said, as the light changed and he started forward. "I see a man who puts up with his father's abuse while still managing to claim an identity in his own small ways, because you know he has no one and relies on you. You subjugate your own desires for his, but because you think it's the right thing to do, to be responsible, not because you fear what he can do to you."

Her vision was definitely different from his. But it wouldn't be forever. He was working on becoming the man she seemed to think he was.

"What about this car? He didn't take it."

"I paid it off last year, but even so, the old

man kindly informed me that I was welcome to keep it."

"He didn't know you'd paid it off?"

"Are you kidding? Nothing happens without him knowing about it. He knew we'd closed on the building before I drove from the closing back to the office. His car remark was just to get a rise out of me."

He waited for her to ask if it had. Any other time she would have.

But he hadn't run to her this time. He'd shut her out.

"It didn't," he said, frowning as he signaled a turn and changed lanes. "Get a rise out of me," he clarified, pushing harder on the gas pedal, increasing his speed to two miles above the limit. Any more than five could get him a ticket, and he didn't have time for that.

"You're really cut off, Liam. When the government freezes assets, they aren't kidding. It means they have some pretty substantial evidence…"

Biting back his irritation—why was it that people couldn't see that he was going to be just fine without his father's money?—Liam said, "I was already really cut off."

"But…"

"And you know what?" He took a corner with enough speed that his tires kicked up gravel.

"When those agents told me that some of his assets were being frozen, my first reaction was relief." She turned and met his gaze briefly before he returned his attention to the road. "Yeah, relief," he repeated, measuring the words for their accuracy and finding them completely so. "For the first time in my life I don't have the weight of that blackmail tool hanging over me. I don't have to fear losing what I've been given, or measure every single one of my decisions by the dictates of my inheritance."

"But—"

"I know, I've still got my trust. And you're right, I am relying on that security while I get established. I get that I'm really lucky…"

"—I was going to say that your inheritance should never have been fodder for blackmail…"

He turned in to the federal building parking lot as her words registered.

"And that trust money was from your mother's family. Designated by your mother's parents to go to you…"

He chanced another glance at her. It was there again. That sense that something was different.

As if she was a woman, not just his best friend.

The idea panicked him far more than the possibility of being wanted by the FBI. Gabi and

Marie…they were the only family he had. He was not going to screw that up.

Most particularly not with baser urges that waned with time. He liked women. He was good with that.

But not Marie and Gabi. He couldn't risk breaking their hearts. Couldn't risk losing either one of them.

And Lord knew he'd never yet known a woman—in a man-woman sense—whom he didn't eventually tire of. He'd yet to meet the woman who could corral his interests…

They'd arrived at their destination.

It was time to see his father. Proud. Strong. Domineering. And locked up.

Liam had no idea how he was going to handle that. But was glad Gabi was with him.

GEORGE COSTAS, CONNELLY'S head corporate attorney, had been present when Walter Connelly had been served his warrant. He'd accompanied his longtime employer and closest friend to FBI headquarters. He'd advised Walter to be completely honest and forthcoming. And then he'd left, promising to get to the bottom of everything.

Gabrielle heard the report from the agent who'd been sent to take them back to Liam's father—Agent Bill Cross. Cross, a man who looked to be about forty-five, was dressed like his counterparts in a suit with a sedate skinny blue tie. His expression grave beneath short graying hair, he led them to a room with a table and four chairs, where Walter Connelly sat waiting.

The first thing Gabrielle noticed through the glass on her way in was that Walter wasn't handcuffed.

"You want to go in alone?" she asked Liam as his old man looked up and saw them standing outside the door.

"No," Liam said. "If you don't mind, I'd like you to come in with me. You're my friend, and a great lawyer. With George's understandable absence, I'd like your take on anything my father has to say. I want to know exactly what evidence the FBI has, what he's been asked and if what he's told them is in any way detrimental. I'll pay you for your time, of course."

She nodded. She wasn't going to take money from him, but they could deal with that later. Right now, the man watching them from inside that room, a man who looked neither aggressive nor beaten, was their priority. Nervous, but determined not to let Liam guess that, she followed him into the room, closing the door behind her. She might not like Walter Connelly's parenting skills, but he was an impressive businessman with an intimidating demeanor.

He'd never approved of Liam's friendship with her and Marie—he hadn't even bothered to say hello on the day of their college graduation. Liam had introduced them. Walter had appeared to not have heard.

"Dad, you remember Gabrielle?"

The old man looked in her direction and then back at his son, giving not a single clue to what he might be thinking. "I do."

Pulling out a chair, Liam sat across from his father, indicating that Gabrielle should join them.

She sat next to Liam.

"I imagine they can hear everything we say," Liam started. Not the first thing she'd have said when confronting an estranged parent in jail, but appearances had always been far more important to the Connellys than she'd ever been able to understand.

"I have nothing to hide," Walter said. His face was no more lined than she remembered from her last glimpse of him three months before— sometime around Thanksgiving—when she and Marie had accompanied Liam to a huge fundraiser at the art museum. Jenna had been out of town and he hadn't wanted to be accompanied by their dads. The expression on Walter's face when he'd seen them walk in had been about what it was now.

"What's going on, Dad?"

Walter clasped his hands on the table and looked his son directly in the eye. "I have no idea."

Liam's jutting chin was the only sign of his frustration. "Look, Dad, I'm sorry I transferred the trust money without informing you. I'm sorry I bought a building without giving you a heads-up. Now let it go. They told me you're under arrest. They're going to hold you. They don't do that for nothing. Tell me what's going on."

Leaning forward, Walter put his nose close to Liam's but didn't lower his voice. "I'm telling you, I have no idea what's going on."

Liam studied his father. He took a deep breath. And studied some more.

Not wanting to interrupt whatever communication was taking place between father and son, Gabrielle sat there. Feeling helpless.

And worried, too.

But she was glad to be there. She didn't want Liam fighting this battle alone.

"So tell me your guess as to what could be going on."

"I've been set up."

"How?" Liam's question shot back immediately.

"I have no idea."

"What evidence do they have that you've done anything wrong?" Gabrielle's voice butted in when she'd told herself she was going to stay silent unless her opinion was solicited.

"Plenty." The older man's steely, intelligent gaze turned on her. She didn't know whether to be flattered or nervous. She was a bit of both.

But determined to remain by Liam's side.

"What evidence, Dad? What have they got on you? Is it legitimate?"

"The files they found containing clients' names and payables exist. The offshore accounts exist. The land that was being used for investment bait exists. That fact that it's worthless swampland, instead of the Grayson development land that it was said to be, is true."

"You sold swampland to our investors?" She didn't need to see the disgusted look on Liam's face to know he was horrified.

"Someone did. That someone was not me."

"Someone in Connelly Investments?"

"Someone using Connelly's name, reputation and client base."

"No one has access to that information except for the top-floor executives."

"I know."

"How many of those are there?" Gabrielle asked.

"Seven, now that Liam's gone."

Finally. Someone had acknowledged the estrangement.

"You and George are out, so that would leave Matheson, Williams, Granger, Donaldson and Buckus." Liam moved right on past any chance at personal conversation. Gabrielle loved his ability to do that. And hated that this was the kind of father-son relationship he'd grown up with. While she didn't see her family much now that they'd moved out of state—and didn't have a lot in common with her younger brothers, as they weren't interested in education or hard work as much as maligning the establishment and hanging with friends—they kept in touch with her. Always called to thank her when she sent money. And called other times, too.

"Dad?" Liam said as Walter just sat there.

"I have suggested to Agent Cross, over and over again, during the several hours I've been a guest here today, that he should be looking at all five of them."

"You aren't a guest, Dad. You're under arrest."

"Perhaps for the moment. George is working on that. I'll be out of here tonight."

Liam looked at Gabrielle, who nodded. If

nothing else, Walter would be out on bail. Best case, they'd have to let him go until formal charges were filed. "He could be considered a flight risk," she said, "but it's not likely, since his entire life is here, and as of now, he still has control of the majority of the company. Only the assets in question have been frozen."

"They've also seized my personal hard drive as well as all of the pertinent Connelly ones, but we'll have use of those again by tomorrow."

His glance made her feel as though she were a bug under a microscope, only not as scientifically important.

And then Liam's gaze met hers. And Walter's dislike of her didn't even matter. "Of the five you mentioned—Matheson, Williams, Granger, Donaldson and Buckus—do you have any suspicions regarding one over the other?"

Mr. Connelly's gaze pinned Liam. "You been talking to *her* about the top floor?"

"Of course not—"

"No, sir, he hasn't."

Gabrielle interrupted only to be interrupted when Liam continued, "I've been telling you for years how smart Gabrielle is, Dad. She has a memory like none I've ever seen. You mentioned the names. Her mind's like a digital catalog."

He'd never said anything to her about seeing her that way. Or having even noticed her mind at all.

Not that she'd needed him to. Their friendship was based on the trust established the night they'd met and on the nightly visits that first year, when Liam would knock on their door and the three of them would rant about classes they didn't like, or homework, or talk about whatever.

And on years of telling each other every good or bad thing that had happened to them.

And on the total acceptance of each other, despite how different they were...

"So is there any reason you can think of to suspect one of the five over another?" Gabrielle asked again, getting her mind back on track. She wasn't a trial attorney. But she handled some minor criminal cases. And had spent her law school years interning with one of the city's top criminal lawyers.

It felt good to be able to offer Liam more than just motherly advice.

"Matheson just went through a nasty divorce," Walter said. "She got everything plus support, and his high school kids have told the court they don't want to see him right now."

"How long has this been going on?"

"Six months. She caught him in bed with her best friend."

"Which makes him not as likely a candidate, because a scheme to the magnitude being described takes a lot longer than six months to be set in motion."

"Doesn't make sense that you'd sell Grayson if you were using the land in a Ponzi scheme," Liam said, looking at his father.

"I didn't sell Grayson." Walter looked down at the table.

"Of course you did. I saw it listed on the sales and acquisitions report months ago."

Walter looked up. Around the room. Everywhere but at Gabrielle. And then said, "What the hell, you're going to find out soon enough. I lost the property at the blackjack table."

Slumping back with enough force to scoot his chair on the floor, Liam stared. "You lost a fifty-million-dollar property playing blackjack?"

"I won a sixty-million-dollar property the next week."

"Delacourte?" Liam asked, while Gabrielle, too shocked to react, looked between the two of them, wondering if they'd both lost their minds.

Who gambled away fifty million dollars in one game?

"You're gambling regularly?" Accusation laced Liam's tone.

"I've taken up the sport again, yes."

"Since when?"

Walter frowned, throwing his hand in the air. "I don't know how long, and I don't answer to you."

Liam's expression became guarded. Withdrawn. And though his face quickly cleared, there was something missing in the depths of his eyes. Not that many others would probably notice. She'd just learned a long time ago how to read him, so she could get back to sleep sooner on the nights he'd visited late.

"So Matheson is the only one you'd suspect?" Gabrielle blurted. She wanted to know anything pertinent that might affect Liam.

"Donaldson took a personal beating when the real estate market crashed back in '08," Walter said, his fingers tapping on the table. They were nicely manicured. "He'd just bought a place for a million and half and in six months it was worth half a million. He bought it on balloon loan, expecting to sell it for profit, and instead went into foreclosure."

"Couldn't you help him out enough to prevent that, at least?" Liam asked. "Buy out the loan for a higher interest thirty-year note?"

"I didn't know about it until it was too late."

"And the others?" Gabrielle asked. Walter's lawyers would get all of this information, track down the paper trail and get the affidavits that would support Walter's claims, if it came to that.

But those were Walter's lawyers. Liam needed his own protection. Whether he realized it yet or not.

And she, who'd only been in college because of a scholarship, who'd been driving a rusted clunker car and wearing secondhand clothes when they'd first met, was actually qualified and able to provide that protection.

"Buckus is an ex-con, of sorts. He had a juvie record that's been sealed. Petty theft type stuff. I've known him all my life. We…grew up…in the same…area. He did his time, cleaned up his act, went to college, went into banking and was a general manager of a major chain branch when I hired him thirty years ago."

"Have you ever had any reason to doubt him?" she asked, including Liam in her question, her glance, as he looked over at her. The appreciation in his eyes lit her up inside.

"Ray Buckus is as good a guy as there is," Liam said. "Keeps meticulous records and makes note of everything twofold. I know this not only from working with him, but I also used to clean his office."

So there'd either be ample evidence to back up the faith both Connelly men had in him or a lack of evidence that might very well point to his guilt.

"Williams is on the top floor but doesn't have

full security clearance in terms of accounts," Walter said then, causing Liam to glance his way.

"I thought everyone up there had clearance."

"Williams is there because I needed his muscle," Walter said. "I'd received threats—that goes with the territory—but one in particular mentioned a bomb…"

Liam's chair flew back as he jumped up. "A bomb! Why wasn't I told about this?" He started pacing.

"Sit down, Liam. Calm down."

Picking up his chair, Liam held on to the back of it with both hands, facing his father.

"You were in college." Walter seemed to relent to Liam's choice not to follow his order to have a seat. "I called the police. A bomb squad came in, gave us the all clear. The note was investigated, but nothing came of it. Larry Charles, chief of police at the time, suggested I get a bodyguard. Williams has a degree in finance and pulls his weight in that area, but he's on the top floor because he's a former Navy SEAL with bomb squad training."

The man neglected to tell his own son about a bomb scare and an employee highly trained to protect them?

"Granger's been with us the shortest period of time," Walter continued, raising an eyebrow to his still standing son. Apparently capitulating, Liam sat. "I don't have any reason to suspect him of anything. I bought him away from Merrill Lynch because I liked him. He's married to his second wife, an internist with a thriving practice, and they have a couple of married kids. As far as I can tell, he lives within his means."

Okay. Well, there was a lot to think about. And…

"Look, I know you have counsel, but I suggest that you get yourself another attorney," she told Walter Connelly. "You're going to need someone who has no connection to you or your company, someone who couldn't possibly come under any suspicion. Someone powerful."

"I'll take care of finding someone," Liam told his father.

"Thank you." Walter nodded.

Gabrielle had to physically restrain herself from letting her mouth drop open. According to Liam, the man never apologized to him or thanked him for anything.

"But I want George involved every step of the way," Walter added.

"I know, Dad. I do, too." Liam was nodding. Looking as if he wanted to say more.

But he didn't. And neither did Walter, as Liam and Gabrielle got up and left.

Head held high, Liam didn't look back as

they calmly made their way down the hallway that would take them back to the elevators. But Gabrielle did. And was disturbed to catch the pained expression on Walter Connelly's face as he watched them walk away. It was gone in an instant.

But Gabrielle had no doubt it had been there.

And no doubt that that look was going to stick with her. Because everything about Liam Connelly seemed to do so.

CHAPTER SIX

HE COULDN'T JUST get on with life. Even if he'd been enough like his old man to turn his back on family, Liam still would have had to find out what was going on. He'd worked at Connelly until recently, had been the heir to the entire corporation and for the past several years had been a top-floor executive. The FBI had been looking at him. He had to protect himself. Clear his name.

Liam pondered long into that night. He didn't go out. Didn't look for a game of chance, a woman or a drink. He didn't run to his confessors. He spent the night investigating, researching, taking care of his own business to the best of his ability.

With the personal list he'd kept of every account he'd worked with during his years at Connelly, and his privately kept contact list—composed of pretty much anyone he'd ever met long enough to exchange contact information—he made more lists. People he could contact. Those he trusted more than others. People he knew trusted his father. People with more money than they knew what to do with. Those who watched their investments more closely. Anyone he knew who was associated with the Grayson development on any level, from tile-laying contractors to investors.

And in the morning, dressed in his best dark suit and a red silk tie and holding a briefcase carrying only a blank note pad and pen, he showed up at Connelly Investments. Fully prepared to be turned away at the door, he was surprised to find himself able to get to the top floor without delay—helped by the fact that the security guard accompanied him.

All the way to George's office.

And back down again, too, twenty minutes later, with an earful from the man he'd once trusted with his life. He'd been told he wasn't welcome. Warned not to return.

He hadn't been given a chance to ask questions. Or express opinions.

He'd never even opened his briefcase.

WITH PURPOSE FIRMLY in mind, Liam drove the BMW he now cherished more than any other possession he'd ever owned—because it was paid in full—away from the upscale part of town that had always been his neighborhood and back to the historic downtown area. He didn't go home, though. After his unproductive meeting with George, he was now working under the dictates of plan B.

A plan that had solidified during the long night.

He didn't call ahead. Didn't want Gabrielle to get any ideas that he was coming to her as a friend needing a shoulder to cry on.

Liam's days of crying on anyone's shoulder were over.

Cataloging every word of the cryptic conversation he'd had with George, telling a story in his mind in an attempt to find clarity, Liam occupied every one of the twenty-two minutes he had to wait for Gabi to finish with her client—a shabby-looking man who looked as if he'd pulled his too-big, ragged jacket out of a trash bin.

"Thank you, Miss Gabi," her client said as she walked with him through the crowded waiting room of the legal aid office.

She'd yet to see Liam sitting there on one of the hard plastic chairs. He watched her, liking the fact that he could observe this Gabi he'd never seen before.

"You're welcome, Jim. You're going to be just fine now, and I want you to come to me anytime, call me anytime, if you need help again."

"I will." The man smiled.

Liam expected the grin to be toothless. And was surprised by the row of even white teeth he saw there.

Those weren't the teeth of somebody who'd lost everything due to drug or alcohol abuse. They made Liam think that at one point in the not too distant past, the man had lived a better life.

Like he himself had?

Was that where he was headed? This time next year, would he be wearing thrift-store clothes?

Gabi and the gentleman were out in the hallway now, out of Liam's earshot.

He stood, ready to approach her when she came back in. He already knew that she was on her last scheduled appointment of the morning—he'd asked at the front desk. She could have an internal meeting, though. With one of her fellow lawyers. Or a prosecutor or judge or...

Hands in his pockets, he left his briefcase on the floor next to his chair and moseyed toward the door, peeking out to see that she was still there.

In her black pants and red blazer, she was garnering attention from a couple of suited gentlemen who'd entered the building. She didn't seem to notice.

But as her client exited, she turned...and noticed him. He started toward her. With composure and confidence. He hoped.

"Liam? What are you doing here?" Pulling her cell phone from her jacket pocket, she glanced at the screen. "I don't have any missed calls from you," she said as she reached him.

"I want to speak with you."

Her frown was instantaneous. "What's wrong?"

"Nothing," he was quick to assure her. But at her look of...was that pity?...he continued, "Nothing other than what you already know," he told her. "Do you have a minute for me?"

"You could have called..." She glanced at her phone again. And Liam noticed how thick and full her short black hair was. How it made a guy want to run his fingers through it.

Wondering if the two men who'd just entered the building had noticed.

His first indication that he wasn't as...okay... as he'd thought.

"I was out anyway. The receptionist said you were on your last appointment." He wanted her to see him as a client.

"I've only got about fifteen minutes," she said. "You want to have dinner with Marie and me tonight? We can all three talk then—all night if you need to."

He wasn't a college boy anymore, needing

absolution. "I'll take the fifteen minutes, if you can give them to me," he said, his tone calm. But serious. "I'd like to speak with you professionally, Gabi. You take on personal clients occasionally, when your workload allows…"

"Yeah…"

"So…do you have room for me?"

"You want to hire me?" Her mouth hung open as she looked up at him. Those silvery-blue eyes familiar—and yet different somehow. "What about George? And the attorney you told your father you'd hire for him?"

That's what he needed to talk to her about. And… "Dad's attorneys will be seeing to him. I'm asking you to represent me." Looking around them, at the people coming and going, passing by, he added, "Can we go to your office?" Surely it had a door. He picked up his briefcase.

"Of course." She led the way with quick steps, glancing back at him to say, "And of course I have time for you. I'd make it even if I didn't."

Liam wasn't surprised at the words. He'd known she would.

He was just a little taken aback by the sudden flood of relief pouring through him.

"GEORGE THREATENED TO have you physically removed from the building?" Gabrielle stopped short of shaking her head, but, in truth, she felt a little dizzy with the turn of events over the past twenty-four hours.

Liam, the one who'd lived the privileged life, was in her office, seeking her help. As though she wasn't just a confessional, she was an equal. Worthy enough to be on the front page of his life rather than tucked into a small space three pages from the end.

Sitting behind her large, but old and scarred desk in a room that might have appeared big enough if not for the floor-to-ceiling bookcases filling two walls and the file cabinets along the third, Gabi asked, "Didn't he get your father out on bail?"

She had windows, but because her office was on the first floor and passersby could see in, she had to keep the blinds partially closed. And because all of the other walls were taken, the windows were behind her.

Absolutely nothing like the office he'd had, with its high-rise view of the entire city of Denver spread out before him while he'd been at his desk.

Upright in the wood-framed chair in front of her desk, he'd be able to see through the windows, though. "Yes, Dad's been released on his own recognizance," he told her. "The prosecutor chose to send the case to a grand jury rather than press charges himself."

She nodded. "In a case like this, I'd expect that. The grand jury is a closed session without the defendant or defendant's lawyers present. The prosecutor presents his evidence, including witnesses, and the jury decides whether or not there is sufficient evidence to warrant charges. Of course, even if the grand jury decides there is not, the prosecutor could still press charges, but it's not likely he'd do so. His chances of getting a guilty verdict from a trial jury would be pretty slim if he couldn't convince the grand jury with no defense being presented."

"It's like a pretrial, then," Liam said.

"Right. It's a way for the prosecutor to present his evidence to a jury without the defense knowing what that evidence is, to see if what he has warrants the expense of a trial."

"How long does that take?"

She shrugged, knowing what Liam needed most was honesty, when what she wanted to do was assure her friend that it would all be over soon. "It could be quick, but in a complicated case like a Ponzi scheme, it could take months. Or longer."

As he sat there looking grim, she asked, "What time did he get out?"

"I have no idea."

"Didn't he call you when he got home last night?"

"I have neither seen nor spoken to him since you and I left him yesterday."

Really.

She did shake her head then. And didn't feel light-headed. Just...confused. "I don't understand. Are you back on the disowned list?"

"I have no idea. Which is why I need you. Something's going on, Gabi. I can do a lot of the investigating, but I need help. A lawyer. You're the only one I can trust."

"Why not call your father? You need to call him, Liam. He needs you. You just have to be the one to capitulate. You know that."

He shook his head. And, strangely, didn't look all that devastated. Determined was more like it.

And kind of...no, quite...handsome.

She sat up. Unsure where that thought had come from. Of course Liam was handsome. He was drop-dead gorgeous. As every one of the twenty or so women he'd dated in college and since had been quick to attest.

His handsomeness just wasn't anything she ever thought about, the way she didn't think about the air she breathed. It was just there. Normal. Until that moment.

Liam was changing right before her eyes. Not

just standing up to his father, but standing up for himself.

He was treating her differently, too. And she had no idea what any of it meant.

She knew what it couldn't mean, though. Whether she noticed how handsome he was or not, Liam would never be more than a very close, very dear friend to her. Not only did they come from completely different worlds, not only was he a self-professed lover of women who didn't see himself being happy with just one for the rest of his life, he was, most importantly, family to her. To her and Marie. Their threesome was sacred. And completely platonic...

"My father is the reason George won't speak with me," Liam said, his elbows on the wooden chair arms, his fingers steepled in front of him. "He forbade it. And gave orders to have me removed from the building if necessary."

"Before, maybe, but not now. Not since yesterday."

"Since last night. According to George, my father emphasized the mandate in the car on the way home. He said I'm not to be trusted."

"What!" She didn't mean to squeal. She glanced toward her door, half expecting to see someone there, checking to see if she was okay.

"I know. It's incomprehensible. He had me escorted up to George's office by security and escorted back down again, too. With no chance to stop off and see him—he's back in his office as usual this morning—or to speak with anyone else."

"Jeez." She let out a whoosh of breath. Wishing she sounded more intelligent. She'd thought nothing Walter Connelly did would shock her.

"Crazy, right?" He seemed perplexed. Disturbed, certainly. But not panicked.

And Gabi realized again that Liam was changing. And, based on his composure now, probably had been for a while. Subtly. Slowly. Without her being aware.

It was as though she was sitting there with a handsome stranger. Who was occupying her close friend's body.

He sat forward. "I have to find out what's going on, Gabi. I have to protect myself. At this point I don't put it past them to somehow hang this on me."

"Your father wouldn't do that."

"I don't think he would, either. But I would have bet my entire trust on the fact that he'd never gamble again, and I'd have lost that one."

"You really think he'd hang you out to dry? His only child?"

"I don't know. I just know that I need your help. I need you to represent me as if I was being investigated. Do whatever you would do to prove my innocence. Tell me what I need to be looking for."

Over the next ten minutes he told her about the information he'd kept in private files, separate from Connelly, the lists he'd made. His thoughts were ordered. Concise. Intelligent. Spot-on.

"Okay," she said, her mind fully focused as he fell silent. She had a pad full of notes in front of her. "I need a little time to sort through this. To do some research, maybe make some calls and to think. Can we meet up again in a couple of hours?"

"Away from the Arapahoe," he said. "I'm probably being paranoid, but I wouldn't put it past my father to have had it bugged by now. He knew we'd closed on the loan less than half an hour after it happened. Clearly he has eyes everywhere."

"You want to skate? We could go to the rail trail." An old railroad track that had been converted into a fifty-mile paved sport path that ran through central Denver and out to the suburbs.

"I haven't had my skates on in a couple of years," he told her. She and Marie had taken up inline skating during college. On a lark. Because Marie had been taking a fitness class and had hated jogging. They'd fallen in love with the sport. And eventually had talked Liam into joining them for some cross-country skates on Saturdays.

"When the weather's nice Marie and I still go just about every weekend. But we haven't been out yet this year. It'll be cold, but the pavement's dry. We could go for a short skate."

"Okay, yeah," he said.

"I'll ask Marie, see if she wants to go…"

He nodded. Gabi smiled. Good. Normal.

But when he stood—a tall, suited man whose looks screamed success—and picked up his five-hundred-dollar leather briefcase, her breath caught.

How could she have just asked this man to go skating with her?

He was Liam, she reminded herself with a mental shake. She and Marie had skated with him more times than she could count.

He grabbed her hand. Squeezed it. "Thank you."

"Of course." She thought her voice sounded normal enough. Hoped it did.

But as he walked out her door with a casual "See ya later," she resisted the urge to rub the hand he'd touched against her jacket. It felt strange. As if it wasn't quite the hand she'd always known.

Which was absolutely ludicrous.

But kind of fit Liam's place in her life at the moment.

LIAM WAS A FEW minutes from home when his cell phone rang. June Fryburg, the editor who'd published his piece on the near abduction—as well as many of his travel stories over the years—wanted him to cover an upcoming court case involving a seventeen-year-old boy who was suing his parents for the right to go off his antidepressants. Unless the boy came up with some surprising medical testimony he was going to lose, but the case was making national news and June, the editor of a small, but gaining-national-attention online news source, thought Liam would give the situation the respectful coverage it needed, as opposed to the sensationalistic handling it would get from their competitors.

He accepted the challenge. He pulled his BMW into its newly designated parking spot behind the downtrodden building he'd just purchased and was about to go in to tell Marie his good news when there was a knock on the window of his car.

Reaching into his jacket was instinctual. And dumb. He didn't carry a weapon. Nor was his cell phone in his pocket. He'd just dropped it on the floor when the knock had sounded.

"Liam Connelly?" The voice was deep. Gruff.

He turned to look. And saw a man, wearing dark pants and an equally dark tweed jacket, staring down at him. The thick neck and broad shoulders pretty much consumed his attention as he reached toward his feet for his phone.

"I'm here via Jeb Williams." His father's former navy SEAL bodyguard.

The man didn't sound threatening. To the contrary, he had his hands out, palms up. Realizing suddenly how he must look—as if he was reaching for a weapon—Liam grabbed his phone. Held it up.

The big guy nodded. Liam dialed.

Williams didn't pick up. His father's employees had undoubtedly been told not to take his calls. George had already told him as much.

He had a choice. He could stay locked up in his car until the guy gave up and left. Or he could open his door and find out why a thug was using Williams's name to seek him out.

Liam opened the door. Got out and faced the man.

"How do you know Jeb?" He went on the offensive because it was better than being intimidated. Or afraid.

"We have much of the same training," the man said, "Personal security and criminal justice."

"What's his wife's name?" Liam felt a bit stupid as he asked. Public internet searches would have listed people with whom Williams was associated.

"Mary Ellen. He met her in college—the

criminal justice training I was telling you about. She has a degree in nursing, though she hasn't worked in years. They have two kids. Heber was born at four in the morning and Faith on Christmas Day."

He hadn't even known Williams had two kids. He'd met Mary Ellen a time or two, at Christmas parties. Knew the couple had kids. Just not how many. Or their names or ages. Williams's specialty had been buyout acquisitions—hostile takeovers, putting people out of work, stripping them of businesses that had been in their families for a generation or more—not a part of the business that interested Liam. He thought there should be another way.

It was an area he and Walter had never agreed upon. Which was one of the reasons he hadn't mentioned the purchase of the Arapahoe to his father.

"I'm Elliott Tanner." The bigger man held out a thick-fingered hand. "I'm licensed and bonded as a PI and also as a bodyguard, here to offer you my services."

"Your services?" He didn't need a thug. Nor could he afford a payroll at the moment.

"I'm in the business of knowing things that technically I don't know. I hear them from sources who pay a lot of money to be non-existent."

"And you want to tell me that you've heard something that leads you to believe I have personal security needs?"

"Your father has Williams."

"My father received threats." Chin high, Liam studied the man, assessing not only what was being said but what wasn't. And why.

"You had a visit from the FBI yesterday."

"How do you know about that?"

Tanner shrugged.

He wasn't going to hire him. Wasn't even considering it, but because he wanted to find out as much as he could about Tanner—namely who had sent him and why—he asked, "Just what is it you think I need?"

"I think that until you find out what's going on with your father's company, there are a lot of people out there who you can't trust. People doing things you can't see."

"But you see them?"

The man was right about one thing—there was a lot Liam couldn't see. Good guys and bad guys and criminally bad guys. So who did Elliott Tanner work for? The good side or the bad? Was Williams a suspect? He was one of the five Walter had named.

But at the moment, Liam wasn't even sure about his own father. A gambling man who'd been adamantly against playing games of chance—to the point that his son, in order to rebel against the old man to the fullest extent, had chosen to play the tables during college—was now playing for dangerously high stakes.

"I'm trained to be the eyes in the back of your head." The man looked at him without blinking.

He was trained for something, that was for sure. Another thing was pretty clear to Liam—if this man was somehow involved in this mess with his father, he wanted to know where the guy was and what he was doing, as opposed to meeting up with him unexpectedly in a dark alley. He wanted a reason to keep tabs on him without seeming suspicious.

"Since you know so much, you must also know that I no longer have access to Connelly finances."

Maybe that was it. This guy was an undercover fed—trying to find out if Liam would somehow find funds to hire him. Funds that Liam had already told them he didn't have.

"I'm aware of that, yes."

"Then you know I can't possibly afford to pay for personal security services." He had a sizable trust, but some of it was designated for Threefold. It was now his only retirement account since his father had taken away his stock options and written him out of his will. It was the money he had to live off for the foreseeable future. Until he could support himself with his writing. He was in the process of doing renovations to his new home—on a much more modest scale than he'd originally envisioned. And bodyguards didn't come cheap.

"I'm here as a favor. I'm willing to take you on, just until this Connelly issue gets settled, for a discounted rate."

He named a fee that Liam could easily afford, but which was ridiculously low for the services Tanner was proposing.

"Someone else is paying you." Liam didn't ask a question. He stated the obvious.

"I'm not denying that fact."

"And you aren't going to tell me who."

"No, sir. And you can trust me to be as discreet in my dealings with you."

"While you report back to whoever is paying you." He hadn't lived with his father his entire life without learning how the man's world worked.

"If, in the course of serving you, I find you involved in something illegal, I might report that."

"So you're an investigator, wanting private access to my life." That made sense. And pissed him off, too.

"I work under contract. The services I am offering you are those of a personal bodyguard. That is the work I will do for you."

"While you investigate me for someone else."

"I didn't say that. I said only that if I find that you're involved in illegal activity, I might report it." He pulled an envelope out of the inner pocket of his tweed jacket. "It's part of my standard contract, issued to every one of my clients, as you'll see here." He held the envelope out to Liam.

Standing in the cold, with numbing fingers, Liam took the time to look over the contract.

"I'd like to have an attorney look at this," he said.

"Gabrielle Miller, I assume."

Eyes narrowed, certain that he didn't want this man to get too far out of his sight, Liam nodded.

Tanner handed him a card. "I'll wait to hear from you," he said. He walked toward the building and disappeared around the corner. He didn't look back.

Liam did, though. He looked all around him as he traversed the short distance between his car and the private residents' entrance in the back of their building.

If Tanner's goal had been to scare him, he'd failed. Mostly. But he'd been put on notice. Made aware.

And he needed to talk to Gabi.

CHAPTER SEVEN

"THAT WAS GREAT."

Taking her eye from the path in front of them, Gabi turned to look at Liam. "Yeah, it was."

Marie, who wasn't fond of skating in temperatures so cold that her nose hairs froze, had opted to stay at the shop.

And she was busy—one of her nighttime part-timers had called in sick. If Liam hadn't needed to have this talk, Gabi would have stayed with her.

They'd skated ten miles at top speed—five out and five back—and were slowly coasting down the path as dusk started to fall. As cold as it was, they were the only two out that afternoon, but she was glad to have had the exercise.

To work off some of the weird tension that had been bottling up over Liam.

But she couldn't shake the guilt she felt about going off with him without Marie. It just wasn't something either of them ever did.

She'd seen Marie's look when she'd waved them off. She'd been smiling. But confused, too.

Gabi would make it right with her. As soon as they got home.

She'd tell Marie how Liam was paranoid and had needed to talk away from the building.

"I'm not going to put the two of you in danger." His breath came easy, even after ten miles.

"We aren't in any more danger today than a week ago," she told him through her scarf. "Your dad's a suspect in a white-collar crime. Not wanted by the Mafia."

In an expensive-looking black jacket over sweats and a black knit cap to match, Liam didn't seem to notice the cold. His cheeks were red, though.

His leather-gloved hand pulled her to a stop as they reached a lighted cement park area where different tracks converged. They faced each other toe to toe.

"I was approached today, Gabi," he said. The seriousness in his gaze scared her. Where was the fun-loving playboy she'd always known? "By a guy wanting to be my bodyguard."

The hissed intake of breath burned her lungs. The sensation dissipated quickly as they stood there, but the shock remained. She hadn't yet told him what she'd found out that afternoon. They'd opted to skate a bit first.

But now she said, "From the inquiries I made today, I can tell you that something doesn't add up. Everything points to your father. Everything."

Liam's chin tightened as he nodded. "So it is him. He's guilty." He spun away from her and then rolled back, scraping the cement with the force of his brake. "The man builds an empire out of nothing but hard work, acumen and integrity, and then throws it all away?" He shook his head.

And for a second there, he reminded her of the young college kid who'd just had his car keys stripped from him.

He started toward the parking lot and his car. Pushing off to catch up with him, Gabrielle said, "That's just it, Liam. It's too clear. Too clean. It doesn't make sense."

He slowed down and she almost ran into the back of him, having to grab his shoulders to steady herself. Even with gloves on her hands, she could feel his warmth.

Or thought she could. Which was crazy.

Even crazier, for a second there she'd wanted to lean up against him, lay her head on his back and just…feel him.

"It's like he's being set up," she said, quickly snatching her hands back before he noticed her weird reaction.

Liam hadn't moved. Nor responded to either her bumping into him or her words.

Glancing across several yards of parking lot, she looked to see what was holding his attention and started to shake. His pristine, shiny black BMW was covered with words written in a white substance, much like a bridal car after a wedding. Except the words definitely were not well-wishes.

Son of a thief.

Ill-gotten gains.

Better off dead.

There were at least six phrases. Repeated more than once.

"Liam? How could someone know we were here?" But it was obvious they'd been followed.

He didn't say a word. Just unlaced his skates, slipped out of them and pulled out his cell phone.

Looking around them, noting just one other car in the lot—a light-colored SUV that hadn't been there when they'd started out. Noting too that the little red car that *had* been there was gone, Gabi didn't see any immediate danger. Relief flooded her anyway as she heard Liam's words.

"I'd like to report a vandalized car…"

He'd called the police.

And she was glad.

HE'D FILED A REPORT. Waited with Gabrielle while a couple of officers checked the area and then, with an escort, driven the few short blocks to their building. When an officer offered to check the area, including their apartments, they'd both accepted. But had the cops look in on Marie first.

Liam had had them check the buildings for possible bugs and they'd reported back that all was clean.

It was a bit of overkill. Still, Liam was the son of a very rich man who'd just been arrested for stealing millions of dollars from innocent people. Gabi had given him one bit of news on that score—according to the arrest record, the Ponzi scheme had been discovered before damages outgrew Walter Connelly's net worth.

The old man could afford to pay back the debt. Which would not only help him in court, but should prevent much of the public backlash he might have received if he'd left investors destitute.

"I'm happy to represent you, Liam, but I need you to put me down as your attorney of record," Gabi said later that evening. The police had left with a promise to do all they could, but Liam knew paint on a car didn't deserve law enforcement resources when there were murders and robberies and weapons in schools.

He'd already called his insurance company.

He'd have a rental car, another BMW, in the morning and his own car back by Monday.

"I get access to a lot more information if I'm representing you," she continued. The three of them were sitting at a table in the corner of Marie's shop, having locked the doors and put up the closed sign as soon as the police left.

"Fine," he told her, then added, "But I mean it, you two, I'm out of here if it looks like this is going to get dangerous for either of you."

"What about that guy you said came by earlier today?" Marie asked. He'd told the police about Elliott Tanner, giving them the information from his card, with Marie and Gabrielle present. "Maybe you should hire him."

"Or maybe he's the one who's behind this," Gabi said. "You said he had an idea you might be in danger. Maybe he got someone to trash your car so you'd think you needed him."

He didn't think so. "He didn't seem like the type of guy to resort to something so...unprofessional." Or like an an out-and-out criminal. "People who run in my father's circles, those who have a criminal bent, tend to be a lot more obscure. They live in shades of gray. Whoever went after my car was pretty clear with his message."

"So call this Tanner guy," Marie said again.

He intended to. Just as soon as he heard back from the Denver police that the man had checked out. He'd pretty much intended to anyway, just to keep the guy close. "Could you check him out for me, too?" he asked Gabi. "You have access to background information."

"No more than the police do, but I'll double-check him for you. And ask if anyone has ever heard of him."

"I'm going to pay you for this," he said now.

"We'll work something out…"

"No." He looked at the two of them. "I'm tired of being given preferential treatment, having favors done for me, being coddled. I will not relent on this. I want to hire you, Gabi. Right now you two are the only people in the world I trust." He fixed his gaze on Gabi. "I'm going to be relying on you to give this as much priority as you'd give any other personal, paying client." Which he knew to be a lot.

Her look reminded him of the one she'd had in college when he'd confess his sins because he knew she'd give him the disdain he deserved. But he didn't feel like that college student now. He wasn't doing anything wrong.

To the contrary, for the first time in his life, Liam felt as though he was in control. Relying on himself to handle what he could on his own and paying for his own professionals to handle the rest.

"Fine." Gabriele's unsmiling expression was a

bit off. Almost as though he'd hurt her feelings. Which was inane. But the feeling remained. Along with a sense that he needed to tend to it somehow. Later.

He'd been about to excuse himself to his apartment. To delve into his own financial files—looking at specific accounts this time—from the list Gabrielle had just given him. The list that was taken straight from the statement of alleged charges the FBI had compiled against his father. His ringing phone forestalled him.

It was the Denver police.

Heart pounding, his friends watching him with concerned gazes, he took the call. And heard that Elliott Tanner was exactly who he said he was. A professional private protector. He had no record. He was licensed and bonded with fingerprints on file with a national database.

At Marie's urging, Liam called the man.

And before he went home that night had his own personal bodyguard.

In less than a month, his entire world had fallen apart, started over and changed again. He'd been disowned, thrown out of his home, found out his father wasn't at all the strong, honest man he'd thought him to be, and he'd suddenly developed some uncomfortable sensitivities where Gabrielle was concerned.

The last bothered him most of all.

"If you have trouble sleeping, give us a call," Marie said when the old elevator bumped to a stop on the girls' floor before continuing on up to Liam's.

He nodded. But knew he wouldn't. He didn't trust himself around Gabrielle any more that day.

And he didn't want either one of the girls figuring out how far he was off his rocker. At least not until he was back on again. And then they could all three laugh about the time he'd thought he was attracted to Gabrielle.

LIAM WAS ONLY being considered a potential witness at the moment, so Gabrielle's investigative rights were somewhat limited. She'd hoped that his father's attorney, George Costas, would offer her some professional courtesy, but hadn't counted on the fact. Not after the way the man had thrown Liam out of the office without even listening to what Liam had to say.

She'd left word with the FBI, requesting full access to evidence supporting the accusations against Walter Connelly, but figured her chances of being granted the right to study the evidence were less than winning the lottery.

And she didn't play the lottery.

She'd hoped to be able to talk to a few of the

people Liam had worked with at Connelly, but had been denied access to any of them.

She could follow his father's case. And had put herself down as Liam's attorney of record with the FBI, requiring them to contact her before approaching Liam.

She needed to do more.

Why she felt so pushed, she wasn't sure. She gave complete focus to all of her clients when she was working on their cases, but Liam was different. And not just because he was a friend. She'd barely slept for thinking about him. For... feeling his pain. In ways she'd never felt for him before.

Which was completely...off.

Even if Liam woke up one morning and suddenly decided he was attracted to her, too, when things went bad—and they would, considering Liam's inability to settle for one woman for more than six months at a time—their friendship would never be the same.

She wasn't willing to lose their family over some latent desire to know what his kiss felt like.

The next morning, on her mandated coffee break at the legal aid office—which she rarely took—Gabrielle took herself outside, cell phone in hand. Naturally paranoid, she was now a bit more so when it came to Liam.

Now that she knew his father had some shady associates, at the very least. And, worst case scenario, was a crook.

The first call she made was to Elliott Tanner. She wanted a list of his clients. Not that she expected him to give it to her. Still, she had to try.

Of course he refused to give it to her without a court order. And would fight doing so even then.

He knew darn well she'd never get that order. Her client wasn't even facing charges.

"If it's any consolation to you, you have my word that I'm going to take good care of him," the other man said, his deep voice sounding more trustworthy than intimidating.

Gabrielle wanted to believe him.

But she took his words with a huge grain of salt. If the man was out to spy on Liam, he certainly wasn't going to come right out and say so. Which meant that Gabrielle and Marie were going to have to be extra diligent about watching his back.

The second call she made was to Walter Connelly. Turning her back to the wall of her building, Gabrielle watched the people walking past. A normal view. On a normal day.

There was no reason for the butterflies attacking her stomach.

She didn't expect to be put through when

she identified herself to Mr. Connelly's secretary. The FBI had finished their investigation as promised, restoring his full access to his computers, and while all accounts relating to the Grayson deal were frozen, Connelly Investments had eggs in many baskets. Walter would be hard at work protecting those eggs.

"Ms. Miller, this is a surprise." Walter Connelly's voice boomed over the line. You'd never know the man was facing a large financial loss. Not to mention possibly twenty years to life in jail.

"Your son has hired me to represent him…"

"The fool's going to sue me? Surely you're smart enough to advise him to drop this ludicrous notion."

"I can't speak to you of Liam's plans, sir, but I can assure you I'm not calling to talk about terms of a lawsuit."

"So why are you calling?"

"To ask you about the alleged charges against you."

"Liam hired you to look into my affairs?"

"The FBI questioned him. He's a natural suspect. I'd be better able to represent his best interests if I had a clue what was really going on."

"As soon as I have one, I'll let you know."

Why she'd thought the man might cooperate with her, she didn't know. If she thought he'd do so for the sake of his son, she was the foolhardy one. He'd written Liam out of his will for buying an apartment building. And Walter Connelly had never made a secret of his feelings where Gabrielle and Marie were concerned. They were common girls. Unconnected. Not good enough for Liam Connelly.

Gabrielle he'd seemed to hate most. Where Marie might get a gruff hello on occasion, he'd looked right through Gabrielle. At least Marie came from a decent, upper-middle-class family. Gabrielle had grown up on food stamps.

She was freezing and needed to go back inside.

"Do you have my number?" she pushed him.

"I do. And I mean what I say," he added. "You should know that about me by now. I do not yet know what's going on, but I intend to. Very soon."

"You didn't do it." Liam had made it clear the night before that he had no doubt to his father's guilt.

"I did not."

"For the record, I didn't think you had," she said. "Not after I read the reports."

"Can I ask why not?"

"Because it's too clean. Everything points to you. If you'd done this, you'd have things pointing in a million different directions."

"And from what knowledge base do you draw that conclusion?"

"I did my homework. The smart way to run a Ponzi scheme is to create a web of trails, intermixing legitimate ones with the phony ones that are then nearly impossible to trace. When it comes to business, you are a smart man."

Her implication—that he wasn't smart in another area—lay clearly between them.

She hadn't called to insult him. But the way this man treated Liam…had always treated him… Gabrielle had to bite her tongue.

"You'll pardon me if I find no merit in your opinions?"

"Yes, sir. Thank you for your time."

She hung up before he could dismiss her as easily as he'd dismissed his son.

Just after three that afternoon, she received a call from Agent Gwen Menard, who told her that she had been granted limited access to their files. Things that they were looking at for any potential connection to Liam. She could pick up copies of the information being made available to her by five o'clock that afternoon.

She was there at four forty-five.

And home, sharing copies with Liam, by five.

He greeted her at his door with a long, grateful look, eye to eye.

She felt it heart to heart. And brushed past him to open her briefcase.

She was there on business. Marie was downstairs. And when Gabrielle had told her she was going straight up to Liam rather than waiting just a few more minutes until Marie could get free and they could bring dinner up to him, Marie had given her a strange stare.

She could be imagining it. But she knew she wasn't. Marie knew exactly what Gabrielle knew about Liam. They'd talked many times about his inability to settle for one woman for long. About how sorry they felt for the women who inevitably fell for him.

They both knew what would happen if either of them were ever stupid enough to fall for him themselves.

And Gabrielle was not going to do anything that would ultimately destroy their family.

CHAPTER EIGHT

LIAM SPENT EVERY minute of the weekend working. Like his father had done when Liam was growing up, he holed himself up in his home office—the newly converted kitchen in his second apartment—and came out only to eat. Sleep. And shower once.

Unlike his father, he didn't have anyone at home needing his time. Anyone he was ignoring.

He spent hours going over Connelly accounts. And then looking at account numbers in correlation with the somewhat complicated trail of deposits and payables the FBI had presented as evidence that his dad was a crook. There were receivables that didn't make sense to him, even understanding his father's business as well as he did. Deposits made into accounts that shouldn't exist, as far as Liam knew.

Certainly there was information that had never been made available to him as a top-floor executive. What the others had known, and kept from him, he had no way of knowing. Not until

Gabi questioned them—if she could figure out a way to get legal access to them, gaining testimony that would be admissible in court if the occasion arose.

Numbers started blurring. His eyes grew weary of following supposed income that showed up as deposits and then disappeared into accounts that weren't used for official Connelly Investments business. He switched gears.

And focused on the work of his life.

These were the hours that slid into oblivion as far as Liam was concerned. He was reading everything he could find on the Douglas case— the teenager who was suing his parents for the right to go off his antidepressants. While there was case history of children suing their parents, there was no case that he could find similar to this one.

He wasn't privy to the closed records, of course. To doctor testimony regarding the boy's mental or physical health. His job would be only to report on the case as it unfolded, and only then on the parts of it that were open to the public.

But as he read, questions formed in his mind. The opening of his article began to present itself.

There'd been a case in Massachusetts not all that long ago. A Boston hospital had filed medical abuse charges against a couple, accusing them of not getting their daughter the medical attention she needed. The parents claimed that they were following the direction from the child's original doctor, who worked for another, equally well-respected hospital. The doctors had differing diagnoses. And the child had spent more than a year in state custody, with her parents only being allowed to see her on supervised visits while the case was in court. In the end, the parents had won.

But not before a nation had become aware of how easily a parent could be robbed of the right to raise his or her own child. For unfair and unproven cause.

Liam's story was the opposite of the Boston case—here, the parents were being taken to court in an attempt to take away their right to seek the medical attention they thought pertinent to their son's health.

Which brought him to yet another case. One of the most well-known, tragic cases in recent American history. A school shooter. One whose mother had allegedly not followed a doctor's recommendation to medicate her son. With horrendous results.

Determining the right or wrong in any of these cases wasn't Liam's job. But knowing the ramifications of both sides was paramount for thorough but impartial reporting.

Finally, after years of slowly building a reputation with human interest travel pieces, he had a chance to write something substantial. For an editor who'd supported him for years and was finally breaking into the big time herself.

Eventually he had to get back to Connelly Investments. Gabi had called a couple of times since her Friday visit to drop off files before Marie brought up dinner and the two of them left together. The first time she'd called had been to ask him to tell her everything he knew about the Grayson project. And then another time to ask about some of the companies that were in Connelly holdings. The FBI had identified a shell company among those holdings. That was already clear. What Gabrielle was looking for, he didn't know. But he wanted her to be free to follow her suppositions and theories wherever they took her.

As he was following his…

The ringing of his cell phone interrupted his concentration sometime after noon on Sunday.

"Yeah?" He picked up without looking at the caller ID.

"I think I stumbled on a smurfing pattern." Gabrielle didn't bother with a greeting, either. He recognized her voice immediately, of course.

What he didn't recognize was the way it brought a flutter of life to his body.

Smurfing. She'd said *smurfing*—a practice of deliberately making deposits smaller than ten thousand dollars, which was the amount banks were required by law to report to the government.

Liam assumed if Gabrielle could find those transactions, the FBI already knew about them. But he asked, "What makes them stand out to you?"

"They don't point to your father. They are the only piece of evidence I've seen so far that doesn't lead clearly to him."

"Meaning what?"

"I'm not sure yet. I just wondered what you knew about them." She named companies. Investors. Money paid into Connelly Investments for services rendered. And he began to see what had caught her attention.

"These are all over the board," he said, rubbing his hand through his hair and realizing he hadn't showered. "Money comes into a company in various ways, but when you're looking at a Ponzi scheme, you're usually only looking at investment income."

"Right."

"Someone really is using Connelly Investments to launder money."

"It looks that way to me."

Thanking Gabi, Liam went back to work with

more energy, looking at the facts and figures a little differently, open to seeing a new angle. He paid particular attention to any monies being moved, deposited, billed, paid out, loaned, written off and even claimed on expense reports in dollar amounts just less than ten thousand.

His eyes were hurting when he realized it had grown dark outside and he hadn't eaten since the cereal he'd had that morning. Looking at the pages of notes he'd compiled, the information collated in various ways, he sat back, discouraged. For all that he'd come up with, he'd wasted an entire afternoon.

And proven nothing. The FBI's evidence was legitimate. Money had come into Connelly Investments, been put into a series of investments in a supposed development community—Grayson Communities, phase two. A bit of the money had actually gone to the purchase of a piece of land—an impossible-to-develop piece of swamp. The rest had been dispersed through what had turned out to be fake records. Invoicing. Balance sheets. All fraudulent.

Staring at the papers, he sat forward. He'd collected a series of deposit authorizations that held his father's signature. They all pertained to deposits made into one particular offshore account. He found no record of any bills being paid out of that account.

So was the money still sitting there?

The FBI suspected there were more offshore accounts. Pieces of evidence that were still being sought. It was believed that information had been deleted from Connelly databases before the FBI's warrant could be served.

A computer forensic team was working on copies of confiscated hard drives, attempting to get the information back.

Picking up his cell while he studied those deposits, all just under ten thousand dollars and made at regular intervals, he pushed speed dial number two—Marie was three—and waited for Gabrielle to answer.

"Can we get access to statements from this offshore account?"

"I've already put in a request," Gabrielle told him. And Liam was glad he'd hired her. He also wished he could see her. Not her and Marie. Just her.

And that's when he knew for certain that something was really, really wrong.

"HE NEEDS TO EAT."

Gabrielle looked up from her papers when her roommate spoke. She'd spread them out all over the living room floor in her attempt to memorize as many of the intricate threads of investments and expenditures as she could.

"Who does?" She knew. She just didn't want to think about him up there all alone. Dealing with all of this by himself. That's why she was giving all of her time to helping sort things out.

Downstairs. Where she could focus on the business at hand.

"Liam, who else?" Marie's tone of voice had a bit of an edge to it. As if she was hurt.

"How do you know he hasn't already?" Gabrielle pretended not to notice.

"You know how Liam gets when he's riled up and focused."

Yeah. He'd gone almost forty-eight hours without a proper meal during finals. More than once.

And when he was on a road trip—at least on the two she and Marie had taken with him to Florida—he'd have driven straight through without stopping for anything but gas if she and Marie hadn't ganged up on him.

He was their friend. They had always taken care of him. "What time is it?" she asked. Marie was still wearing her coffeehouse apron. It couldn't be that late.

"Almost seven."

Oh. "And you're just coming upstairs?"

"I didn't want to disturb you," Marie said, her smile tinged with a bit of sadness. "You're a lot like him, you know." Maybe. Probably.

"I have to work hard right now. I just invested

most of my savings in this building." Not to mention the call she'd had from her brother earlier that day, asking for a couple hundred dollars to get his car fixed. Again.

"You're going to work like a fiend to help him."

"Like I'd do for any client."

"If you say so."

"It's true."

"What about your rule to quit by noon when you work on Sundays?" Marie sounded peevish. And Gabrielle knew what that meant. Her friend was bothered and wasn't going to let it go.

Because she couldn't. When Marie's heart hurt, she listened to it.

And she was right. Gabrielle did have her Sunday rule. Everyone needed a time to refresh in order to be their most productive.

"I've just taken on a rather large case, and I have very little time to get up to speed."

"Liam isn't even a suspect. Technically there is no case."

Feeling tension build, Gabrielle figured maybe Marie was right. Maybe she'd worked too long for a Sunday.

"What are you getting at?"

"I don't know. It's just, you've been…different. With Liam."

"I have not! I'm helping him. Just like I'd help

you." She was lying to her best friend. She hated
how that made her feel. "He's our friend." She
continued on her collision course, an edge to
her that didn't pop up often with Marie. "You'd
do the same."

"I'd be there for him." Tendrils of Marie's
blond hair had escaped from her ponytail after a
full day of working over steaming pots. "But…
you've gone off alone with him, twice now, and
in twelve years you've never done that before.
Plus I've seen you look at him. It's like…how a
woman looks at a man. And your voice changes
when you talk to him these past few days."

"I do not have a thing for Liam!" The idea
was absolutely preposterous. "You're imagining all of this."

"You've never lied to me before." The disappointment in Marie's voice was something she
never wanted to hear again. Ever.

Jumping up, Gabrielle walked right across
the top of her piles of papers, regardless of any
mess she might make, and helped herself to a
diet cola from the refrigerator. Only then did
she face her friend.

"I am not falling for him," she said. "I'm not
going to risk us—the three of us—ever. And
falling for Liam would do that. Big-time."

"You know I love him, too," Marie said. "I'd
give my life for him. He's a great man. But

we both know how he is with women. He's monogamous, always faithful, but he moves on. Even with Jenna. He stuck with her longer than most, but…"

"I know."

"But?"

"But nothing." In the years they'd all been friends, Marie had never even intimated that she thought there was anything other than friendship between Liam and either one of them. "It's just…"

Marie's face fell, her gaze filled with worry. "It's happening, isn't it?"

"No." She wasn't going to let it happen. "I just… He's changing," she said. "Haven't you noticed?"

"He's finally standing up to his old man, if that's what you mean."

"And carving a life for himself. By his own sweat and blood."

"And the help of his trust. None of which has anything to do with what we're talking about. You're attracted to him, aren't you?"

Gabrielle tried to deny the charge. But this was Marie. And she'd just told herself she wasn't going to lie again. "I don't know. Maybe. But it will pass."

Shaking her head, Marie looked as if she

might cry. "I sure hope so. He'll break your heart, Gabi. And then where will we be?"

The threesome. Their family.

"I know."

"Does he know? Has he said anything to you?"

"No! Of course he doesn't know. And even if he did, Liam wouldn't ever do anything about it. He's our protector. The older brother neither of us had."

"Except he's our same age."

"You know what I mean. And no. He has no idea that…well, anyway. It doesn't matter. It's going to go away as quickly as it came. Don't worry. Nothing's going to change as far as the three of us are concerned."

Marie studied her a minute more and then said, "So how about we make a grilled chicken salad and take it upstairs?"

She'd never have suggested it herself. Not after the conversation they'd just had. But with Marie at the helm—Marie, who always had her back and didn't want anything between her and Liam any more than Gabrielle did—she didn't mind chopping veggies and making her honey mustard dressing. And she was perfectly happy to take the flight of stairs up to his apartment to spend an hour sharing a single glass of wine and a salad with Liam Connelly. Just as friends.

And with Marie at the helm.

BASED ON THE number of times Marie had asked him how he was really doing, she wanted him to spill his guts. Liam couldn't blame her. He'd been doing so since the night they'd all met. Had established a pattern—one upon which their friendship was based. And she knew he had more to spill now than ever before.

In a weird kind of way, he owed her that.

But as he sat in his apartment Sunday evening, enjoying the fresh salad and bread they'd brought, Liam couldn't find words to convey what was going on inside of him.

Truth was, he didn't want to find the words.

He wasn't a kid anymore. Didn't need to spill his guts.

He was glad Marie was there. That both of his friends were there. Was very glad for their company. The three of them. Together. Just like always.

Glad that he didn't have to spend time alone with Gabrielle while he was so tired.

What he needed was a few hours supine in his new master suite. Which, while not as roomy as any he'd had before, had turned out quite nicely after he'd had three rooms—two beds and a bath—joined as one.

"What do you make of that one offshore account?" he asked Gabrielle, as they sat at his solid cherry dining room table and listened to pipes groaning as they ate. "Why wasn't it deleted with the rest of them?" Between the two of them, they'd brought Marie up-to-date regarding the case.

"According to Gwen Menard, the FBI's theory is that they got there with their warrant before whoever was doing the erasing had a chance to finish, so that one account was still there for the FBI to find."

Made sense. But the girls hadn't brought food up for a business meeting. "You and Gwen are getting pretty tight, huh?" he asked in his attempt to not talk business.

"She's willing to share information with me as long as I do the same with her."

"But you can't, really, can you? If you were to find something that would incriminate me, you can't pass it on to her."

"Correct, but I can share anything else we find. With your permission, of course. I took for granted I had your permission, as it was the only way to get what we needed."

"I gave you carte blanche. You know that."

Marie tapped her knife on the table. "Hello! Did you two forget we're all friends here? What's with all this 'correct' and 'your permission, of course'? Since when do we talk like that?"

"Sorry," they both said at once. Liam looked

at Gabi. Her head was bent. Which was just as well. For a second there he'd forgotten that Marie was at the table. An unforgivably self-ish act on his part. She was as much his friend as Gabrielle was. The only good meal he'd had that weekend, the one they were sharing, had been Marie's idea.

A particularly loud thump, squeal, hiss and bump came from a pipe beneath them, distract-ing him from his guilt. They spent the next cou-ple of minutes talking about the building. Men had been working on the elevator all week. It was still slow. Still jerked to a halt on some floors. But it was safe and reliable. The heating system was next on the list.

Liam agreed to start calling around for quotes. And his phone rang.

He recognized the number, a new one on his caller ID, and glanced at Gabrielle again as he answered. "Tanner, what's up?"

He'd wanted to ignore the call. Not a pru-dent or responsible thing to do under the cir-cumstances.

"You haven't left your building all weekend."

"I know."

"I just want to be clear that you don't have to fear going out."

What kind of a wimp did this guy think he was? He'd grown up rich. Not soft.

"I've been working all weekend," he said now, very aware of the two women at his table who'd stopped eating and were unabashedly listening to every word he said. "I work from home."

"Understood. I'd like to go over your schedule for the coming week so I can be as prepared as possible and thus be more likely to guarantee no bumps in your road." The man's voice was deep, but not the least bit thug-like.

"I'm due in court at eight o'clock tomorrow morning." He named the courtroom in the downtown courthouse where a seventeen-year-old boy would be fighting for his right to go off his medication. "My schedule from there depends upon what happens in court. I'm following the story wherever it takes me."

"I'll be by to get you at seven thirty."

"Wait. What? I don't need you take me to court."

Gabrielle's gaze sharpened.

"So what do you suggest I do to earn my fee?"

"I'm not paying you much of a fee."

"The point is I've agreed to keep you safe. You've already been vandalized once. It could be a one-time occurrence. It could also be the beginning of escalating events. The guy wrote *better off dead* on your car. As the FBI contacts investors who are victims of the swindling, and your father's arrest makes the news, you, as his son—and as far as the world knows, his heir—could be a target. These first few days are critical."

"You just told me I didn't have to fear going out."

"You don't. Not as long as I'm with you."

Liam wasn't going to buy into the panic. The guy had to be working for someone else. He didn't just appear out of the blue, offering his services to Liam under his own auspices, not at the low price he'd quoted. He'd say whatever he had to say to get Liam's compliance. "My father was arrested on Wednesday. The car was defaced Thursday. Nothing has happened since."

"You haven't been out, other than to go to the car dealership."

"You've been watching me?"

"It's what you're paying me for. And by the way, whoever left those messages on your car had to have been watching you, too. What's to say they haven't been doing so all weekend? Maybe the reason nothing further has happened is because you haven't been out of your home."

"You're trying to tell me I'm not going anywhere without you for the foreseeable future?" Two sets of eyes, one big and brown, the other silvery-blue, glistened with concern.

"I'm letting you know where you stand, from a personal security viewpoint."

His defenses dropped a notch. "I appreciate that." A smart man understood that he couldn't do all things all the time. And Tanner was of more use to him than not. "I would just as soon drive myself to and from court. I don't want to give people any ideas that I need a bodyguard. I do not intend to start looking guilty. But if you happen to follow me when I'm out, then fine."

Marie took a bite of salad. Gabrielle nodded. And Liam was satisfied.

CHAPTER NINE

MARIE'S CELL RANG just minutes after Liam hung up. Edith Lawson, the seventy-year-old widow in 503, needed someone to come get Gordon Brinley, her ninety-year-old neighbor, out of her bathroom again. Gordon was a bit senile, but everyone watched out for him. Grace stopped in to give him his medications. Leon made sure he bathed regularly. Elise was in charge of arranging meals for those who couldn't cook. Most of the residents had known each other all of their lives.

But at that moment, Gordon Brinley was of the opinion that Edith's bathroom was his own.

"Remind Edith that if she'd keep her door locked, Gordon couldn't wander in," Gabrielle told Liam as he headed up.

"If she keeps her door locked, there's no telling where he'll pee," Marie blurted.

"If she keeps her door locked, he might wander to the stairwell and get hurt," Liam added as he headed out the door.

"You worried?" Marie asked, frowning as she

looked between Gabrielle and the door that had just closed behind Liam.

"Of course I'm worried. There are clear possible dangers facing him." They weren't talking about Gordon. Or Edith.

"Edith asked me if the Walter Connelly who was just arrested is any relation to Liam."

They hadn't kept Liam's identity from the residents. They'd just never exposed it, either. Because when Liam came around them, he was just Liam. They'd always been his escape from the high-powered, wealthy existence he'd been born to.

"I heard you tell Edith you'd talk about it later. Was that what you were referring to?" Gabrielle had only eaten half of her salad, but she'd lost her appetite.

"Yeah. Liam should be the one who decides what he wants everyone to know, and we couldn't very well have a discussion about it with Gordon upstairs relieving himself."

The old man had been out in the hallway without his pants on once. It could happen again. If he ever became a danger to himself or others, they'd call the authorities, but until then, everyone watched out for him so he could stay in the home he'd shared with his now-deceased wife for sixty years. The home where he'd raised his only son, a soldier who'd been killed in Iraq.

Marie was pushing the remainder of her food around in her bowl. Liam's salad sat at his place at the table, the fork still in the bowl. And there the two of them sat. As though the meal couldn't go on without him.

Because their lives couldn't go on without him?

The thought bothered her. Brought a sharp pain of tension to her stomach. They couldn't count on Liam to be there forever. He was destined for greatness. And all Gabrielle had ever wanted was enough money to sleep at night without running bills and income through her head. Enough money so she didn't have to worry, and not so much that she had to worry.

The life Liam led—where nothing was ever completely private, where someone always wanted something from him, where he never knew whom he could trust or who was after his money, where when things went wrong the whole world had an opinion about it—wasn't for her.

Not that he'd ever offered. Or would offer. Not that she'd want him to.

Because even if his father ended up destitute and Liam really had lost his entire inheritance, he still had close to a million dollars in his trust. And if he lost that, he'd make more. Liam Connelly was one of those men who was going places. One of those chosen few who would be successful at whatever they tried to do.

He was a very special man.

She was glad to have his friendship.

Not because of the money. But because of him. He was a part of their lives. And she wasn't going to get all weird and make it uncomfortable for him to continue to be with them. Their little family was vital to all three of them.

Far more important than any curiosity about how well he kissed.

LIAM RELUCTANTLY AGREED with Gabrielle and Marie. The residents of Threefold's newly acquired apartment building should know the truth about his identity.

Gabrielle wanted them to know because knowledge helped prevent misconception that could turn to rumor and then dangerously wrong statements, should any of them be interviewed by the FBI.

Marie thought they should know because they were family, and family watched out for each other. She figured with Grace and Edith and the others home all day, watching everything that went on, someone up to no good would have a more difficult time creating havoc for Liam.

Liam figured they were both right.

All three of them concurred that it would be best if Marie and Gabrielle called a gathering of the residents and told them the basics of what was going in Liam's life. They thought it best that he not be present so as to forestall the questions that would likely bombard him if he was accessible to them. The women were going to let everyone know that Liam was understandably stressed, so it would be very much appreciated if everyone respected his need for silence at this time.

He wasn't so sure the few younger residents they had would respect that stance. But he was fairly certain the older ones would. And since all but two of the rented apartments were currently rented to that older population, he wasn't all that concerned.

He didn't see Elliott Tanner behind him on his way to court on Monday. Nor did he see him in the courtroom. He thought he caught a glimpse of him in the foyer on the second floor of the courthouse as he came out of the courtroom just before noon, but couldn't be sure.

Truth be told, he didn't spare a lot of thought for the guy. The story unfolding before his eyes was consuming him. He had a seventeen-year-old boy who wanted to know himself, to find out who he was and what he was capable of accomplishing without being dumbed down, as he put it, by the antidepressants and anti-ADD medications he'd been on since elementary school.

His parents, who clearly loved him and were hurting for him, understood from his medical team that to take him off the medication could very likely make him a danger not only to himself, but to others.

He argued that they couldn't know for sure what he'd do as he wasn't off the medication long enough to find out. He wanted to drive. To date. But how could he ask a girl to love a freak like him? Someone who might flip out if he missed a pill?

His parents didn't see him as a freak. They saw a gifted and capable young man who had some chemical flaws in his makeup. Flaws that could be completely managed by the medications he was taking.

Both sides had compelling arguments.

The expert witnesses who were going to be testifying were believed to side 100 percent with the parents. The boy's legal team, who were responsible for Liam and other reporters in the courtroom, were counting on the sway of public opinion to make a difference.

Liam wasn't sure it wasn't some kind of bullying tactic. He also wasn't sure it was.

He was going to be in court for the rest of the week.

He had a missed call from Gabi. He'd turned his phone off in the courtroom. But he returned her call as soon as he was out.

"Did you get my message?" she asked, picking up after the first ring.

"No, I just called you back. We're on lunch break. Court is due to resume at one and go until three."

"The case is just being heard by a judge, right? No jury?"

"Right." But she hadn't called him about his story.

"I got the bank statement you asked for." There was an odd note in her voice. Excitement. High energy. And a bit of doom, too.

"And?" he asked, dread filtering over him like a dark brown cloud, encasing him in a haze through which he couldn't see clearly. If his father was guilty of fraud, then so be it. Liam couldn't change the truth.

"It's a private account, Liam. As in personal. There's no tie to the Grayson monies. And no sign that the monies being deposited into it are being filtered back out again in little less-than-ten-thousand-dollar increments like we saw in the other accounts. They're deposited that way. But they're being spent by debit card, in amounts that appear to be normal living expenses. Eating out. Groceries. Shopping. They range from ten dollars to a few hundred."

"What are you telling me? That my father isn't guilty of fraud?"

"I'm telling you I don't think this particular account has anything to do with the rest of it. You know as well as I do that there's ample proof of fraud in Connelly Investments. You saw the same reports I did. You've even verified some of them when the FBI hadn't yet been able to."

Gabi had pointed that fact out to him the night before, after he'd come back from rescuing Gordon. Or Edith, depending on how you looked at it. After they'd finished dinner, before the two had left together, he'd given Gabi permission to tell Gwen everything he'd told her.

"But maybe he's not guilty of money laundering," Liam said now, the courthouse halls a bit busy with the various courts adjourning for lunch. What was with him? Still trying to believe in the old man...

"It's a personal account, Liam. Being used by someone in Florida. Do you know anyone in Florida who your father might be sending money to?"

"Of course not."

"No long-lost aunt or uncle? Or even a grand-parent? Someone from Walter's past he might not want you to know about?"

"My father grew up in the foster system. He has no family." Confused, coming down from a professional high to land back in the mud of his life, Liam walked to a deserted alcove at the end of the hall and stared out into the street. His phone in one hand and his briefcase in the other, he stood there in his silk-lined trench coat over one of his newer hand-tailored suits, feeling at a total loss. "Is there a name associated with the account?" he asked, which should have been an obvious first question.

"No. It's in the name of a trust."

"But someone's drawing money from it with a debit card."

"It looks that way."

"Wouldn't there be a name associated with the card?" There didn't have to be. Necessarily.

"It's in the name of a corporation."

"Let me guess. One that doesn't exist."

"One that no one has been able to find as of yet."

"But you're going to keep looking?"

"Gwen and her team are at it as we speak. I'll join back in when I'm through with my afternoon appointments."

He nodded. Feeling stupidly relieved. Gabi had his back.

And because she was there for him, he could go back to work. He'd been gifted a reprieve of a few hours. He'd worry about his father—about his life—later.

GABRIELLE WAS ALONE in the apartment, pacing, at five o'clock that night.

Liam had said he was going to be out of court at three. She'd expected him to come straight home. She'd been there waiting for him. And he hadn't shown up.

She'd started to worry. Then to think he'd decided to have a night on the town to get away from his troubles, or maybe to grab a beer with someone he'd met in court… She just hoped Tanner was with him.

In case he'd slipped his bodyguard, she'd started to worry again that something had happened to him. So she'd called. Just to make sure he was okay. And he hadn't picked up.

Because he was with a woman?

He didn't need her getting all female on him. He was a man with a full life of his own. He didn't answer to her.

Nor should he.

So she'd hung up without leaving a message. And paced.

Tanner had been pretty insistent that he

wouldn't leave Liam alone. Which would mean that it wasn't likely he was in danger.

She had to face facts. He was with a woman. She just knew it. Beautiful women had always fallen at Liam's feet. All of them drop-dead model gorgeous. A lot of them with enough money to make up for any of his father's losses. It was no wonder he'd never been able to settle for just one.

It had always been that way, from the time they'd first met. There was no reason for her to feel…put out. She was neither rich nor gorgeous. Never had been. Never even particularly wanted to be. And she'd never, ever wanted to be one of his women.

They came. And they went.

Gabrielle was with him to stay. She wanted that far more than she wanted to know what his kiss tasted like.

She jumped when her phone finally rang, just before six. It was him. She was shaking as she pushed the button to answer.

"Sorry, I just got out of court. There was one hell of a scene and things ran over…"

She wanted to hear about it. As soon as she quit acting like a ninny and was back in her right mind.

"Gabi? You there?"

"Yes, of course."

"So what did you find out? I assume that's why you called."

No, she'd been home, waiting to break the news in person. She'd called because she'd been consumed with visions of… "Call me when you get home and I'll come up."

"You found out something."

"Just let me know when you're home."

"Gabi, don't do this to me. If you know something, just tell me."

She couldn't. Not over the phone. Not while he was working. Because she was not only his attorney, she was also his friend.

"Seriously, Liam. I'm…working on something else right now, but I'm home. Call me when you get here and I'll bring you the stuff I got today so you can go over it yourself."

She held her breath. She hadn't lied to him. She just hadn't told him that his life was about to change forever.

Again.

That had to be why she'd been so emotional over him the past couple of hours. Because she knew his heart was going to split at the seams and she wished she could hold it together for him.

"Will do," he said, sounding so much like his old chipper self that she almost reconsidered meeting him so he could have a night as his old self. Her news would be the same in the morning.

Except that he'd be back in court then. And she had a full day of hearings ahead of her on Tuesday.

"I feel like Chinese," he said, and she could tell by his breathing that he was taking the stairs out of the courthouse rather than the elevator.

A dumb thing to do when one could be being followed.

If Tanner was a good guy, he'd be in that stairwell, too…

"I planned to stop on the way home. You and Marie want some?"

"Marie has a date tonight," she told him. "Burton."

A safe, completely boring guy who liked the theater as much as she did. Someone with whom she'd never fall in love. Or need to trust with her heart. Which, sadly, fit Marie, who trusted no man but Liam, and not even him when it came to women.

"How about you? You feel like Chinese?"

She didn't feel like food at all. Or being alone with him, either. Especially not tonight. "Sure. The usual."

She'd said the words before. More times than she could count. Tonight they sounded intimate. Because tonight Marie wasn't included. And when she found out that Gabrielle had had dinner alone with Liam, in his apartment, her fears would grow again.

But aside from her bizarre reactions to Liam's manhood lately, there'd been another major change in Gabrielle's relationship with Liam. She was his legal counsel. And tonight she had news that she had to tell him without Marie present due to attorney-client privilege.

He told her he'd be home in twenty and hung up. While Gabrielle stood at the window, worried by her earlier jealousy at the thought of him being out with someone else.

This had to stop.

CHAPTER TEN

"THE GATE OUT in front of your father's house was splattered with eggs this morning," Gabrielle told him as soon as he opened his door to her that evening. He'd just set the table with plates and silverware. The cartons of Chinese weren't even opened yet.

"I'm assuming he called the police." He'd shed his suit coat, and now loosened his tie and undid the top button of his shirt.

Setting her briefcase on the chair that Marie had used the night before, she started dishing up their dinner. "He's hired a security firm to watch the place twenty-four-seven and a member of that firm called it in."

"He's got security cameras. It shouldn't take them long to find the culprit." Liam came from the kitchen with iced tea.

"They've already got the guy."

"Any chance he confessed to spray painting my car? I got it back today, by the way, had it delivered to the courthouse, and it looks good as new." He waited for her to sit and then joined her.

"No, he says he didn't spray paint your car. His beef is clearly with your father. He's twelve and lives down the street and says that his dad gave your dad a lot of money and now they have to move. And I'm glad you got your car back."

She was eating only little nibbles from the end of her fork. She'd said she had stuff to bring him. He assumed that whatever it was was in the briefcase. And based on her seeming inability to look him in the eye, it wasn't good.

He didn't call her on it, though. Dinner was good. Eating it alone with her was…nice. Just having her there made the day better. He'd feel guilty for being glad that Marie wasn't with them when he allowed himself to think at all. Right then, he didn't want to spoil the moment.

GABI WASN'T SURE how to tell him. After dinner, for sure. No reason to spoil his appetite as well as her own. And then, before the table was even cleared, Marie called.

Sam, one of her full-time employees, had called her just as she and Burton had been sitting down to a preshow dinner.

Sometime in the past hour, someone had left an envelope for Liam on the counter at the coffee shop. Sam had found it in the far corner, with a napkin holder half on top of it. Marie was on her way back to the shop.

Liam called the police, who told him not to open the envelope or even touch it again until they arrived. As he and Gabrielle waited for the elevator, he dialed Elliott Tanner. And by the time the two of them were in the shop, Tanner was there. He asked the remaining two customers to leave and locked the front door. Gabi was getting ready to send Sam home when Marie arrived and by then the police were inside the shop. They spoke with Sam first, and then he left. Marie spoke with Tanner while Gabrielle and Liam talked with the police, a different pair than the ones who'd answered the spray-painted-car call. And then everyone spoke in one group. The officers didn't think there was anything dangerous about opening the envelope, but in light of recent events, suggested that they take it with them and have it opened in the lab. Liam readily agreed.

A report was made. Liam signed it. And they were gone. Again.

"Elliott didn't get here until Liam did tonight, but he said he's been outside since Liam got home and didn't see anything suspicious," Marie told Liam and Gabi.

Elliott. Gabrielle noticed her friend's reference to the bodyguard—who was still Tanner to the rest of them. Marie, who'd had bad luck with the men in her life—starting with a deceitful, unfaithful father—had a tendency to size them up before she felt entirely comfortable.

"The shop was open," Tanner said, looking like a businessman in black pants and a dress shirt, as he stood behind Marie. "Customers came and went."

"Sam said he didn't notice the letter until he was wiping up after a rush."

"The police didn't seem all that concerned," Liam piped up, his voice light. "And it's not like we're looking at death by letter here."

"I'll feel better when we know what it says," Tanner said. But he didn't sound all that alarmed, either. Liam suggested that the other man go home. Most particularly if he was going to insist on hanging out at the courthouse again the next day.

Gabrielle had to give the bodyguard credit. He appeared to be taking his job of protecting Liam seriously. For whatever reason.

He might be looking for dirt on him. She was confident he wasn't going to find any. And if he kept Liam safe in the meantime…just in case there was someone out there looking to harm him…

"The police said they'll be doing extra patrols tonight," Liam reminded the other man. "And there's been no indication that I'm in any physical danger."

He was right on both counts. Gabrielle was the one who was afraid. For him. Beyond what was called for.

But then, she wasn't just worried about his physical safety. There were a lot of ways to hurt a man. She seemed to be feeling any pain that might hit Liam, and there was a hit he didn't yet know about.

It took another five minutes of rehashing, but the bodyguard finally left. Burton, who'd apparently been waiting outside and had seen the man leave, popped in to tell Marie that they still had time to make it to the showing of *Phantom of the Opera* that they'd paid an exorbitant amount of money to see.

With a long, concerned look at Liam and Gabrielle, she allowed herself to be led out. There was no viable reason for her not to go.

Gabrielle knew her friend didn't want to leave her alone with Liam. Marie had her back. And she needed her to. But they couldn't very well explain that to Burton. Most particularly not in front of Liam.

Liam was going to go back upstairs. It was the natural thing to do. He'd expect her to follow. Their business had been interrupted.

She didn't trust herself to be up there alone with him. Until she knew that whatever was in that envelope addressed to Liam was not unfriendly, she had to assume that it was. That danger might be escalating against him.

And she was falling for him. Tensions were high. Something could happen to him.

Before she ever knew what it would feel like to be held by him.

"Can we sit for a minute?" Her tension must have shown on her face as she blurted the words.

One glance at Liam's expression told her that.

Until the past few weeks he'd been like a brother to her. Always. She'd been immune to his good looks. To his manliness. And now she wasn't. The irony of that, in light of what she was about to tell him, didn't escape her.

He took a seat.

Gabrielle pulled a thin file out of her brief-case. She placed it in front of him.

And then sat.

He didn't touch the file. "Tell me."

She nodded toward the file. "I think you should look at it." She'd been trying for hours and just couldn't figure out a way to tell him.

Her job had always been to pick up the pieces. Not to cause him to shatter.

And she'd never felt the pieces so personally.

Liam crossed his arms.

He could also be stubborn and pigheaded. She used to get frustrated sometimes when he did that. Now all she wanted to do was pull him to her. To kiss him until nothing else mattered.

So she reached into the file without fully opening it. Pulled out a photo.

Placed it in front of him.

Gabrielle had been touched by the sheer natural beauty of the teenager smiling up out of that picture. She had Liam's blond hair, though hers was a shade lighter. His blue eyes, too. But her features were more round. Much softer. He stared. Frowned. Shook his head.

"Have you ever seen her before?"

"Of course not. Who is she?"

"She's your half sister." Wow. Never in all of her rehearsed scenarios had she just blurted out the news like that.

He pushed the photo away. Shook his head again. "There's been some mistake," he said. And then, arms on the table, he leaned toward her. "Come on, Gabrielle. You know my entire life history."

She couldn't hold him. So, heart crying inside, she said, "Her name is Tamara Bolin. She's fourteen. A freshman in high school. She's on the swim team and has a four point zero GPA."

Chin jutting, Liam looked at the picture from the distance he'd given himself from it. His hands, still on the table, were trembling. Gabrielle had the urge to cover them with her own.

And didn't feel as out of the world as she had when the urges had first started happening. She couldn't begin to accept them. To let them feel...normal. She and Liam didn't touch like that. Not with...that kind of emotion attached...

"She lives in Florida." Gabrielle kept talking because she didn't know what else to do. The empty coffee shop felt suddenly like a morgue with most of the lights off. There was more. A lot of it. He'd ask when he was ready. For the next several minutes Gabrielle sat silently. It was what friends did, she told herself. They sat in the fire with you. Hurt for you.

"Does she know about me?"

His question came as a relief. And increased her tension, as well.

"Yes."

"Since when?"

"She's always known."

"You've spoken with her, then?"

"No."

He nodded toward the file. "It's all in a report? That she knows me?"

"I spoke to her mother, Liam."

He had to have done the math. To know that his father had been unfaithful to his mother during the last months she'd been suffering so horribly with the disease that had ultimately claimed her life.

The word that softly came out of his mouth was not one he'd be proud of saying. Most particularly in reference to his father. But she didn't blame him.

"Who is she?"

"Someone he's been in a relationship with for more than fifteen years. He's been supporting the two of them all along. Until three months ago he was still seeing them."

His steely gaze settled on Gabrielle and the skin of her face felt as though it had been touched. "That account I found—it led to this?"

She nodded. Using every bit of her self-control to keep her tears from falling.

"Tamara has always thought that you were ashamed of her existence," Gabrielle said softly. Hoping she could do this right. For two people who hadn't asked to be born and seemed to carry similar hurts in their hearts where their father was concerned. "She didn't know until today that you never knew about her."

"He never told her he was keeping her a secret."

"No. He just told her that she was not to contact you. That she had to wait for you to contact her first. She has a picture of you in the back of her diary."

He blinked. His nostrils flared. And he stared at the picture.

"She wants to meet you, Liam. Her mother, Missy Bolin, said that your father kept business files in the office he used in her home when he visited. She said that you're welcome to them, too. Apparently she was shocked and hurt when he broke things off with her and now, with the arrest, doesn't want any of his stuff in her home. She wondered if the files would have something to do with the FBI's investigation and doesn't want to get in trouble, but she doesn't want to just hand them over, either."

"Why would he leave files there after he broke up with her?"

"I don't know. But I'd sure like to find out. Wouldn't you?"

He picked up the picture.

"It's not her fault, Liam," Gabrielle said quietly, leaning toward him, getting as close to a touch as she could allow herself with the strange feelings wrestling inside of her.

He nodded.

"Missy said they're free this coming weekend."

He sat silently for another long couple of minutes and then looked up at Gabrielle. "Will you come with me?"

Her first thought was that Marie wouldn't be able to get away from the shop on such short notice. She and Liam had never traveled together without her.

"Of course." The words that came out of her mouth created all kinds of problems.

She was too eager to go with him to take the words back.

CHAPTER ELEVEN

LIAM SPENT THE week in court. Just before the noon recess on Friday, the judge, who'd been expected to take the matter under advisement, ruled in favor of the parents of the seventeen-year-old Douglas boy.

He had deep compassion in his tone as he told the young man that while his convictions were important, the unfortunate truth was that he had a physical ailment that required medication. Liam wasn't surprised by the ruling. He'd hoped that it wouldn't come until at least Monday. He and Gabrielle were booked on a flight to Fort Lauderdale at eight o'clock that evening. Now, before packing and preparing to meet the sibling he'd never known existed, he was going to be writing about another teenager's heartache.

But even if he didn't have time to pack properly, he was going to meet Tamara. The thought had been creeping into his thoughts on and off all week. As he'd sat in court, he'd wondered how much she was like the teenagers taking the stand to testify to the character of the boy suing his parents.

He bade goodbye to his bodyguard via text as he and Gabrielle went through security at the airport. He hadn't seen Tanner at the airport, but he was getting used to knowing that anytime he was out of his home, he had a shadow.

Nothing had come of the letter that had been left at Marie's shop. The threat it conveyed hadn't been specific—a wish for him to suffer as he and his father had caused others to suffer.

His father had apparently been getting hate mail on and off for years. Stood to reason that now that Liam was understood to be working at Connelly Investments, he'd inspire some of the same anger.

Whatever, it wasn't something he was going to worry about.

"She's probably going to think I'm an old fogy," he told Gabrielle as they stood at their gate at Denver International, waiting to board the plane. He was flying coach for the first time.

"She knows how old you are." Crowds were closing in on the door as the time to board grew closer, but they had no need to join in. Gabi had relented and let him pay extra for priority boarding.

He could still be in the lounge if he wanted to be. He'd never wanted to be.

For that matter, he could certainly afford to fly first class if he'd wanted to do so. But Gabrielle couldn't. And she wasn't allowing him to pay for her flight.

He was going to, when he paid her bill at the end of the month, but she didn't know that.

And cutting corners where he could, financially speaking, wasn't a bad thing. It had become very clear to him that money didn't last forever.

The surprising part about this discovery was that he was really doing just fine. With the financial changes in his life at least.

He wasn't so happy about the weird bit of excitement that had accompanied thoughts of this trip all week—aside from that associated with meeting his little sister. No, he'd also been het up about the fact that he was going to be sitting alone with Gabi in the plane. Traveling with her alone.

They were going to be spending the entire weekend together....

"Knowing someone's age and building an image of them in your head are two different things," he said, forcing himself back on track.

He was going to have to make sure that he didn't do something stupid on this trip. Like try to kiss Gabi on the beach under the moonlight.

No matter how much the desire to do so was starting to plague him.

"You're worried she's not going to like you?"

"No." Of course he was.

"The only thing I can recommend is…be nice to her mother."

To date, Liam had refused to speak with the woman, leaving Gabrielle to make all of their travel arrangements, down to the two rooms in the medium-priced hotel she'd booked for them not far from Tamara and Missy's modest beach cottage.

He didn't reply now.

"Whatever else she might be, whatever choices she's made, she's been a good mother to your half sister," Gabrielle said, her tone reminding him of sitting in that beanbag in her college dorm, confessing his sins.

"Besides, you don't know her story. Maybe she didn't know he was married when their affair started. Maybe she didn't know until after she was pregnant and she found out he couldn't marry her."

He turned his head, trying to read those silvery-blue eyes that hid so many things. Things he was finding himself more and more curious about.

"Is that what she told you?"

"I didn't ask."

"But she told you."

Gabrielle cocked her head. "Maybe. In a roundabout way."

The woman was maddening. He was paying her. She was representing him. Not Missy—probably short for Melissa—Bolin.

"I'm here to help you collect information that could impact the potential charges against your father and thus might affect you," she told him. "Your personal business is your own."

Yes. But he didn't want it to be. He wanted her to share it with him. All of it. Down to the soap he used in the shower.

The thought brought him up short. And, though he wasn't proud of himself, he did what guys sometimes did. He went on the attack.

"Why don't you date?" he asked her.

"Funny question from a ladies' man who hasn't been on a date in weeks."

"I just broke up with Jenna." And she knew why he had.

"I'd expect you to be playing the entire field at this point. You used to flirt all the time when you were out with Marie and me."

His past behavior had earned him the comment.

"Jenna would be humiliated if I started being seen with other women so soon after dumping her."

Even though, on that last night, she'd begged him to break up with her. She'd met someone else. Someone she was in love with. She was just waiting the appropriate amount of time before she started seeing him publicly.

"Anyway, quit trying to divert a question by putting it back on me, counselor. My love life has nothing to do with the fact that you haven't been out in more than a year." If she'd just hurry up and get herself hitched, it would decimate this growing threat that he might screw everything up between them due to his sudden feeling that she was the only woman alive.

"It's been about two months." Her dry reply didn't thrill him.

"Two months? Who did you go out with? I didn't know about it." And now he was jealous?

"You don't know a lot of things about me, Connelly," she said, her words softened by the grin she gave him. "He was a cop. A detective. I met him in court. We went out a few times."

"But it didn't work out." Too bad.

"He wanted to get serious, and I'm serious about my work."

She hadn't been in love with the guy. Just like she hadn't loved any of the other men she'd dated since he'd known her. The thought gave him an odd sense of security.

Because she was a good woman. Honest,

morally upright. The kind a man could count on to be true to him. The kind he'd want to take home to his parents. To raise his family.

His thoughts were off-the-wall. Out there. Aged. Chauvinistic. Because in reality, there was no hint of old-fashioned family values in his life. He was plagued with the surreal knowledge that at eight o'clock the next morning, he was going to meet his sister. After thirty years of thinking himself an only child, born to parents who'd loved and been faithful to each other. Putting up with his father's harsh, autocratic ways had been bearable because he'd been so certain that, at heart, his father was a good man who loved him.

And had adored his mother. A man his mother had adored. Enough to give him a second chance when he'd gambled away his fortune.

Whatever. He wasn't a kid anymore. He was a grown man with his own life. It was up to him what he made of it. And it was time to get on with doing it.

GABRIELLE HAD GIVEN Missy their itinerary. They knew where they were staying. Missy had chosen the restaurant for their initial meeting Saturday morning.

The plan was to have breakfast and then go on

to Missy's to sort through Walter's files. Liam could keep them or dispose of them. Missy just wanted them out of her house.

If all went well with the meeting between Liam and Tamara, they'd spend Saturday evening together before Gabrielle and Liam's flight back to Denver Sunday morning.

Sitting next to Liam in the middle seat of a fairly empty plane to Florida, Gabrielle concentrated on the details of their trip. Doing a mental rundown of times. Locations. Goals.

A pretty young flight attendant stopped beside his aisle seat, asking if they wanted anything. He ordered them each a coffee and Gabrielle faltered. His arm was up against hers. Brushed hers as he placed her steaming-hot cup on the tray table she'd lowered from the seat back in front of her.

Giving the impression that they were together. As in *together* together.

The waitress smiled at him as he thanked her. And his eyes lingered on her as she passed on up the aisle.

Did she notice?

Gabrielle felt like secondhand goods for the brief instant it took her to remember that Liam was free to exchange glances—and phone numbers and anything else he wanted to exchange—with anyone he wanted.

No matter how it might look, they were most definitely not *together* together. Nor would they be. Even if he fell in love with her, it wouldn't work. His flirting with the flight attendant was a perfect reminder of that. And she wasn't the type of woman who dated casually. Which was why she didn't date much.

If she and Liam were ever to have a personal, intimate, *together* together relationship and it ended, her heart would be irrevocably broken. Things would never be the same between them again. Marie knew it. And so did she.

They were Threefold. A family. If something went wrong between Liam and Gabrielle, Marie, who loved them both, would be caught in the middle. She'd suffer right along with them. She'd eventually have to choose, and based on Marie's difficulty in trusting men, she'd choose Gabrielle.

Which wasn't fair, either.

Bottom line was, she and Marie needed Liam too much to risk losing him. And he needed them, too.

For the next several minutes, as Liam's arm touched hers and sent little shivers of awareness through her, Gabrielle tried to concentrate on the pretty attendant parading up and down the aisle, smiling as she passed. Noticed the way Liam's gaze had followed her again. And told herself, quite strongly, that she wouldn't ever, ever want to be his woman. And when he leaned over and spoke to her, his breath on her neck urging her to turn her head to taste his lips, she forced herself to remember the things he'd said during late-night talks in their college years, about being attracted to other women while he was in a relationship.

If he was hers, and looked at another woman like he'd just looked at the attendant…she'd never be comfortable around him again.

So…maybe right now, dodging her burgeoning feelings for him was hard.

Losing him as a member of their family would be hardest of all.

"LIAM?" THE VOICE was soft. Hesitant. He heard it, but it didn't register immediately. He and Gabrielle were standing, arm to arm, at the baggage claim carousel. Glued to each other's sides so they didn't get lost in the busy Florida airport. He knew for certain she hadn't said a word.

Fact was, she hadn't said much to him at all since shortly after takeoff. She'd said she was concentrating on the papers in front of her. Knowing her as he did, he didn't question the statement a bit—at first. But when he noticed her staring at a page—a biographical report on Donaldson's real estate deal gone bad—so long he'd practically had it memorized himself, he knew that she wasn't working.

"Liam?"

The voice came again. Gabrielle spun around, looking just over his shoulder.

"Oh!" Her mouth formed a circle with the word. She turned toward him, glanced at his face, and then behind him again.

"It's Tamara…"

The hair on the back of his neck stood on end. He felt as though spiders were crawling up his spine.

Turning so quickly the long black trench coat over his arm tangled between the legs of his suit pants, Liam pasted a smile on his face.

Whatever his feelings about the girl's conception might be, she was not going to pay for his father's sins where he was concerned…

He saw her and lost his breath.

Her eyes…looking into them was like looking into a mirror. The doubt there—he could read it as clearly as he'd grown up reading his own. Was he wanted? Was he good enough?

Their father had a lot to answer for.

A slender redheaded woman stood behind the girl. She moved forward, as though to protect her. Liam didn't give her a direct glance.

"Tamara?" he said, his smile growing so much that it hurt his face. "Oh, my God, look

at you!" he said, holding out his arms to her.
"You're beautiful."

She was a baby. A child. A young woman.
His little sister. And when she flung herself into
his arms, he grabbed her and hung on for dear
life.

GABRIELLE WAS UP two hours before she was due
to meet Liam to head out for breakfast the following morning. Their rooms weren't adjoined
in the high-rise beach hotel where they were
staying. She hadn't spoken to him since they'd
said goodnight outside the elevator the night
before.

But she'd been thinking about him nonstop.
She'd asked if he wanted a snack or a cup of
coffee before they'd turned in. If he wanted to
sit and chat for a while. She was a bit nervous
doing so without Marie, but, after her talk with
herself on the plane, she felt a little more confident that she'd stay on the right path.

And she could always text Marie if she decided she couldn't trust herself.

Still, disappointment had flooded her when
he'd shaken his head and said he just wanted
to head to their rooms. The emptiness he had
left behind kept her up much of a night that she
should have spent resting.

She'd finally called Marie. Who'd strengthened her resolve to keep things on a friends-only basis with Liam. She'd told her to be ready in case Liam tried to change things.

Which sent Gabrielle into another tizzy. Was it possible Liam really did return her feelings? Was he finding her attractive, too? Looking at her in new ways?

At which point Marie had come down uncharacteristically hard on her. Reminding her that going into a tizzy was not the way to stay strong and follow through on her decisions.

And Gabrielle had asked, "If Liam were different, if he was a one-woman type of guy and could have made one of us happy, do you think he would have split us up?"

"No. If he was that type of guy, and one of us was the one for him, he'd have expressed that interest and the other one of us would have supported that choice."

Gabrielle had thought so, too, but... "So, if things had been different and he chose me?"

"I'd have been fine with it, Gabi."

"You've never had any of *those* kinds of feelings for him?"

"Never. I go for tall guys, you know that. Crazy, since I'm the short one. But there you have it."

Gabi had had a sudden flash of Marie telling them what "Elliott" had said that first night she'd met him. And knew that the bodyguard had been spending some time in her shop over the past week, since the threatening letter had arrived, rather than just outside in his car. Marie had mentioned him in passing more than once.

Could it be that her friend was falling for someone? That maybe she'd finally met a man who could get past the barricade around her heart?

She'd been about to broach the subject, but Marie had wanted to know everything about Liam's sister. About the surprise meeting.

Gabrielle hadn't had a lot to tell her because the moment had lasted all of five minutes— just long enough for the two to meet and say hello so, Missy had explained, Tamara would calm down and get some sleep. Marie had had to go then. She'd only had a few hours to sleep before getting up to meet Grace downstairs, to bag and tag the baked goods the older woman made every morning before opening the shop. Certainly not enough time to deal with Gabrielle bringing up the tough subject of Marie's love life.

Saturday morning, after showering and dressing in the light-colored linen pants and tailored button-down short-sleeve top she'd brought, Gabrielle slipped into a pair of low-heeled pumps, fluffed and sprayed her short black hair, put on some makeup, and delivered herself to her laptop. She'd spent part of the night going over files in the Connelly case, specifically the files Gwen Menard and her team had compiled on the five top-floor executives Walter Connelly had told them about—people with the security clearance to have run a Ponzi scheme with Connelly funds.

She was so focused that she jumped when Liam's knock sounded on her door. She'd actually lost track of time. And lost the opportunity to stress anymore about the upcoming day.

Liam would get through it just fine. She'd advise him where his father's papers were concerned. And then they'd head home. Back to Marie. Their apartment building. Normalcy. Back to Liam confiding in both of them. And Chinese takeout for three.

The thought was completely obliterated by the warm smile he gave her as she opened her door to him. But she gathered it back around her as quickly as she could, shrouding herself in determination as she locked her door and let him slide his arm through hers as they headed down the hall. If Marie had been there, he'd have joined his other arm with hers.

Like he had for college graduation pictures, her law school graduation, and when he'd taken them both to a charity event before the holidays.

Liam was facing what had to be the hardest time of his life. He needed her and Marie more now than ever. Marie wasn't there to do her part.

So Gabrielle was going to have to do it for both of them.

CHAPTER TWELVE

LIAM DIDN'T UNDERSTAND how it was possible to feel so fiercely protective and to love someone so completely in such a short space of time, but by the time he and Gabrielle had finished breakfast with Tamara and her mother, he knew his little sister was going to have a place in his heart—and his life—forever.

She'd wanted to ride with them in the car he'd rented the night before for the short trip from the restaurant to her home—saying she could direct them if they got separated from Missy in traffic—and he was glad to have her there. Glad, too, that she'd chattered the whole way about the places they were passing—regaling him with her memories of having grown up in the Florida suburb—showing him a life that was at once completely different from his and relatively happy as well.

"She's a great kid," he said to Gabrielle as they stood together in the third bedroom—which served as a sewing room, with Walter's desk and a filing cabinet on one end—in the small beach cottage his father had bought for his mistress and their daughter. Tamara had gone to help her mother get iced tea for them.

"She adores you." The warm look in Gabi's eyes stopped him for a moment. So he looked past her.

"I'm not sure why," he said, though he couldn't deny that Gabi's words appeared to be true, judging by how many times he'd looked up to find Tamara watching him, smiling. "She doesn't know me at all."

"On the contrary, she knows you very well," Missy said, carrying a tray with four glasses on it. Tamara was behind her with the pitcher of freshly brewed tea.

"Dad talked about you to Mom," Tamara said, her eyes clouding as she set the pitcher down on her mother's cutting table. "And she'd tell me things. When I asked. I didn't blame you, by the way, even when I thought you didn't want to know me. It had nothing to do with me. Mom made sure I understood that. It was just about you being your mom's child and Dad not…"

She broke off. "Anyway," she continued, her face reddening. "I just… Mom said that Gabrielle is your attorney, but it seems like you're… friends…too. It's cool that you'd bring her here to meet me."

She was looking between him and Gabrielle

as if there was something to see. And in that instant, he wanted there to be. Suddenly uncomfortable, Liam pulled at the collar on the sport shirt he'd paired with designer jeans that morning.

"We're just friends," Gabrielle piped up, helping herself to a glass of tea. Her formal attire reminded him that she was there on his payroll. Working. Because of the mess his father had made of his life.

Of all of their lives.

"We have a third friend, my roommate Marie, and we've all been hanging together since college. She would have come with us this weekend. She's eager to meet you, too, but she owns a coffee shop and couldn't get away."

"I live in an apartment upstairs from them," Liam added.

"In that apartment building you said you'd just bought?" Missy asked.

"The one that Dad disowned you for buying?" Tamara's words left no doubt that her feelings for his father—their father—bore resemblance to his own.

"Yes, that apartment building. I just can't get used to hearing you say *Dad*, referring to the man who fathered me," he told her. And then sent an apologetic glance toward Missy. Tamara was still a kid.

He had no business laying his adult griev-
ance at her feet.

"It's okay to talk openly in front of her,"
Missy said. Holding his gaze. It was the first
time he'd looked directly at her.

She had kind eyes.

And he wondered how she'd felt when she'd
found out, after she was pregnant, that the father
of her child was married with a child of his own.

"What did you call him?" Tamara asked.

"Old man, mostly." He said the first thing
that came to his mind. "Or Dad. It's just…" He
shook his head again.

"Weird, huh? That I'm the kid and yet you're
the one who was treated like one."

The dart her words shot into his heart took
any breath he'd have used to respond.

"Are these the files you want us to go through?"
Gabi asked Missy, saving him.

Again.

Someday he was going to have to thank her
for that. Her and Marie. Meeting Tamara, finding out that his own father had formed a family
separate from him, not even letting him know
they existed, made him realize even more how
much his friendship with the girls meant to him.

Not only more valuable than money—but far
more important than any pressure his senses

were sending him to explore a more intimate relationship with Gabrielle.

Family was forever. Liam's love liaisons were not.

As IT TURNED OUT, Tamara was the most help to Gabrielle. The girl had an organizational eye that rivaled her own and between the two of them, they had the files sorted within an hour.

"These are identical to the files the FBI pulled out of Walter's desks at home and at work," Gabrielle said late in the morning.

"He had copies of all of his home files and his work files here?" Tamara asked.

"He had file folders with these same labels in both desks back in Denver," she told the room at large. Missy was at her sewing machine table, going through a midsize moving box of things. Presumably Walter's.

Liam had left to clear out his father's side of the closet he'd shared with Missy. She'd asked him to do so.

Gabrielle had watched Liam all morning, her heart aching for him, the need to hold him growing stronger with every hour that passed.

"It would have been hard to keep track of everything if he had different filing systems everywhere." Tamara interrupted her thoughts.

"I'm surprised he didn't just use the computer," Missy added. "I kept telling him that he could keep things in the cloud and have access to them wherever he was."

"People who are doing illegal things aren't going to put their stuff out on a cloud, Mom. Everyone knows clouds can be hacked."

"We don't know for sure he's guilty." Gabrielle felt oddly compelled to remind the girl. "He swore to me that he's innocent."

Tamara looked up, a sweet, vulnerable expression in her gaze. "Do you think he's being framed?"

"I don't think so," Liam said softly, coming into the room carrying a large suitcase, which he put down as he crossed over to Tamara. "You and I are proof of his duplicity. All these years, I've had a sister, and he didn't tell me. If he can rob us of a relationship, he's certainly capable of robbing investors…"

With one hand on her shoulder, he looked over at Missy, who'd stopped what she was doing. A small pile of mementos: ticket stubs, photographs, brochures, even a room key, lay beside her. "You said I could speak freely?" Liam asked.

"Of course. I'd prefer that we hear things from you rather than on the news. Some of Tamara's friends have met Walter. They might recognize him if his picture gets out there."

"They'll recognize his name, won't they?" Gabrielle asked.

Missy shook her head. "When Walter was with us he was just… Walter," she said.

"He said he could just be himself when he was home with us," Tamara explained, looking from Liam to Gabrielle.

"It seemed really important to him."

Gabrielle had wondered about the nice, obviously costly but quite small cottage that Walter had called home when he'd visited Florida. She'd assumed, until that morning, that he'd stayed in the hotel suite he'd rented every time he came to Florida. She'd seen the bills…

"Yet he wouldn't let me have a normal life," Liam said. "He took away my car for a year because I wanted to live in a dorm."

"You were his golden boy, Liam," Missy said. "You were everything he was not. You'd been born to money. Raised to know nothing but the good life."

He looked at Gabrielle. She'd never needed so badly to wrap her arms around him. And pushed the sensation away. Far away. "It makes sense," she told him. "He left his harsh beginnings behind when he had you."

"Except for Buckus," Liam said.

Gabrielle picked up the Florida file she'd found on the man, eager to get a look inside.

Based on what she'd seen in the Colorado file the night before...

"I think they were closer than you realized," she said, getting ready to tell him more when Missy interrupted.

"Ray Buckus?"

"You know him?" Liam's gaze was sharp as he glanced at the other woman.

"Who's that?" Tamara looked between her mother and newfound brother. At just five feet and in skinny jeans and a T-shirt, the blonde looked vulnerable enough to be blown over in a big storm.

"He works for your father," Missy said.

"He grew up with him." That was from Liam.

Missy's hands were trembling. "I didn't know that."

"So who *is* this Buckus guy?" Tamara asked, her tone giving no indication of the obvious nervousness in her gaze as she looked at her mother.

"Have you ever met him?" Gabrielle asked Missy.

The older woman shook her head. "I thought he was an accountant. Walter told me he had no family, other than Liam, that he grew up in foster care and has no ties to that part of his life. Why wouldn't he have told me that he'd known Ray all his life? Who is this guy?"

"He's a financial broker at Connelly," Liam said. "He and my father—" he glanced at Tamara "—our father," he corrected, "grew up together. Ray got into some trouble, did some time in juvenile detention. I've wondered if maybe Dad was involved in whatever it was and Ray took the rap for both of them. All I know is that Ray straightened himself out as soon as he got out. Because he'd been a juvenile offender, his record was sealed. He went to college and was working as a bank manager for a major chain when Dad offered him the job at Connelly thirty years ago. Ray was as eager to leave the past behind as my father was. I've known him all my life. He's a good guy."

"He sent you checks." Gabrielle jumped in when Liam finished. She was looking at Missy. But didn't miss the sharp turn of Liam's head as he aimed his steely gaze at her. "I spent part of yesterday and last night going through files the FBI sent over on the five top-floor executives at Connelly. I noticed that Buckus had made a couple of deposits into your offshore account."

Missy nodded, looking slightly sick. "When Walter was out of the country. I just thought it was his accountant making the deposits. Walter told me his name because he wanted me to have someone I could call if I ever needed anything and couldn't get in touch with him."

"Did you ever call him?" Tamara asked.

"No."

"But you knew my father was paying you through an offshore account." Liam's comment bordered on accusation. Tamara slumped down to the rocking chair next to her mother's cutting table.

"I did."

"And you didn't find that suspicious?" Gabrielle was interested in the answer, as well.

"He told me that because Connelly does global business, some of their accounting is in Switzerland. It had to do with tax breaks."

Liam's expression smoothed a bit, which indicated to Gabrielle that Missy's answer was plausible.

And as a lawyer, she had some questions.

"Did he ask for his stuff back?" She'd been wondering why Walter hadn't already made arrangements to collect his files and other personal items from his ex-mistress.

"No."

"And you didn't find that odd?"

"Truth be known..." Missy was choking back tears.

"Dad broke my mom's heart," Tamara said, her tone gaining an edge now. "She's barely been able to work."

"What do you do?" Liam asked.

"She's a registered nurse. She works for a doctor's office here in town. When Dad called and told her they were through…"

With a hiccup, Missy said, "It's all right, sweetie. I'm fine. I'll be fine." She turned to Liam. "I loved your father—blindly, apparently. I was so shocked when he broke things off."

"You two weren't having problems?"

"No more than we ever did. It was hard, with him having two lives…"

"Did you ever suggest moving to Denver?" Gabrielle asked.

"Of course. Walter valued our anonymity as a family too much to give it up. And then there was Liam…" She glanced his way.

"Did he tell you why he kept you hidden from me?" Liam's chin jutted forward as he shoved his hands in his pockets.

"He said you'd never understand…because of your mother. And then, later…we were years deep in our secret. He said that telling you would cause problems that we didn't need."

Gabrielle watched the expressions chasing themselves across Liam's face. He might have made trouble. His father still should have trusted him. And told him even if he didn't. Liam had had a right to know.

Gabrielle stepped forward around the desk,

easing closer to Liam. "So you didn't wonder why Walter didn't send for his things?"

"He's a billionaire. Nothing here he couldn't replace. He even had copies of his files…." She looked into the box she'd been sorting through. Probably figuring none of the memories meant anything to Walter.

And she could be right.

The man had cut Liam out of his life, out of his will, for buying a building. It was conceivable that if Missy and Tamara had grown to be a problem for him, he'd cut them out completely, as well.

"If you want to know the truth, Mom thought Dad had found someone else," Tamara said. She was talking to Gabrielle. Avoiding Liam's gaze.

"As far as I know, he didn't," Liam said. "But then, I haven't known about you two all these years…"

"There's no indication from his finances that he'd started traveling somewhere new," she offered, seeing the pain on their faces.

Walter Connelly had much to answer for. Far beyond possible criminal fraud charges.

"And he was still sending you money. I saw a deposit into the account less than two weeks ago."

"Some of it goes into my college fund," Tamara said.

"But he supports you, right?" Liam asked his sister.

"He bought the cottage outright years ago," Missy said. "And had it deeded in my name only. I pay all of the bills. The money he sends is all spent on Tamara or put in savings for her."

"The FBI thinks that Buckus is involved in the fraud. They think he and Walter are working together." Gabrielle tried to steer the conversation into less painful areas.

"What do you think?" Tamara asked, sitting up on the edge of the chair.

"I think that if Buckus was in on it, he'd have wiped away evidence of your mother's account. He was the only one, besides your father, who knew about it. Why leave it there? Why leave that money in danger of being seized? It doesn't make sense. I think that the account was left because whoever cleared all incriminating evidence from Connelly computers didn't know about it."

"Which means that our father didn't wipe away those files."

"Or he got stopped before he could finish," Liam said, but Gabrielle was already shaking her head. Missy was, too.

"Walter would have wiped that one first," Missy said.

"So, what?" Tamara asked. "You guys are saying that Dad didn't do it?"

"We know he's been duplicitous," Liam said. "And I know he's been gambling again."

Missy's catch of breath told its own story. "You didn't know that," Liam said.

"No. I didn't. He told me he'd had trouble with it when he was young but had soon seen how destructive it could be and stopped."

So why had he started up again? Unless he knew that he was in financial trouble. Unless he had been trying to get back funds that had been spent, funds he needed to pay those wronged investors without other arms of his business being tapped to pay the debt.

"If he didn't wipe away evidence of Mom's and my account, then he didn't do it." Tamara latched on to the piece of evidence that was uppermost in Gabrielle's mind as well.

"I'm not ready to believe that," Liam told his sister. And Gabrielle wondered if he ever would be ready to trust his father again.

Walter Connelly might not be fraudulent in his business deals, but the man had committed some pretty hefty wrongs, just the same.

CHAPTER THIRTEEN

BY LATE THAT afternoon Liam was wishing his father had never been born—except that would have meant neither he nor Tamara would be in existence, either. Spending time with his little sister was phenomenal. But the unwelcome specter of their father kept popping in.

Whether Missy had been totally duped by Walter and had not been aware of the part she'd played in his father's adultery or she'd known that she was sleeping with Liam's mother's husband was unclear to him.

He didn't want any of it to matter.

But it did.

"Wait a minute." He glanced at Gabrielle, who was riding with him in the leather backseat of Missy's newish four-door sedan on the way to the pier where the four of them would be boarding a boat to have dinner on the ocean.

"What?" Tamara, dressed in black leggings and a pretty white blouse, turned around from the front seat beside her mother.

"I was just going through these papers," he

said. A folder of his father's that hadn't matched any of the ones he or Gabrielle had seen in Denver.

"The folders of papers he hadn't filed yet," Gabrielle said.

"That's what we thought they were. I mean, the forms all match transactions and accounts that we know about, so there was no reason to keep them separate," he said.

"But now you think there was a reason?" Tamara asked. She was one smart girl. A chip off the old block, not that his old man deserved the credit for that.

"Look at these." He pulled out papers and handed them to Gabrielle. She studied them with that focused look she got when she was fully engaged in something.

She was being such a great sport. Traipsing along with him for the weekend. Putting up with the drama his father had created for so many people.

Was it any wonder he loved her?

"They're all signed and dated by him," Gabrielle said, looking at him. And for a split second he had no idea what she was talking about.

He loved her? Not like he'd always loved her and Marie, but…he *loved* her?

"Signed in ink, not computer-generated or electronic signatures." She stopped talking.

He stared at her. As though somewhere on her person was the clue that would let him know that he was wrong. She was just Gabi. One of his two best friends in the world.

Instead, he wanted to kiss her. In the worst way. In a way that prevented anyone from ever taking her away from him...

"Are you feeling okay?"

Her concern, more than her words, got through to him. "Yes." He looked away. Breathed in deeply and out again. Escaping the emotion threatening to overwhelm him as he'd learned to do at the foot of his father.

She'd been talking about forms. Signatures. "Dad insisted that all investments and payouts be signed in ink," he said. "By him or George."

"So we're to assume that all of these were done while he was here? He'd have scanned them and sent them back, but still kept the originals." She was still looking at him oddly.

And as she handed him the folder, leaned into him.

He took the folder. And kept his shoulder pressed against hers as he opened it. "That's what I'm thinking. He's got copies of transactions in the other files, open transactions, just like he does at home. These are set apart because they're originals."

"I can tell you every time he's been here in

the past fifteen years," Missy said, looking in the rearview mirror as she made a turn that had them heading toward the ocean. She'd changed into black jeans and a sequined sweater and put on more makeup. She wasn't a beauty, but there was something quietly pretty about her.

He could see what his father might have seen in her.

He didn't approve of any of it. Not when he thought of how hard those last years of his mother's life had been. How hard she'd tried to be the wife his father had needed her to be, to make appearances and host dinners and always look her best, in spite of the pain she'd been in. Or the lack of energy she'd had.

"A list of those dates would be good to have, Missy, thank you," Gabrielle said beside him, and Liam was ashamed for his bad manners. "If you could just email it to me?" All four of them had already exchanged email addresses before they'd left the cottage that afternoon.

"I have the list, too," Tamara said. "At least for recent years. I made him sign my diary every time he got there and write me a note in it before he left. I told him it made him feel more real to me during the times he was gone."

Liam felt as though he'd been sucker punched. His father had written in this child's diary? To comfort her?

This child had craved their father's presence while Liam, who'd taken it for granted, had wished him gone much of the time.

"How often did you see him?" He asked a question that should have been first off his tongue.

"Only a couple of times a month, a couple of days each time, when you were home. But since you went away to school and lived on your own, it's been more often," Missy said.

"More often since Tamara was little." He was glad to know.

"I don't remember the couple of times a month." The teenager turned to look at him again. And smiled that sweet vulnerable smile that had him in the palm of her hand. "Mostly it was at least a week each month. Used to be even more than that, when I was in elementary school."

It wasn't as though Liam would have noticed his father's absences. Certainly not when he was in college and working nights in Denver. And in later years, they'd both traveled so much, lived in separate homes, spoken only when they had pertinent information to pass along.

He wanted to ask what they did when his father was there. Something held him silent.

"Look at this." Gabrielle pointed to a particular line on a transaction sheet. It held a code that identified the person who'd generated the sheet: George, not that Gabrielle had reason to know that. And not that it mattered. His father's attorney filled out paperwork for him all the time.

Her body pressing more completely into his mattered more than anything at the moment.

He didn't want anyone snatching that beautiful body away from him. Gabrielle's attention was addictive.

And he had to get a grip on himself before he lost his place as family in her heart.

"Look, Liam," she said, sounding a little irritated. He'd never realized how much he liked that tone. It told him she cared.

"I am looking."

"Every one of these sheets deals with transactions we now know were fraudulent. They were sent to your father down here for signature, which clearly means that he wasn't at work generating the business. And every single one of them was initiated by the same employee code."

"It's George's code."

It didn't mean anything. Except that George had been covering his father's ass while the old man lived his double life.

And maybe… "George knew what was going on," he said as Gabrielle nodded.

He wanted to be glad that they were uncovering evidence. As more things came to light, they were getting closer to the truth. Closer to having the whole thing resolved and behind them.

But George?

And was Ray Buckus in on everything, too, as Gabrielle had said Gwen Menard suspected?

Was anyone trustworthy?

"Who's George?" Tamara asked.

"Your father's corporate attorney," Gabi answered for him.

And he had his answer. He knew two people who were completely trustworthy: Marie and Gabrielle. But if he went after Gabrielle, tried to date her, he could likely lose Marie's trust. And if things didn't work out for him and Gabrielle in the long run—if he got the urge to move on that had hit him at some point in every relationship he'd ever had—then he'd lose Gabi, too.

Lose the only two people in the world he knew he could really trust.

A man would be a fool to jeopardize that.

Shaking his head, Liam chalked up his rush of emotion for the woman at his side to the emotional turmoil his father had wreaked the past weeks. And the complete change in his personal circumstances.

Obviously, whether Jenna was ready to come out with her new boyfriend or not, it was time for Liam to start dating again. Before he blew the best thing in his life.

His friendship with his business partners.

DINNER WAS WONDERFUL, if a bit uncomfortable. Gabrielle loved being around Tamara. The young woman was smart and way more astute for her age than Gabrielle had been. She was also kind.

And a bit bossy, too. Most particularly when it came to her mother.

Missy was a nice woman. Obviously in emotional crisis. But Gabrielle trusted her.

The discomfort came from the man sitting beside her. In jeans and a polo shirt he looked… as great as Liam always looked. She was just seeing him differently.

He seemed to be looking at her differently, too.

And more than usual. Far more. Every time she turned her head, she caught him looking at her.

Making her self-conscious about the skinny jeans and knee-length open sweater she'd pulled on over a jeweled long-sleeved T-shirt. He'd seen the outfit before. It wasn't as if she had a closet full of clothes. But maybe he thought she should have dressed up more?

Or was too dressy?

222 ONCE UPON A FRIENDSHIP

Not that his surreptitious looks gave off any hint of disapproval. To the contrary. They were making her want to stand on the deck in the moonlight and kiss him.

The cruise around the harbor was sold out and included live entertainment, but when there were opportunities to talk, the conversation centered around Tamara. The fault of all three adults there, not the child's.

It was as though they were all avoiding any negative topics—until the teenager asked them about Denver. She wanted to know about the mountains and the malls. About the Connelly Investments building and the home Liam had grown up in.

A home that could possibly be seized by the courts if Walter Connelly was found guilty of fraud. At the moment, Liam's father was still living there.

"I texted Dad earlier," Tamara said when they were just finishing their meal. "I asked him if I could come to Denver."

"You did?" Missy said with shocked displeasure. And Gabrielle wondered if it was the first time the girl had texted her father since the breakup.

"I know you told me to wait for him to contact me, but I just wanted to see what he'd say."

"What did he say?"

"No."

"That's it?" Liam asked.

"He said that he's busy with work right now and wouldn't be able to show me around or spend time with me."

Gabrielle figured it was the best answer of any he could have given, unaware as he'd be just what Tamara knew about his current situation.

"So, I was thinking," the girl went on. "Maybe I could come stay with you two?"

"With us?" Gabrielle looked at Liam.

"Wait," Liam said, sitting back and scooting his chair a bit farther from the table. A bit farther from Gabrielle. "I thought we made it clear. We aren't… We don't live together. We're friends. Period." His statement sounded so… final…it hurt Gabrielle's feelings.

"I know. But you're pretty much living together," Tamara said as Gabrielle breathed through the pain inside of her. "You're in the same building."

"In different apartments," Gabrielle said before Liam could express any more discomfort.

Tamara spent the next ten minutes or so asking Liam about things they could do together in Denver. And Gabrielle breathed a sigh of relief.

To cover any inexplicable and completely inappropriate *disappointment* that hung in her midst.

ELLIOTT TANNER WAS waiting for them as they came through security. Marie was with him. And they seemed to have become quite good friends over the past couple of days, based on the ease with which Marie was conversing with him.

"It's crazy," she said as soon as she was in hearing distance. She went right up to Gabrielle, gave her a hug hello and then turned to Liam. "The Colorado district of the federal prosecutor's office made an official announcement this morning—on a Sunday—that a grand jury indictment is being sought on several federal criminal charges against your father, and reporters are everywhere. George is just saying 'no comment' and 'not guilty,' and your dad hasn't been seen out. So this afternoon they showed up at the coffee shop, waiting for you to show your face. I called Elliott right away."

"According to my source, someone looked at public records and saw that you'd just purchased the Arapahoe," Tanner said, keeping them all within the big reach of his shoulders, as though he was their umbrella.

Liam shrugged his carry-on over his shoulder, filled with adrenaline. He was a freelance reporter working for peanuts from his apartment. But no one was going to care about that. They cared that he was his father's son.

"I'll get a room at a hotel," he said. Thinking clearly.

Marie was there.

His time alone with Gabrielle was over.

They'd made it safe and sound.

And right then he cared more about his friends' safety than anything else. Once he drew attention away from them, he'd find some way to get to his father. The old man had a lot to explain.

Liam wasn't going to put up with Walter's refusals to speak to him. Not anymore.

"You absolutely will not leave."

"No way." Marie and Gabrielle spoke simultaneously. "You're going to come home. We can figure out ways to get you in and out when you need to go," Marie continued.

"Then they'll just hound you," he told them.

Gabrielle was walking beside him. "I'll be happy to give them our statement."

As his attorney. He'd forgotten about that for a second. "And think what the publicity could do for Marie's business," she added, her words hitting him hard.

Not because of what they said, but because she knew just what to say to calm his concerns. He wanted to go home. To be in the building they'd all bought together. She was giving him a way to do so and still live with his conscience.

As soon as they had their luggage—including the suitcase of Walter's things—Tanner herded them to an elevator farthest away from baggage claim. "I don't think anyone knows we're here," he said. "There were only a couple of die-hards parked out front when Marie and I left out the back. And I'll be around to make certain that no one gets in to bother any of the three of you."

"You're one body," Liam said, still not convinced.

"They're reporters, not bandits with guns." Gabrielle's laconic reply brought a smile to his lips. And there he was wanting to hug her. To loop his arm through hers. And feel her shoulder pressing up against his.

He wanted to know that when they all went home, when all goodbyes had been said for the day, Gabrielle would still be with him.

Not downstairs with Marie.

And that thinking was going to get him in far more trouble than any reporter could.

Tanner held the elevator door for the three of them, waiting to board last. "I plan to hang out at the coffee shop," he said. "And I'd suggest, for now, the three of you hire a security guard to cover the private entrance in the back. You don't want someone getting aggressive with any of your older residents as they come and go."

"It's probably all going to die down in a day

or two," Liam said aloud, allowing himself to believe it. Glad to focus on something besides Gabrielle. "News's shelf life is shorter than a gallon of milk's these days," he continued. "I'm assuming there have been no more mysterious letters left, or new paint jobs?"

"Until the reporters showed up this afternoon, all was quiet," Marie told them. She'd reported the quiet part both times Gabrielle had called from Florida.

The three of them agreed that Elliott should find twenty-four-hour security for the back of the property for at least the next week. And then Marie spent the rest of the trip home bombarding them with questions about their weekend. Most particularly about Tamara.

All in all, Liam figured it was good to be home, despite Denver's thirty-degree drop in temperature after Florida's balmy winter weather. There was no snow on the ground. He was in a warm car. There were groceries in his cupboards. And he had good friends.

The only blight that he felt more acutely than was called for was his jealousy of Marie, who was in the backseat with Gabrielle. In Florida, that had been his place.

And he'd liked it there.

CHAPTER FOURTEEN

GABRIELLE MADE IT to bed late due to Marie's continuous questions about her weekend. She was happy to share everything but her inappropriate feelings for Liam. They'd disappear with time.

She also didn't mention his obvious distaste at the idea of his little sister thinking there could ever be anything romantic between Gabrielle and him. That memory was for her alone. To pull out anytime she started to daydream about his kisses.

Or get jealous about his girlfriends.

Or feel the hurts in his heart as though they were her own.

Dressing with care the next morning—in a short, slim black skirt, a white blouse and a jacket, with a black-and-white polka-dotted scarf—she applied more makeup than she normally did for work and slipped into pumps that she'd bought for a Christmas party one year. She did it all with one thought in mind—not embarrassing Liam.

She was glad she had as she avoided the back entrance she normally used, veering through the coffee shop and then out onto the street. To say there was a barrage of reporters would have been overstating the matter, but there were four of them, talking to each other, cameras around their necks. Looking for the insignia of one of the major news sources, she was glad to see none.

Things weren't as bad as they'd all feared coming home the night before. Liam was not being targeted.

Feeling Marie's, her staff's and Elliott Tanner's gazes on her back from just inside the store, she approached the loiterers.

"Ladies and gentlemen." She addressed the reporters. "I'm Gabrielle Miller, counsel for Liam Connelly. Mr. Connelly would like everyone to know that while he is deeply saddened to hear about his father's arrest, they are not currently in contact, nor is he employed by or associated with Connelly Investments in any way."

"Yeah, right up until he pockets his inheritance," one young man grumbled. He was dressed in jeans and a sweatshirt—could use a shave and a haircut, too. His attitude matched his appearance.

"Doesn't Liam Connelly stand to inherit whatever might be left of his father's significant holdings after investors are paid back and Walter Connelly is in jail?" another man asked before Gabrielle had a chance to acknowledge the under-the-breath comment. The second guy bore a badge that said he represented Detector Online, a fairly well-known internet news source.

There was someone there from their local community news as well.

"No, he does not." Gabrielle's smile was genuine. She realized that Walter Connelly, while autocratic, unbending and sometimes cruel, had actually done his son a favor in disowning him. "Liam is not in his father's will."

"So why does he have counsel?" the jeans-clad attitude asked.

"To deal with people like you." As soon as the words were out of her mouth, she regretted them.

"People like me?" Attitude asked. His camera had been whirring since she'd first addressed them.

"People who look for dirt where there is none," she said. This punk thought he was going to make Liam's life miserable just because he could? Without caring at all about the innocent people he was affecting? "If you did your homework, like a good reporter should, you'd see that Liam has never appeared directly with his father in any of the society pages. Even when they traveled in the same circles, they didn't travel together. If you think being the owner's son gave him any power, you're wrong. Unless you think making social appearances and overseeing small accounts does that. Liam, by the way, is a freelance reporter. Maybe you could read the article he did on last week's Douglas case and get some pointers about covering real news rather than looking for some to make..."

Three reporters were staring at her with open mouths.

The fourth, the target of her inappropriate diatribe, shut his.

No one was going to care that this was her first press conference. That she was a public lawyer who represented people who'd never make it on the news unless they were dead. Or committed a heinous crime against someone like Liam.

All they were going to care about was that she'd just allowed herself to be cajoled into screwing up.

Bad.

LIAM HAD WRITTEN his article, submitted it and left town. He'd been greeted at the airport late Friday night by the sister he'd never known and not given more than a fleeting thought to the professional project. The night before, after leaving Gabrielle and Marie's and making it up to his own apartment without incident, he'd purposely avoided the internet. He didn't want to see what might be waiting there.

But Monday morning, after a hard workout on the equipment he'd had installed in the bedroom next to his own—and a very late breakfast—he went online to see how bad his father's press was getting.

How much of it there was.

To determine his own plan of action.

As a reporter and as a son.

It wasn't as bad as he'd thought. All of the major news sources mentioned another billionaire businessman allegedly being the next in line to take a fall. A basic overview followed: development land was sold to investors who later found they'd invested in swampland when the land they were supposed to have invested in was reported as a holding of a senator who was taking a political hit for illegal campaign managing.

And Connelly Investments had continued to take investment dollars for Grayson Communities when Connelly no longer held that commodity.

He just couldn't believe his father had been that stupid. Nor could he get bogged down by that stupidity.

When he'd avoided it as long as he could, he typed in the web address for the news source carrying his own article, hoping that it would have an impressive amount of hits. And worried that it wouldn't. For himself.

And because he'd had a thought. Maybe he could convince his father to let him write a series of articles about him. His climb up from nothing. The years of integrity in the community and success that had followed. He was going to offer to help preserve his father's good reputation in any way he could. To write articles that were fact based, instead of sensation based, to counteract the bevy of press that had arisen in the past twenty-four hours.

He wanted to do it for Tamara. For himself. And, if what Gabi and Tamara believed was true—that his father really hadn't committed fraud—he wanted to do it for the old man, too.

He just needed to be able to prove to his father, in a way that was measurable, that his own articles would carry weight. Hits on Friday's article could be that proof.

He was planning to be armed with the offer to write the article when he demanded an audience with the old man. The idea could have merit if his article had a respectable amount of hits.

The editor had given him administrative rights over his content so that he was able to see what most viewers could not—the page's statistics.

Sitting back, he stared. But only for a moment.

Over a hundred thousand views in a single weekend.

He could hardly believe it himself. That should get the old man's attention.

With a couple of deft moves of his finger, he'd made and printed a screen shot of the page. He tightened the knot of his tie and, throwing his trench coat over his arm, picked up his briefcase and was on his way.

While waiting for the elevator, he remembered to text Tanner.

And was moderately impressed when the man was already in place, his SUV running and waiting for Liam as he stepped out the back door.

IT WAS LUNCHTIME before Gabrielle had a chance to think about the morning's gaffe. She'd tried to call Liam about it on the way to work, to warn him, but he hadn't picked up. She didn't leave a message, figuring it was better just to tell him about the episode in person, when she could profusely apologize for representing him in such an unprofessional fashion, for letting the reporter get to her and make her antagonistic, for making Liam look like a buffoon with a groupie.

A tearful client, one whose husband was suing for shared custody of her kids and hadn't returned them after his scheduled weekend visit, had been waiting for her when she walked into the office, and her focus had been fully engaged the rest of the morning.

Now Terri, the paralegal Gabi relied on most, found her in the hall staring at a vending machine of day-old sandwiches. "Gabi, I've been looking up your name all morning like you asked. Something just popped up a few minutes ago."

"It's bad, isn't it?" She could tell by the worried look on the young brunette's face.

"Well, you better take a look." Pulling Gabrielle by the arm, Terri took her into the office she shared with several other paralegals and sat her at her computer.

Gabrielle was thankful the room was empty except for the two of them when Terri clicked on an icon on the bottom of her screen and the site Terri wanted her to see came up.

Attitude had published it. She recognized him in the small headshot. His moniker was right there beside it: Tarnished Truth.

What Man Wouldn't Die for a Hot Attorney Like This? was the headline. And there followed a streaming video of her inelegant speech. Watching herself, Gabrielle wanted to crawl under the desk. It was worse than she'd feared.

She was worse than she'd feared. A she dragon defending her fold.

Only Liam wasn't her fold.

And she'd just made a fool of both of them.

"DID YOU LET your attorney know you were going to be seeing your father this morning?" Elliott Tanner clearly didn't like where Liam was having him take him.

"No. She's working. I'll tell her later today."

The bodyguard's frown gave his opinion. But there were some things that were between just a father and his son.

It was more a given that they wouldn't have contact since the old man had cut him off and then had him thrown out of the Connelly Investments building.

Liam had tried two ways to get inside his father's home. He had Elliott Tanner punch Liam's access code into the gated entrance. When that didn't work, he called up to the house and was told by the housekeeper who'd helped his mother raise him that his father wasn't home. When he asked to be admitted anyway, he was told again his father wasn't home. Cajoling didn't work. Charming her didn't work. His father wasn't home.

So, in spite of the fact that he was ruining a good suit and a new pair of shiny leather shoes, and with his bodyguard in tow, he resorted to the one way he knew for sure he could get in. The way he'd used to sneak in and out of the mansion when he was a kid. Through a group of trees, past a thick patch of shrubbery, to an old gatehouse on the back of the property. When his father had had the security fencing put in, he'd left the old gatehouse, building the fencing right up to it.

Because Liam's mother had asked him to. She'd loved that old gatehouse. Had painted it several times.

Luckily for Liam, Walter Connelly wasn't into gatehouses and had no idea that his son had stashed a key to that one under the cement foundation.

But all the effort gained him was a face-to-face conversation with a very nervous housekeeper.

"Your dad doesn't want you here," she told Liam, standing between him and the front hallway. She'd opened the door to him. He took that as a good sign.

She was also looking very nervously at the silent dark-haired giant dressed all in black behind him.

"Don't worry about Elliott. Dad sent him to

me," Liam said, mostly convinced the words were true. "He's here to protect us."

"Your father doesn't want you here, Liam. I'm so sorry. But I can't let you in. I'll lose my job…"

And how was a sixty-year-old spinster who'd spent her entire adult life serving one family going to find a life outside of the Connelly mansion?

Which she was going to have to do if Walter was convicted.

"I want to help him, Greta," he told the not-so-handsome German lady who'd come to live with them before he'd been old enough to remember. "I don't care about Connelly or being written out of the will. But he's my father. He needs my help. You know how stubborn he gets…"

"I can't let you in. I can't talk to you." She glanced behind her. Hands clasped in front of him, Tanner shifted. "If you come back, he's going to take out an order of injunction against you."

"Is he here?" Liam asked, trying to get a glimpse into the house, to whomever she feared finding out that she was breaking Walter's mandates. He wasn't going to be threatened or bullied.

She leaned forward, whispering, "He's had cameras installed all over in here. Video and audio. Now go."

"Is he here?" Liam asked beneath his breath. Greta shook her head and shut the door.

By two in the afternoon, the next time Gabrielle had a break, Attitude's video had gone up on Facebook and YouTube. All thanks to him, she was certain.

And one of the less reputable national news sources was showing it on their site, as well.

Sitting at her desk with the door closed, Gabrielle picked up her cell phone to call Liam. It was probably too late. Chances were he'd already seen it.

Stupid of her to give some unknown journalist a chance at the big time by walking right into the nationally breaking story of Walter Connelly's imminent trip to the grand jury.

She should have taken a page from George, an experienced and successful corporate attorney, and just said Liam had no comment.

She should have called Liam at lunch.

But she'd hoped the little worm's story wouldn't be seen by anyone who wasn't looking for it.

She'd three missed calls. All from Liam.

He'd known the old man was vindictive. But Liam had never, ever, in a million years expected this. Sitting in a jail cell with Elliott Tanner right beside him, he had to hand it to the old man. At least if he was going to have his son arrested, he'd made sure that his bodyguard would do the time with him.

He was putting Liam in danger. And protecting him at the same time. As if that somehow made it all okay. Made him a better man.

"You should've called her office phone," Tanner said, sounding not quite peevish, but close to it. "She told you that she turns the ringer off on her cell when she's with clients or in court."

Yes, Gabrielle had said that. "She's with people who need her more than we do," he said. "People who can't afford to hire another attorney."

Which was why he'd told Tanner he'd fire him if he used his own phone call to try to reach Gabrielle on her office line.

Besides, it seemed he had more of his old man in him than he'd thought. Let Walter stew when he didn't hear that his son was out of jail. It wouldn't hurt for him to know that his son was sitting in a jail cell. Like Buckus had so long ago.

For him?

Gabrielle had been going to phone Gwen Menard that morning on her break. To fill her in on what they'd found over the weekend. To hear if there was anything more to report on the investigation against his father.

Liam would rather she use her break time for

the more important work. As long as they were out of jail before bedtime, he was fine.

"These investigations take months," he said aloud, mostly to drown out Tanner's breathing down his neck.

"We are not going to be here for months."

"I was talking about my father. Years, even."

Would Gabi continue to represent him all that time? Would he be able to keep his growing passion for her in check? Or would it fade, leaving them in peace?

And their little family happily together forever. The girls would marry good men. They'd have kids. And Liam would be their honorary uncle...

The thought of Gabi having another man's children made him start to hyperventilate. So he thought about Marie's kids.

And had no problem at all.

"You're going to get pretty bored hanging around me for years," he said to Elliott. He couldn't think about Gabi, clearly. Not until this was all over and he was more himself.

Elbows on his knees, his head hanging, Tanner turned and looked at Liam. "If today's anything to go by, I doubt it," he said.

"So you plan to be around?" Liam asked, more to goad the guy. To get him to admit that Walter was behind his employment with Liam.

"No."

It was all the man said. Clearly all he was going to say. So Liam asked, "What do you do when you aren't watching me?"

"I watch other people."

"Here in Denver?"

"Yep."

"So if I look you up…" He'd have done so already, if not for the fact that Williams had sent him. And the police and Gabi had both checked on him, as well.

"You'll find my LLC duly registered and my taxes paid."

"You think we'll make the evening news?"

They'd left the Connelly mansion as soon as Greta had verified that his father wasn't home. And gone straight to the lion's den. Connelly Investments.

At which point Walter, who'd expressly forbidden Liam access, had called the police.

The reporters outside Connelly Investments had been only too happy to snap flashes in their faces as they'd been escorted out of the building in handcuffs.

Another dry look from Tanner. "You can count on it." The man was rubbing his hands together. As though he'd like to be grinding something between them.

"You got family?" Liam asked. Someone

who'd be alarmed to see him on the evening news in handcuffs.

"An aunt and cousin out in California."

"You see them much?"

"No."

"Ever been married?" He figured Tanner for around his own age, thirty, thirty-one.

"No."

Receiving the loud and clear message that the subject was off-limits from the other man's tone, Liam asked, "You don't like me much, do you?"

The silence in the jail cell left too much room for thoughts that needed action. Like getting together with June Fryburg while his article was hot and finding out if she'd give him a chance to write about the Connelly case from his own perspective, even if his father wouldn't cooperate.

In the meantime, talking would pass the time.

"I like you fine, Connelly," Tanner said. "Now would you shut the hell up so I can listen to what's going on down the hall?"

Neither of them was going to be there long, Liam was certain of that. As soon as Gabrielle got free and listened to her messages, she'd be there to bail them out.

His old man would drop the trespassing charges...this time.

But Liam had gotten his message, loud and clear.

He wasn't going anywhere near Walter Connelly again. Ever.

But he would be going through Connelly's files again, paying close attention to a timeline of everything George had done.

He had to know if George was in on the fraudulent investments with his father. If Buckus was. Or if the old man had acted alone.

He had to figure out a way to secure Greta's future in the likely event she found herself out of work.

He had money in his trust. Nothing by his father's standards. But if he invested well and started to earn substantially, he could possibly afford to take on a housekeeper. As long as she'd work for less than his father was paying her.

One thing was for certain. When it came to making money, to finances and investing, Liam knew a lot.

Because he'd learned from the best.

CHAPTER FIFTEEN

As soon as she heard Liam's first voice mail, asking her to meet him at a particular city jail on a particular street, Gabrielle packed up for the day and ran for her car. In pencil-thin two-inch heels. She dialed his number on the way and hung up when it went straight to voice mail.

Luckily she didn't trip and kill herself.

By the time she was buckled in, she had Marie up on the Bluetooth in her car—an inexpensive after-factory model that her brother had installed for her when she and Marie had driven to New Mexico to see her family two years before. "Are you with Liam?" Marie asked as soon as she picked up. "Oh, my gosh, Gabi, I just saw the news and..."

"It's all over the news now?"

"Of course it is! Based on the footage I'm looking at there were at least thirty members of the press there when they took him away."

Wait. What? Maybe she should have listened to Liam's next two messages. She'd been too impatient with her voice mail system, needing

her to choose whether to save or delete. His first
message had said to meet him at the jail. She'd
thought Walter had been arrested again.

"Who took who away?"

"Liam! He was arrested! Right outside of
Connelly Investments! Elliott was, too! The
news says that Walter Connelly had them arrested for trespassing!"

"You've got to be kidding…" Gabrielle
wanted to cry. To scream. To rant at a mean
and vindictive sixty-year-old man.

She wanted to be surprised.

But she wasn't.

More than anything she wanted the man she
loved out of jail. Immediately.

Loved. She hadn't just thought that. Or rather,
she had, but loved like… Marie loved him.

"I can't believe he went down there," she said
now, pushing aside her personal feelings as she
focused on the case. That was all that mattered
at the moment.

The case. Who was guilty and who might be
being framed.

Not who loved whom.

"I'm on my way to the jail now," she told
Marie. While Gabrielle would have liked to
hang up to concentrate on the hour ahead of
her and the legalities involved in getting her

client out of jail before dinner, Marie, who was understandably wound up, needed to talk.

Gabrielle told Marie about her morning screwup. Asked Marie if she'd seen anything on the news about it. She hadn't. Which meant it hadn't yet made national news.

With any luck, it wouldn't.

"Grace has been fretting most of the day," Marie said next. "She's bothered by all of the reporters. Several of them are."

"I'll bet Janice thinks the whole thing's exciting," Gabrielle said, calming as she pictured the residents who were depending on the three of them to keep them securely in their homes. "Maybe you should call a meeting after you close the shop," she suggested. "Just let everyone know what's going on and about the security company we've hired to ensure that they can come and go without hassle or fear."

"I had Sam hand deliver memos to every single tenant first thing this morning," Marie told her. And Gabrielle knew she should have thought of it.

Marie counted on her to be Threefold's legal advisor. And that morning she'd been too busy thinking about how she was going to look as she represented Liam when she walked out the door to think about anything else.

Like keeping her head about her as she took

on media representatives who were out to use the Connelly misfortune to their own benefit.

Liam was consuming her. Not just her mind, but her emotions. And those emotions were clouding her thoughts.

That had to stop.

HE SAW THE gorgeous woman standing in the lobby of the police station first. The two-inch heels clicked prettily as she walked, drawing his attention. His gaze traveled from there up over slim ankles, long, perfectly shaped legs, a black skirt and a tailored jacket with bow-shaped silk buttons at the waist, and the police station, the afternoon faded away for that split second. He was himself again. Taking interest in a woman he'd yet to meet...

"I'm sorry it took me so long to get here."

At first he recognized the voice as if he was in a fog. Recognized the heels walking toward him. It was as though he'd known already.

And didn't want to know.

"Are you okay?" The heels were toe to toe with his smudged dress shoes. "Your pants, they're stained. Were you in a fight?"

The beautiful woman was his attorney. He'd been ready to flirt with Gabrielle.

"Don't worry about the time," he said, infusing so much cheer in his voice he convinced himself that he was fine. "I could have called your office phone, but I thought it would do my father some good to spend the afternoon knowing that his son was in jail. Until now it's been the one place he forbade me to go that I didn't."

"I apologize that you had to make the trip down here," Tanner said from just behind Liam.

"What happened?" Gabrielle asked as they walked with the officer who'd escorted them from the holding cell toward the window where they could sign to have their things returned to them.

"I insisted on seeing my father." Liam could do his own talking. "I stood outside and called his phones, cell and office, more than once, leaving a message on his office recorder, letting him know that I wasn't going anywhere, so he might as well pick up. When none of that worked, I went inside."

"Liam told his father he wanted to help him," Tanner butted in. "Next thing you know there's three squad cars pulling up and we're both in handcuffs being carted away."

Liam was shown to the window and signed for his wallet, briefcase, belt and cell phone. Tanner did the same.

"It's all over the news," Gabrielle said softly as, with officers watching them, they headed out into the cold.

Liam wasn't sure he cared at the moment.

More pressing was the woman walking with him to her car. She looked so…feminine. And it felt so good, having her there rescuing him. As if he was hers to rescue…

Suddenly this moment, not the one when he'd been cuffed and pushed down into a squad car, was the scariest part of the day.

It shamed him, this inexplicable need to be tied to her. She was there to help him. As his attorney. She was one of his very best friends. She trusted him.

And suddenly he was picturing what it would be like to kiss her.

It was unacceptable.

Wrong.

And going to stop.

THE NUMBER OF reporters outside the coffee shop had doubled since that morning. As Liam drove down the street that cornered the front of their building, instead of pulling up out front, Gabrielle eyed the batch of them and groaned inwardly when she recognized Attitude. She'd yet to tell Liam about that piece of bad news in his already horrible day.

Driving around back, Liam pulled her car right up to their entrance and turned her keys over to the security guard who would park her car, leaving her to wonder how she was going to get her keys back.

"Your keys will be delivered to you upstairs," Liam told her, as though he could read her mind now, too, in addition to knowing her order for Chinese without having to ask.

"I've taken the liberty to arrange for twenty-four-hour security both in front and back of the building," Elliott said quietly as they left the car and went straight into the building.

Security was keeping paparazzi off the back lot, but cameras had zoom lenses and Gabrielle didn't want to take any more chances of having any part of her splashed on the news.

"I'll be heading home," Elliott continued as they walked with purpose toward the elevator that would take her straight to her apartment. Where she could assess the damages while Liam got cleaned up.

She'd heard, in the car on the way home, how he'd come to be smudged. And had been glad that she'd been in the backseat, having asked him to drive, so he couldn't see her sudden smile. The antics—gaining access to his father's estate through the old gatehouse—reminded her of the Liam she'd known in college. That boy had been nearly dauntless when it came to reaching a goal.

"For the next few days, I'm going to insist

that you call me before you leave the building," Elliott was saying to Liam.

"I'd rather you follow Gabi." Liam stood tall, briefcase in hand, as they waited for the elevator. "People saw her come bail us out. She's been inadvertently put into the limelight now, too. I won't have her harmed, or in any way hassled..."

"Forget it, Liam," she said dryly. She wasn't one of his fragile hothouse flowers who didn't know how to change a tire. Or shoot a gun. She didn't need his protection. "You're the one they want. You're the one who's had a threatening letter and a vandalized car. You're the one with a billionaire father who's been arrested for stealing from people."

"I can't be two places at once," Elliott said, looking at Liam. "If you want to stay put here with the security in place, I can make sure Gabrielle gets to and from work without mishap."

She opened her mouth to tell them that they were being ludicrous, but the elevator doors opened and in those two seconds, Liam said, "You've got a deal. Have a good evening," and ushered Gabrielle in.

She was not going to be watched. She wasn't one of the rich and famous.

"I liked it when Marie and I were just nobodies." She said the words, somewhat peevishly, as they traveled slowly up to the second floor. She was going to call Elliott Tanner before morning and tell him to stick to Liam.

Just because he'd said he'd stay home didn't mean he would. And if today was anything to go by, he clearly needed watching more than she did.

The man had no radar when it came to putting himself in danger. Growing up privileged seemed to have given him a false sense of security. "Thank you for all you did for me today," Liam replied. "You're going to see a bonus on your check."

The words were just the slap in the face she needed.

She might be Liam Connelly's friend of more than ten years, might even be inadvertently falling in love with him, but right now she was just his paid attorney.

It would do her good to remember that.

ALL SHE REALLY wanted was to have a salad alone, in peace and quiet. Texting Marie to let her know she was home—a safety habit they'd fallen into in college—she kicked off her shoes as soon as she was in their door, picking them up to carry them back to the shoe holder hanging in the closet.

Liam had asked her to meet him upstairs in

half an hour. And even if he hadn't, she'd have had to see him. She still had to confess her idiocy of the morning.

And pray that he didn't figure out that after more than ten years of being his platonic friend, she'd suddenly developed intense, nonplatonic feelings for him.

They had to talk about the trespassing charges and how she was going to go about working with his father to have them dismissed. They had no time to deal with personal drama. Walter could play hardball all he wanted, but she had too much on him for him to refuse to drop the charges. She'd already figured out that much. All she had to do was threaten to expose his affair as more evidence of his overall duplicitous nature, adding in that he'd been carrying on with Missy while his sick wife was still alive.

She'd never follow through on such a threat. But if playing rough with Liam's father was the only way to get him to drop the charges against his son, she'd do so.

She was intending to convince Liam to sign an agreement to stay away from his father in exchange for Walter's dropping of the charges. Hopefully, Walter would respond well to the polite and rational plea. Surely he didn't really want Liam to have a criminal record.

Reaching for a pair of old sweats—Liam had

seen her in her pajamas enough times to make standing on ceremony with him completely unnecessary—Gabrielle changed her mind at the last minute and grabbed a pair of black pants and a white sweater, instead.

The night ahead was not going to be a time among friends. She was going to be working. And as long as she kept her mind on her job, she'd do it well.

There would not be a repeat of the morning's unprofessional lapse. Nor would she allow herself to think about Liam as anything other than a client.

There was just too much at risk to do otherwise.

LIAM PURPOSELY WAITED for Gabrielle to arrive before turning on his computer or television set. He'd listened to his voice mail, though, and found that June Fryburg, the editor he'd called, was not only willing to have him do his own version of the Connelly story, one based in truth rather than speculation and innuendo, but she'd already sold it to a major news source.

Her first big coup. And his, too.

His father was inadvertently giving Liam what he'd always wanted most. Success as a journalist. The only thing he wasn't sure about was if June had made her call to him before or after he'd appeared on local news in handcuffs.

He told himself that it didn't matter, that journalists who went to jail trying to get a story were often more sought after for having done so. And he could in good conscience say that he'd been at Connelly Investments that morning with the express purpose of getting this particular story.

He wanted to help his father before public opinion, through the press, crucified him. Even if by some chance the grand jury didn't indict him, which Liam seriously doubted, his reputation would be ruined. There would be doubt in people's minds when it came to Walter's trustworthiness.

In the investment business, a lack of trust was the kiss of death.

Something he had to keep in mind for himself, the small voice inside of him reminded. Financial investment was the business he knew in his sleep. It was his fallback. His security net.

He couldn't be going around breaking and entering or getting himself arrested anymore. His reputation was his security.

There was a message from Tamara as well. For both of them. She wanted to come to Denver. To see their father. And to see him and Gabrielle again and to meet Marie. She had a week off at spring break and enough money saved to buy a plane ticket.

She failed to say whether or not Missy would approve of the adventure. As much as he wanted to see her again—and he did, he missed her already—he was not going to come between a girl and the mother who was loving and committed to giving her child the best chance at a good life.

And, ironically, the last message was from a Denver police officer, following up on his two threat reports—the letter and the car. The two reports had been joined into one case, assigned to a Billy Wilton. Liam was to contact Billy about any further incidents or if he had any more information on the previously reported crimes. Other than that, there was nothing to report. Officer Wilton left both his office and cell phone numbers.

Liam wondered if Billy Wilton knew about Liam's arrest.

He was out of the shower, but still with wet hair, in jeans and with a towel around his neck when he heard Gabi's knock on the door.

Looking forward to a kicked-back evening where he could just be himself, he didn't bother going for a shirt before he answered. She'd be in the sweats she put on when she was in for

the night. They'd be right back on even footing.
Friends for life.

Where they belonged.

He, for one, couldn't wait.

CHAPTER SIXTEEN

LIAM HAD THE professionally dressed Gabrielle who'd arrived at his front door sit at his computer. With a hastily donned black T-shirt on with his jeans and shoes on his feet, he leaned over her just enough to see without a glare.

So much for a kicked-back evening. His attorney was tense. To say the least.

They both knew that his arrest had made the news. It was wise to find out how much of an issue the press was making of the situation. He'd done a stupid thing. A couple of them. In hindsight, he wasn't proud of himself.

Gabrielle was his lawyer, being paid to assess the situation and then advise him how to proceed. It was her job to clean up his mess.

He'd already signed on to the internet, but left his home screen up. His executive desk chair seemed to swallow Gabi as she sat there. Clicking.

The only reason he noticed how slender and... feminine...her fingers looked as she placed them on his keyboard was because he was used to seeing his own thicker hands there.

"Liam?" Her hands dropped back to her lap as she turned her head just enough to see him.

"It's okay, Gabi. I'm prepared. Whatever it is, we'll deal with it." He hadn't told her about his idea for the article yet, about his editor's positive response. First, because, though he'd called, he hadn't been able to reach June to make certain the offer still stood in light of the day's events.

And secondly, because they had to figure out the day's repercussions before he socked her with another issue. Gabi was best at one thing at a time. Always had been. She'd studied for one final at a time. Ate food off her plate one item at a time. Paid her bills one at a time on the day each was due.

"No...there's something else..."

His stomach lurched. Had she noticed the way he'd first looked at her when she'd walked toward him at the police station? Did she know that he was developing extremely uncomfortable feelings where she was concerned? He was pretty sure he'd kept them to himself. But...

She hadn't worn her sweats, as if she was trying to keep distance between them. Or wasn't comfortable around him anymore.

She wasn't saying anything. The pained expression on her face was enough to keep him rattled.

He could bring up what was happening. Talk

about finding her irresistible all of a sudden. But what good would it do? They both knew what they'd be risking by starting anything between them. Assuming she even had an interest in trying to date him. Marie would be hurt, left out. A third-wheel situation didn't usually work well for long. Plus, he was rich. Gabrielle had never hidden the fact that she wasn't comfortable around so much wealth.

But, most importantly, if his interest moved on—and though he couldn't imagine it at the moment, the reality was, based on his history, that it probably would—there'd be no way to go back to the "them" they'd been. He'd have lost his family.

So maybe if they talked about it—agreed that neither of them wanted to pursue anything—the allure would die a natural death.

It was possible.

The elephant in the room and all that.

"Look," he started, having no idea what was going to follow, knowing only that he had to take accountability and somehow make this right before it was too late.

"No... I... There's..."

"Gabi, it'll all be fine—"

"I screwed up." She blurted right over him, as though the falsity of his assurances was so strong it had blown her reticence right out the door.

Liam stepped back. Away from the emotion that flooded him as he looked into those pain-moistened eyes.

Wait. What was she talking about? He was the one who'd gotten himself arrested.

He was the one who'd somehow fallen for his attorney.

Her eyes filled with tears. "I'm so sorry. I wanted so badly to help you, and instead I've made everything worse. At a time I didn't think it could get any worse."

His system stopped for a moment. Total shut-down.

Gabi was crying? For him?

Marie was the emotional one. Not Gabrielle…

The agony in her gaze hit him anew. What-ever she'd done…it must be bad.

"What did you do?" he asked, the question infused with dread. Had she agreed to move away? Taken a job somewhere? Was she leav-ing him?

"This morning. Out front. I was going to make that 'no comment' statement to report-ers, if there were any out there. Like we talked about on the way home last night."

In the cacophony of his day, he'd completely forgotten that little detail.

"So what happened?" He was trying to look stern but wanted to smile. Gabi wasn't used to his life, to having reporters at charity functions or having her picture in the society pages now and then. She'd probably chickened out, gone out the back way. She was, after all, the reserved one of the bunch. Unless she was in court.

"This jerk…" She glanced away then, as her voice, full of anger and disgust and he couldn't tell what else, continued on. "He was out to nail you to a cross. He'd already made up his mind about you—certain that you're in as thick as your father is. He was just looking to get me to say something that he could twist to fit the spin he'd already put on his story."

Interesting. Apparently she hadn't chickened out. "And?"

"I said more than 'no comment.'"

"You did." He wanted to take this seriously. Gabi was a smart woman and not disposed to drama. The fact that she was upset usually meant something was legitimately upsetting. And he wanted to hug her, too. He never should have sent her out there, a small fish in his big diseased pond.

She'd been so sure she could handle it. It had seemed so important to her the night before when they'd all discussed their plans, that as his attorney she should be the one to make the statement. Marie had thought it a good idea. So had Elliott Tanner, not that he had enough history on them to know what he was talking about, except from a safety standpoint. Tanner hadn't thought Gabi would be in any danger facing any reporters on her own. To the contrary, it had seemed the least dramatic way to go...

With her hands clasped in her lap like a schoolgirl, she said, "I got defensive, Liam. I said more than I should have."

"What did you say?" He was still just merely curious at this point.

Another glance up at him and she turned back to his computer. "You can see for yourself. The jerk put it up on YouTube."

Liam's first clue that Gabi had real reason for concern hit him when she mentioned that the video was online. His second came as soon as her fingers hit the keyboard. She knew right where to go to find what she was looking for, which meant she'd already seen it. And knew it was bad.

The third was the number of views the video had had. Almost as many as his article. In less than a day's time.

She'd gone viral.

"IF YOU DID your homework like a good reporter should..."

Liam watched the scene unfold on his computer screen, completely entranced. No one had ever…ever gone to bat for him like that.

He'd had no idea Gabi had so much lion in her.

Or that he'd be the one to inspire such a passionate response from her.

And there was that black suit again. And more makeup than he was used to seeing on her. Makeup that had mostly worn off by the time she'd come to get him from jail that afternoon.

Her back to him now, she faced the screen the entire time the video played.

When it finished he didn't say a word. He was too moved to trust himself not to say something he'd later regret.

One thing Liam had learned at a young age was that there were times to hold your tongue.

Gabi was typing again. The name of a rag internet news source. He was familiar with it. And would rather work for his father than write for them.

She clicked, quickly clicked again and a bold black headline filled his screen: *What Man Wouldn't Die for a Hot Attorney Like This?*

Gabi thought the hideous scumbag had made up a lascivious, insulting, disgusting story.

In Liam's mind the lowlife reporter managed to hit right on the truth.

"I'm sorry." She was still looking at the screen.

She was sorry? Did that mean she wasn't on to him? Hadn't noticed that he'd fallen for her?

Could he still salvage this?

"I'm not sorry," he said, complete seriousness behind every word. "You stood up for me, Gabi. You are not responsible for the fact that one man's brain took him straight to a dirt pile. What you said is completely true. My father and I are not only not close, he never even let me associate closely enough with him at work to have the ability to be instrumental to a scheme like this. You aren't to blame for this reporter's cheesy attempt to get a lot of press."

"I should have said 'no comment.'"

Possibly. But he was glad she hadn't. However, Liam quickly determined that now wasn't a good time to tell her how completely wonderful her defense of him made him feel.

Because in the end, the way he felt wasn't wonderful at all. Not when it meant risking Threefold and the family they'd grown into.

FEELING THE WEIGHT of her failure on her shoulders, and in the heat in her cheeks, Gabrielle closed the window on the incriminating article and sat there. They had to move on to the big news of the day—the reputable news sources—

but ethics required her to turn around to him first.

"I fully understand if you'd like to seek other representation, Liam. It won't hurt my feelings, and it won't affect our friendship." She looked him straight in the eye as she spoke. "This was my mistake. I let you down."

"Stop." He looked as though he was going to come closer, but didn't. "I told you, this is not your fault. I need you, Gabi. I trust you. And right now you and Marie are the only people in this world I can say that about."

"You're sure?"

"Positive."

The glow his words—his look—gave her made up for a lot of the angst she'd been carrying around all day.

And instilled a new commitment within her to give Liam the absolute best representation he could hope to have.

It also nudged the growing need to have the right to take care of him, in every way, forever. The feelings had to stop. Because if she couldn't get this under control, if she continued to feel jealous just thinking about him with another woman, she was going to end up making all of them uncomfortable.

Putting a breach in their friendship that surely

wouldn't survive as they all eventually married and had families of their own.

Most particularly if she was jealous of the mother of his children…

He was watching her. She had to focus. To concentrate. And do what she knew she could do well.

"Okay, so let's see what the media has done with you today and move on," she told him, instilling her voice with the confidence she gave to all of her clients.

With sure strokes, she typed in the URL for a national news source before looking at the local news, which they already knew had full coverage. "If you're not up here, we're ahead of the game," she said as she typed. Pushed Enter. And waited.

Watching the local coverage would be much easier for him when he knew that the scope of the broadcast was limited.

The headlining story, complete with a picture that covered the top left quarter of the screen, had to do with the newest twist in an ongoing global political battle. She scrolled right by it and down to the bolded list of links that represented the current news. Liam wouldn't be there. Hopefully Walter wouldn't be, either. They could get to the local stuff and formulate a plan.

Namely, her plan to get Walter to drop the trespassing charges.

She scanned quickly and then came back up the list from the bottom to the top.

Behind her, Liam hadn't moved. Didn't even seem to be breathing.

And then she saw what he'd obviously already seen, the second item, under breaking news: A Twist to the Breaking Connelly Investments Case. Beneath that, Son Liam and Attorney Girlfriend Go to Lengths to Direct Press Away from Father.

With a feeling of dread like lead in her stomach, she clicked on the link, hoping the story would be short and indicative of the fact that there was no real news to report where Walter was concerned.

It took a second for the link to load. A picture was coming up.

Gabrielle turned to look at Liam. As if he'd been waiting for her to come get him, he leaned in closer, their cheeks side-by-side as they watched the photo slowly load.

"It's probably just a stock photo of your father," she told him, but she knew, even without seeing, that was wishful thinking.

"It's going to be me in cuffs," he told her. He sounded as if he thought things could be worse. "Wouldn't you know it, the one time I show up at Connelly with smudges on my suit is the one day the press notices me…"

She turned her face, needing to see the smile she knew he'd be wearing, and their gazes met. The press had just called her his girlfriend.

She hadn't allowed herself to entertain the thought. Knew she couldn't now.

"How do you do it?" she asked him.

Their mouths were so close she could see the small lines in his lips as he said, "Do what?"

"Stay so upbeat all the time. No matter what someone says or does to you, even if they knock you down, you come up with a smile. Or some positive way to spin it."

"I didn't know I did."

"It's what drew me to you from the first time we met," she told him. "You'd just been kicked in the teeth by your father when Marie and I knocked on your door. And you were all about having us help you make your bed since you'd never done it before. You were excited to sleep in a dumpy room with not a single luxury— unless you counted the running water and flushing toilet in the bathroom—just because you could."

He was still watching her, not the screen, so she continued to hold on, too.

"What would you have had me do?" She watched his lips move.

"Exactly what you did." She almost smiled, but couldn't quite. "It's just that I was…"

"Horrified?"

"Something like that. I see danger everywhere, pitfalls and risks. Life has always been a minefield to me. Then I spend time with you and I see flower beds."

"My father raised me to expect the best out of any situation. I think I probably segued a bit from his initial intent, but I learned early, probably from Mom and growing up with her sick, that the best way to get through anything tough was to look for the good. In every moment. It's not like I stand around looking for it. I think she showed me how to find it naturally. Like she showed me how to brush my teeth and use the right silverware," he told her slowly, his gaze seeming to devour her face.

"I would have liked to have met her." She licked her lips gone terribly dry.

"You met me instead."

Yes. Yes, she had. He moved an inch. She didn't. That was why his lips touched hers. Because he'd expected her to back up and she hadn't. It was accidental. And the shock held her still.

Until his lips moved on hers. And she responded.

CHAPTER SEVENTEEN

IT TOOK LIAM less than five seconds to know he'd made the most major error of his life. Jerking back from Gabrielle, he became a six-foot-tall mass of panic.

What had he done? How did he undo it?

For every way in, there had to be a way out.

He came up blank. So he turned to the computer screen.

And saw the picture.

Emotions exploded like a burst dam, coursing through his system with a force that threatened to drown him.

Anger. Excitement. Fear. First and foremost, fear.

There in front of them, staring out at them… was a picture of him and Gabi.

His most private shame that day was right there for the world to see. Him and Gabi as a couple.

Why he'd made such a serious error in judgment, why he'd so inappropriately crossed the line, breaking the trust that he and Gabi and

Marie had established in each other so many years before, he had no idea.

But the fates were mocking him, calling him on it, right then and there. For all the world to see.

Obviously taken with a telephoto lens, the photo depicted the two of them sitting together, alone, leaning in toward one another, eyes meeting, at a little café table. The background showed a large window, and outside, darkness.

"That was taken at the coffee shop." Gabrielle's voice sounded choked as she spoke beside him. The photo made it look as if they were a couple, intimate. Splashed on the national news.

Liam had no idea what she was thinking. He couldn't look at her to find out. But he knew her well enough to know that she'd see all of this in the worst light possible.

Knowing too that once there, she'd set to finding a way to protect them from the harm. Because that was what Gabi did. She looked for the dangers and then either prevented them or tended to them...

"He, or she, must have been out front. The background is the side window..." He focused on the picture. Not on the kiss he'd just instigated.

Not on the fact that she'd responded.

On the fact that a kiss had never rocked him so deeply...

"It was the night the letter came to the shop," she said. "That's when we were sitting at that table, just the two of us. After Tanner and the police left, and then Marie went with Burton, we were the only ones in the shop..."

He wasn't surprised she'd gone straight to analyzing. He'd moved as far away from her as he could while still having a good view of the screen. They'd both continued to stare only at it.

If they ignored the fact that they'd just kissed, would the fact disappear into the ether as though it was just another of the dreams that had been haunting him the past several nights?

"We have to find out who took the picture," Liam said.

"My guess is it's the same person who sent the letter. I'm thinking he sent the letter to set us up. To bring us both down there. With the hopes of getting a good shot of the two of us together."

"Why would anyone want a shot of the two of us together?" The surprise brought on by her statement had him staring at her before he knew he'd broken his vow not to look at her again. "We weren't branded a couple until you spoke to that reporter this morning..."

Gabi's brow furrowed, and for the first time

since he'd known her she looked lost. Completely and truly lost.

Had his kiss done that to her?

The idea shouldn't please him.

But it did.

DIZZY WITH CONFUSION, Gabrielle attempted to swallow to counteract the dryness in her throat. She looked back at the computer, attempting to find a rational explanation for the way her mind had spun a scenario that didn't exist.

Her life was based on reason. Understanding allowed the ability to affect. To change. To make better...

"You're right," she said when she could trust herself to sound professional. "The photographer wasn't looking for us in particular, he was watching you and I just happened to be there. It fits. The news of your father's arrest had hit, but there was no mention of the grand jury indictment yet at that point. He was betting one would be coming, that it would be big news, and he was going to be ready when it hit. I'll bet he took hundreds of photos so he'd have an arsenal to choose from when the time was right."

She was back on her game. Her mind was working. She just had to focus on the job. The one thing in her life she could count on. Her security. And her greatest satisfaction. Her source of happiness…

And pray that Liam let go of her jumping to such an inane conclusion. Lest he figure out that she was also inanely rattled around him.

Lest either one of them be forced to mention the kiss that they needed to forget ever happened.

Liam pointed to the screen, farther down in the article, and she realized he'd been reading.

His finger was on her quote from that morning and she started to lose grounding again. Shaking inside, cold and feeling pressure in her chest, she knew her worst nightmare from that morning had come true.

She'd embarrassed Liam on a national level. Made his situation worse by feeding the media fodder the American public would gobble up.

He scrolled down. And the picture of him being arrested came into view.

The news was sensationalistic. The national source's handling of it was not. Only the facts were being told. But the implications couldn't be missed.

As soon as Walter Connelly had been arrested, his son and his longtime best friend, attorney Gabrielle Miller, had hit the streets with their separate little dramas. One had to ask, according to the story, why the couple who'd never been together in the media before both hit on the same day. Could it be that they were trying to detract media attention from the FBI investigation?

Trying to protect Walter Connelly by having his alleged sins be less public?

The article intimated that the couple, in light of the newly exposed picture of them taken the week before, were clearly an item. The pieces were all coming together: Liam Connelly's broken engagement. His father's arrest. And then the exposure of his longtime affair with Gabrielle.

Both Connellys were of the same cloth—men who appeared honest and trustworthy but led secret and not so honest lives.

The implication was that Walter Connelly was already assumed guilty. Before he'd even been indicted.

The press was busy judging the family's way of handling being found out, not questioning if a man with as many philanthropic endeavors as Walter had would have committed such a crime. They'd already been judged.

Other pictures were there. One of Liam and Elliott by the door in the back of the apartment complex and several of Walter—stock photos and a couple of more recent ones.

There was a paragraph about the twelve-year-old's egging of Walter's gate, exemplifying that not only investors had been hurt by the Connelly scheme, but also their families and their children.

The American public was encouraged to stay tuned and find out what other secrets would be exposed in the course of the investigation.

Gabrielle wanted to throw up.

LIAM WANTED TIME to himself. He'd kissed his best friend. Lies about his life were all over the news. And his father was about to be indicted on charges that could put him in prison for the rest of his natural life.

Liam couldn't let the night end this way, though. No telling what Gabi, with her worrying and X-ray vision when it came to danger, would do with that kiss undiscussed between them. By morning it could have grown into a mountain that would keep them from ever seeing each other again.

And that was his worst nightmare.

She closed the internet browser. "The first thing we have to do is get your father to drop the trespassing charges," she said, proceeding in a very calm, determined fashion to lay out her plan to get his father to capitulate.

"It's a good plan," he told her, settling his butt on the corner of his desk. A couple of feet of heavy wood between them wasn't much, but it was better than standing close enough to feel the heat coming off her body.

Or smell the scent of her skin.

"You know my father well," he told her, not displeased by that fact, either.

"Comes from more than ten years of watching you deal with him," she said. She chuckled, but there was no mirth on her face. Nor was there when she looked at him.

"You're good at sizing up your adversary and cutting to the quick," he told her. Because he didn't want her to size him up and cut him off, he had to deal with this.

Had to make things right between them.

"Then we have to figure out how we're going to handle your publicity, Liam. Do you want me to make a formal statement? Do you want to stick with the 'no comment at this time' routine? How do you want me to play this?"

She wasn't quitting him. He switched gears a bit. To give himself time to figure out what to do with her. For her. For them.

To figure out how to not only preserve their friendship—his and Marie's and Gabi's—but to prevent any more of the rash and inappropriate feelings and actions emanating from him without his will.

"What do you suggest?"

"In my opinion, the less said, the less anyone has to twist or use against you."

Then she probably wasn't going to like what he'd deemed his good news, either.

"I could break up with you—publicly speaking, of course," he said. It had worked for Jenna. Got them apart in the eyes of her father without making her look bad. Making her the victim and him the bad guy.

That, at least, would take off the pressure of having the press make this nightmare any worse. Or shine a light on reality in their fantasy. A light that Gabi might actually begin to see.

"Why would you do that? It would only keep the gossip growing. Gain more attention. You'd have more reporters watching you. Everywhere you go. Everything you do. Just so they can be the one to see you with yet another woman. To…"

He got the picture.

"With my history, they'd easily believe that I'd moved on. I was trying to get them off your back."

"Let me worry about my back, Liam. I've gotten pretty good at it over the years."

"You're probably not going to like what I have to tell you next," he said. Might as well disappoint her all at once. And then find some way to do damage control.

The muscles in her cheeks dropped. "What?"

"I've sold this story." He told her about June Fryburg asking for an exclusive.

"Wait, what? What story?"

"My father. Connelly Investments. The truth. A father's journey as told through the eyes of his son."

"You don't know the truth." Was there doubt in her voice?

"That's why I was at Connelly Investments today. To get my father to agree to let me help him." He told her about his idea to present the good sides of Walter Connelly. To tell the truth. In the hope that if an indictment came back, his father would get a fairer trial than if he'd been completely harangued by the media.

"You thought he'd just confess his guilt and leave you to get him a lighter sentence?"

Maybe. Something like that. In part. But there was so much more to it. "I'm hoping to preserve his reputation in the event that he doesn't get prison time and still needs to support himself," he said.

She studied him. Nodded. "I think it's a good idea."

Was there no end to the shocks that were hitting him that day? "You do."

Sitting back in his chair, looking like a professionally dressed waif siren, she crossed her hands in her lap and said, "While my natural inclination would be to stay silent, I think, in this case, silence would be more like an admission of guilt. The media is going to believe what they choose to believe, and spin whatever fodder they can find to fit their version of the truth. If you put your truth out there, at least people will have a different version to believe if they choose to do so. If nothing else, the media will have a harder time building their case against your father because they'll have to refute your facts rather than just making stuff up."

He liked having an attorney on staff.

"There's only one problem to all of this."

Maybe he liked having an attorney on staff.

"What's that?"

"Getting your father to agree. Especially after we've just agreed that you'll stay away from him in return for his dropping the trespassing charges."

There was that. "So I'll start the series by telling the truth that I know without his help. I can talk about where he came from and how he built his empire. He did that with hard work and integrity, Gabi. I'm certain of that."

"There's another issue you need to be prepared to deal with, Liam. Two of them, actually, if you hope to build any kind of trust in your integrity as a reporter—your father's gambling and Missy. And, as a result of Missy, Tamara."

The sincere concern shining from her eyes pinned him. And had him wanting to kiss her all over again.

"My father gambled when he was young," he told her. "It's not something we ever talked about."

"But it's why you took up the sport in college..."

"Yes."

"I can write about what my mother told me about the situation, how she told me and why," he said now, saying out loud some of what he'd already clarified in his mind regarding the article, or series of articles, he'd proposed. "That way if his current gambling comes to light, we've already, in a sense, dealt with it."

"But you won't bring his current gambling to light."

"Of course not. How would that help Dad?"

She nodded. Didn't let him in on her thoughts.

So he moved on. "I'm not sure what to do about Missy and Tamara. It's not my story to tell. And I have no intention of doing anything that will bring any harm or discomfort to that kid."

His sister. His little sister. Every time he

thought about her it was like discovering the best present under the Christmas tree was for him.

"You're right, it's not your story to tell, but you might not be able to do anything about a disruption to Tamara's life. The FBI knows about Missy's offshore account. It's only a matter of time before someone else finds out. Look how easily that account led us to Tamara. Others are bound to get there eventually.

"And while I know your father kept a low profile whenever he was with them in Florida, it's still possible that someone might recognize him with his photos being plastered all over the media."

She was right, of course. Always. It was maddening. And comforting.

"I suggest you call them," Gabi said, still drowning in his oversize office chair. "Decide between the three of you how you're going to handle that part of it."

Lips shut, he nodded again. Glad to have her advice. To know that she was going to be there. That he could trust her…

"We have to talk about it, Gabi." He looked her straight in the eye. Because if they didn't, that kiss was going to grow a wall between them.

This time it was her gaze that disconnected.

Turned to the side. Slightly off center. So he couldn't find her. "No. We don't."

"Yes, we do."

She stood. Arms crossed, she left him alone in the office and returned to the dining table where her things waited for her. By the time he caught up to her she had her purse over her shoulder. "I'm not talking about this, Liam."

He hadn't even said what this was. But they both knew. That kiss had already grown so big it had smothered them out of the room.

"I'm sorry." He didn't think it was the right thing to say. But it stilled her departing movements.

He took that as a good sign.

"I had no right to do what I did. I can't even honestly tell you why I did. I've been sitting here trying to figure it out and I just don't know."

Picking up a folder, she held it against her with both arms. "Then let's just put it down to the stress of the day and forget it ever happened."

He wished. "Are you honestly going to tell me that you're going to forget?"

She turned her back on him. And then, with a sigh, swung around again. "I can tell you I'm going to try."

Something about the look on her face, now

that he was close to her, struck him. Several things occurred to him at once.

If Gabi had no feelings for him other than friendship, she'd be laughing this off. Like the time a bozo friend of his had tried to convince her to make out with him just to show him how it was done. She'd told the guy if he touched her she'd knee him where it counted and then sue him—and proceeded to beat the guy at a game of pool. Later, when they'd all been out together at a party, the guy had apologized to her and they'd all laughed about it.

Another flash that landed was her reaction to the reporter that morning. She'd defended him as though she'd had ownership in him. As though the guy's erroneous assumptions affected her personally.

As everything started to add up, he started to sweat.

Was it possible that Gabi was falling in love with him, too?

"You know me, Gabi," he blurted. "I last six months with a woman. A year, tops. And afterward, things are never the same."

"Tell me about it." She was walking toward the door. Keeping her expression to herself.

"You and Marie…you're my real family. I'd rather die than lose that."

She stopped but didn't turn around.

"I just want you to know...what happened tonight... I won't do it again."

Her bent head felt like a nail in his coffin.

CHAPTER EIGHTEEN

GABI WANTED TO curl up and die. Or to sleep for a very long time. But she knew Liam. When he charged forward, he wasn't going to stop until he'd reached his goal.

She also remembered that he was usually right when he got that way.

She turned to face him.

"I don't want my relationship with you to change," she said with total honestly. "I don't know how to be more clear on that."

He came closer. Held out a hand to her and then let it drop.

"We're good together," he said. "The three of us. You and Marie and me."

For the first time since she'd arrived that evening, she took in a completely easy breath. Held it. And relaxed as she let it go.

Then she looked into Liam's blue eyes and wanted...more.

"Our friendship is my rock." She laid it on the line for him. And meant every word, in spite of a longing she couldn't explain. "Romantic involvement... If it didn't work out, there'd be no way to go back to what we had."

Her cheeks burned as she heard the words come out of her mouth. No one had said anything about romantic involvement. They'd kissed. Almost chastely. For a second or two.

"But...you responded to my kiss. You feel things...between us...too."

Her breath left her body at his *too*. But too much was at stake. "It'll pass, Liam. It's just all the change. You moving in here...like Tamara said, we're practically living together." Not that the proximity seemed to have had an effect on Marie. Or him with Marie. "And with you being disowned, kicked out of your apartment, losing your job...and me taking on the biggest case of my life. I've never represented anyone who even came close to making the front page news before. Plus there was the car vandalism and the threats. And then the fact that with me representing you we're spending time alone together. And that's not even taking Tamara into account. That was a really emotional thing for us to share. It's natural that we'd get a little out of whack."

"It's messy," he said, sliding his hands into his pockets. So he wasn't as sure of himself as he wanted her to believe.

The knowledge brought a bit of comfort to her.

"So…if we're both aware of the situation, we've talked about it now and we both agree that we don't want to take it any further…we're good then. Right?"

He didn't answer quickly enough. And her heart started to rush again.

"I can't ever be one of your women, Liam. I would never be okay with you looking at other women—wanting them—when you're with me. And even if you weren't, I'd probably think you were…"

He didn't flinch. "I'd let you down, and you'd get hurt and I'd get hurt and things would change."

She nodded. "So we're good? It happened. We kissed. And it's done."

"We're good." He smiled.

She tried to. "We've been through a lot these past few days, Liam, and with me as your attorney, we're experiencing it together rather than just you experiencing it and me hearing about it later. That's all this is, you know. They call it proximity."

Was she trying to convince him? Or herself?

"I'm sure that's all it was." He crossed his arms, his shoulders more relaxed.

And as if a dam had been built, preventing her from seeing him as anything but a friend and a client, Gabi suddenly remembered something else. "I meant to tell you, I talked to Gwen Menard today."

He chewed on his lower lip like he did when he was starting to focus on something.

"She said that Matheson's attorney came forward this morning with a financial report that would rival anything the CIA could have built. He's been taken through such a wringer by his ex-wife, in her attempt to take him for all he has and keep his children from him, too, that there's no stone left unturned in his life. He's no longer a person of interest."

"I can't say I'm happy to hear that. But I'm not surprised, either. I can't keep pretending my father's a man of integrity."

"That doesn't mean he's a thief, Liam." It was as though they were back in college. He was in their dorm room, needing something no one else gave him. And she needed to give it to him.

They were back. Her and Liam. With room for Marie.

"So, we're agreed that the way to handle the press is to say nothing to them directly, and I'll write my articles," he said. "And you're going to get with my dad tomorrow and get him to drop the charges."

"Correct." Relief flooded through her. They were good. She could do this. Life was going to be just fine.

Liam's hands were back in his pockets. He was frowning. "I have to be honest with you, Gabi. Just in case…well…so we don't get messed up here…with our…understanding and all."

Her heart started to pound. Again. "Okay."

"I agree with you completely. I want and need only friendship from you."

"I know, Liam. Believe me. That's what I want, too." It was. She was certain of that.

"But when you smiled just then, I thought you looked beautiful."

Her entire body flooded with sensation. Warmth. Pride. Something that made her want to smile inside. And dread, too.

Before she could come up with any kind of response, Liam continued. "You remember when I told you that even when I'm in a committed relationship, and completely into it, I'm still sometimes attracted to other women?"

Of course she remembered.

"Well, just so you know, when I'm with you, that hasn't happened. On the plane. That flight attendant. She was a looker. I tried to feel something. And I couldn't."

Blood pumped through her veins with such force she heard wind in her ears.

"Don't worry, it's only happened a time or two, that I don't feel things for other women, but it's not like I've been around many since we've been spending so much time together. I'm sure it'll pass, and I'll be back to my old self, finding everyone hot, but… I had to be honest with you, just in case…"

"In…case?" The words stuck in her throat. She wanted to run.

"In case… You just have to understand. What you mean to me…it's far more than any romantic relationship in the world would ever be worth. I can't afford to lose that."

A butterfly spread its wings inside of her.

"So…we're good?" he asked, frowning.

Gabi nodded. "We're good," she said. And hoped to goodness that when she had some time to sit down and process what had just happened she'd still feel that way.

AFTER SPEAKING WITH June Fryburg first thing the next morning and then heading downstairs for a cup of coffee—mostly to make sure that Marie treated him exactly as she always had, which she did—Liam was heading upstairs to start on his article when Grace called out to him.

She had a toilet that wouldn't stop running. She'd picked up the part she needed, she just couldn't get the bolt undone to replace it.

Because their current budget only allowed for

them to call a handyman when things went really wrong, rather than keep someone on staff full-time, he ran upstairs to take a look. They stood there together, staring at her john. He'd pulled off the lid, could see little bubbles in the bottom of the water-filled tank, could pretty much ascertain that they had to do with the running water sound, but he had no idea what was causing them.

The water was clean. So was the inside of the tank.

"You've never fixed a toilet before, have you?" Grace asked him.

He thought about prevaricating. But looked at her and shook his head. "Nope. Truth be told, this is the first time I've ever looked inside one."

Just hadn't been on his to-do list.

"See this long screw thing here? That controls this float that controls the water level. This whole thing is called a fill valve. It opens this rubber thing to let new water in when you flush. This is what needs to be replaced. You have to unscrew this from under the tank and I just can't get enough strength out of these hands to get it done."

There was a wrench on the floor. A pipe wrench he remembered from his shop class in high school.

"You've changed one of these before?"

"Yep. Used to be I'd just watch, but since my Bernie died so young…" She shrugged. "Anyway, we have to turn off the water." She started to reach under the toilet, and Liam reached in front of her.

"Let me get that."

"I can do that part," she said as he turned the water valve. "I did it last night."

She stood back as he straightened up.

"You flush the toilet to empty the tank. I did that, too, but when I couldn't get the bolt undone, I had to refill it so I could use it in the night."

He flushed. The tank didn't empty completely. But almost.

"Here." Grace handed him a towel. "You'll need this under the tank. The rest of that will empty through the hole when you remove the bolt."

On his knees, and then his back, Liam found the bolt. With very little effort he got it undone. And got sprinkles of water on his face, too. Clean water. Still, the shock of it stopped him for a moment. But with an eighty-year-old woman watching him, he quickly got moving. Following her instructions, which were impressive, he had the fill valve changed and the toilet flushing without error in less than half an hour.

He'd have to tell Gabrielle. She'd get a kick out of it...

His thoughts stopped. Why not tell Marie? She'd appreciate it, too. Heck, Gabrielle probably knew how to change a fill valve.

Because she knew everything about taking care of herself.

"You're a good boy," Grace told him as he finished.

He'd been about to roll his sleeves back down but stopped, deciding to head straight upstairs to the shower.

"I just want you to know, whatever the papers have to say, I don't believe them. Except maybe the part about you and our Gabrielle. Do you two really have something going? Because I have to tell you, if anyone deserves a fairy tale romance, it's her."

He handed Grace's wrench back to her. Washed his hands. And turned to her.

"Gabi and Marie and I...we've been friends for a lot of years and I don't want us to lose that. You understand?" He spoke gently, but waited for her silent nod before he continued.

"The things the papers are saying about us... they're lies. And they're hurting Gabi. I need you to tell the other residents that Gabi and I... as a couple...it's not true. They listen to you.

And maybe, at least here at home, we can end this craziness and have some peace."

Her face fell, her lips completely losing their smile.

"You're sure, Mr. Liam? I know she's a bit too serious, but Gabrielle's a beautiful girl. Inside and out. And loyal. You'll never meet anyone more loyal than that one."

Liam chose to avail himself of his Fifth Amendment rights—staying silent so as not to incriminate himself—all the while cringing on Gabrielle's behalf. He could just hear the string of words that would come from her mouth if she were hearing this.

"You're sure there's no way you could fall in love with her?"

"I'm sure she doesn't want me to."

"You've talked to her about it, then?"

"Yes, ma'am. And she is as emphatic as I am about the whole thing." He could look her in the eye with that one. "So can you spread the word for me?"

Seemed like a fair trade for fixing her toilet.

"Yes. Of course," Grace said, but Liam had a feeling he'd just ruined her day.

GABRIELLE'S CALLS TO Walter Connelly went un-answered. She left two messages and a third with his secretary. When she'd still had no response by lunchtime, she grabbed the tuna sandwich she'd brought from home and ate it in the car on her way to the swank part of town where the Connelly Investments office building stood—still in business. Regardless of the pending grand jury indictment, the arms of the company not included in the FBI's investigation were still open and available for business. Because only one series of investments was involved in the investigation, that left the majority of the company's holdings to run business as normal.

There'd been a run on accounts since Connelly's arrest. But he had a lot of interests in companies that didn't bear his name. Most people would never know those companies held ties to him. Certainly those whose lives were wrapped up in the companies he'd invested in wouldn't want people to know. They'd go down with him.

She made it in the front door because she knew Liam's relationship with the security guard and introduced herself as his lawyer. With a little persuasion, she made it upstairs to the top floor, too. Escorted, of course.

Coming off the elevator, not sure where she wanted to head, not sure which office was Walter Connelly's, she glanced both ways.

And saw a familiar someone, his back to her,

going in an office two doors down. An unusually tall someone who would be hard to mistake.

Elliott Tanner.

He hadn't seen her. But she'd seen whose office he'd entered.

"Right this way, miss." The security guard pointed in the opposite direction of the office Tanner had entered. And for the moment, she put the man out of her mind.

In the large scheme of things, he was small.

Liam had told her enough about the woman who guarded his father's office to get a word in with her.

"I'm sorry, Ms. Miller, as I told you on the phone, Mr. Connelly is not going to speak with you. And he certainly has no interest in seeing you."

"He has to speak with me," Gabrielle told the older woman sitting so pompously behind her desk. Liam had fondness for the woman—though at the moment Gabrielle couldn't figure out why—so she smiled and said, "Gloria, I'm sorry to be a problem, but I'm Liam's attorney of record and Mr. Connelly has filed charges against my client. I could speak with George, of course, but I suspect Mr. Connelly will want to conduct this business directly with me. Tell him that Liam and I spent the weekend in Florida."

The man was going to force her to play dirty.

Which didn't help her opinion of the coldhearted adulterer at all.

Gloria took one look at the security guard standing just off to the right of the doorway and slipped through the door leading to the company president's office. Did that mean she knew about Missy and Tamara? Or had Gabrielle been convincing enough that she thought she should consult her boss?

She was back before a full minute had passed. "You can go in," she said.

The guard moved forward as Gabrielle did.

"Alone," Gloria said. "Mr. Connelly said to send her in alone."

That was that. Gabrielle knew even before she'd stepped through to the inner sanctum that she'd won.

"WHAT DID HE SAY?" Liam asked her as she called to tell him that the deed was done. She'd be back at her office with five minutes to spare for a bathroom break before her first afternoon appointment arrived—an obese thirty-four-year-old man with a chemical imbalance who needed her help applying for social security disability.

"He said okay," she reported, glancing in her side mirror as she switched lanes and sped up. "I walked in, he asked what I wanted and I told him our terms—your agreement to stay away from him as long as he dropped all charges against you. And he said okay. He told me to wait while he had Gloria draw up the paper, which I did. He's already signed it. I'm to get your signature, deliver the form back to him and it'll be done."

"Just like that? You didn't have to threaten him?"

"I asked Gloria to let him know we'd spent the weekend in Florida."

When he didn't respond, she wished she could see his expression. "He and I never mentioned Tamara or Missy, Liam. But I'm sure he knows now that you know about them."

And still, Walter Connelly didn't have a word to say to his son.

While Gabi had dreamed the night before that she'd married him and given him a real family.

Liam was at home Thursday afternoon, two days after Gabi had met his father, putting the finishing touches on the first article in what was now going to be a series on financier Walter Connelly as told by his only son.

Gabi had delivered his signed copy of the agreement between father and son the same day Walter had had it drawn up. Though he'd stayed in the car, Liam had ridden over with her—with

Tanner somewhere behind them. Liam hadn't been out of the apartment building since.

He'd gone down for coffee each of the past couple of mornings. Visited with Marie. Her concern for him was nice. And he wanted to make certain that Tanner was good for his word and was seeing that Gabi made it to work safely, that security was still watching the place and that no one was bothering Marie or her business.

When he looked outside his window just before dusk on Thursday evening, he didn't see a single reporter left downstairs. He'd been checking a couple of times a day.

He didn't kid himself. They were in the wings, waiting to squeeze out the next drops of juice. But for now, all was quiet. Liam appreciated the silence.

Tanner had checked in each day to ascertain that his services wouldn't be needed. Liam had no idea what the man did after that.

There'd been no word from his father.

He hadn't seen Gabi since the elevator had stopped at her floor after their errand late Tuesday afternoon. Hadn't spoken with her in more than twenty-four hours. That hadn't stopped him from reliving their kiss.

Over and over again.

And each time, he'd turned back to the computer screen and started writing about his father.

When he hadn't been writing, or going through personal files for pertinent dates and reminders of time with his father, he'd been going through Connelly files, pulling out anything and everything having to do with George.

Something was bothering him about his father's attorney. He just couldn't find anything to give meat to his hunches. Or to give to Gabi to give to Gwen Menard.

Standing at the window, feeling like a prisoner, he remembered an episode of an old sitcom he'd seen with the girls a time or two. *Frasier* had been one of their favorites. He'd found it boring at best.

But there'd been a time when Martin, the ex-cop father of a couple of uppity psychiatrists, had been obsessing over a case he'd failed to solve while on the force. As Liam remembered it, everyone thought Martin was nuts. But he wouldn't give up. Gradually others started to help him look for clues in the files he had spread all over the table, more to humor him than anything else.

His sons moved the files around on the table. And that's how Martin finally found the clue he'd been missing. By looking at everything in a new light.

Seeing something that wasn't in the mix before. Not a new item, just a new perspective.

Liam returned to his Connelly files. There was a pile for items that had to do solely with George. Another pile for those in which only George and his father had been involved. And another that involved George and anyone else on the top floor.

He rearranged. Keeping his father in one pile, George in another. But started to split up the files involving other top-floor executives. Separating out ones that both George and his father had been involved in.

His name came up pretty much never.

Until he came to an account he'd forgotten about—the Schlotsky family. A deal he'd handled years before, because he'd been the only executive on the top floor when the brother investors had shown up to close a deal with Donaldson. Only top-floor executives had the ability to close deals. And the Schlotsky brothers were an important one. It had been when Donaldson was out a lot, dealing with his house and trying to figure out a way to prevent the inevitable foreclosure that was going leave him and his family homeless. The other man had apparently completely spaced on the appointment. While Liam had never actually closed a deal before, he'd witnessed more than a hundred of them.

So he'd done what he had to do for the good of the company. He'd found the file. Presented the papers that needed to be signed. And had signed his name as an official company representative.

A week or so later, it had turned out that some numbers had been changed on the form—presumably by one of the investor signers—and Liam hadn't caught the mistake. Liam knew darn well nothing had been changed. He'd stood over the two men, watching like a hawk as they'd signed. And delivered the papers straight to George, who'd later caught the mistake.

His assumption—and he'd told George, who'd said he'd check into it—had been that Donaldson had made the mistake in drawing up the papers. He'd never heard what Donaldson had to say about the incident. George had contacted Liam a day or two later to tell him that the problem had been fixed and that they never had to speak of it again. The investors had re-signed papers with the correct figures. He'd told Liam that he was not going to tell Walter about the gaffe.

And to Liam's knowledge, he never had. Walter, who would have ripped into him for making such a novice mistake, had never mentioned the deal to Liam.

So why was he looking at his father's signature as the witnessing representative on the voucher that admitted that this was the second set of forms and that the first had been destroyed? A voucher that had been signed by both investors and their attorney, as well?

He called Gabrielle immediately.

MARIE HAD INVITED both Liam and Tanner to share dinner with them.

Tanner had had another engagement, escorting an out of town client, and Liam had declined. But Gabi had said she'd come up. And when he heard a knock at his door shortly thereafter, he pulled it open without checking to see who was there.

"Mr. Liam Connelly?" the jeans-clad woman asked. How had she gotten past security? Was everyone else okay? The thoughts flew through his brain.

"Yes," he said, wishing he'd put Elliott Tanner's number on speed dial.

"I'm Officer Warren from the Denver police," she said, pulling her badge out of her jacket pocket. "I'm here to serve you with this order." She held out an envelope.

An off-duty cop doubling as a process server?

He didn't have to take the envelope. He wouldn't be served with whatever it was until he took it…

Liam took the envelope. The cop was gone before he'd finished opening it.

Reading the officially stamped document with his door still open, he didn't care that the cop had left. He had no business with her.

His business was with his father.

CHAPTER NINETEEN

"THIS IS A matter of public record." Liam paced between the stove and the dining table in the girls' large eat-in kitchen. Pointing at the restraining order he'd thrown on the table, courtesy of Walter Connelly.

Gabi, leaning against the counter, watched him. Marie was making tea while dinner warmed in the oven.

If ever there'd been a time when he needed to be alone with Gabi, right then was it. This crazy thing he had for her. It wasn't getting better. It was getting worse.

"What's he trying to do here?" he asked, taking his frustration out on the matter at hand. "He's making us a laughingstock. Just think what the media will do with this. I just don't get it. Why would he do this? I already agreed to stay away from him."

He turned. And Gabi moved enough to avoid his running into her.

When what she wanted to do was hold him in her arms until his hurt went away. Liam would be just fine without his father in his life. Better, probably.

But he still, on some level, wanted him there. And at the moment, that was what mattered to her.

When Marie had told her he was at the door, she'd quickly changed from the work clothes she'd still had on into a pair of her oldest and baggiest sweats and an oversize gray sweatshirt.

Clothes that would hopefully put them back on normal footing.

She'd been supposed to meet him upstairs.

"Maybe he heard about the story you're doing," Marie suggested, looking cute in her new jeans and black sweater. Maybe Liam would notice how good she looked.

No, that wasn't any better. For any of them.

She didn't need Liam with another woman. That would hurt too much. She just needed to quit caring for him in that way.

She'd done fine for more than a decade. "The order prevents him from derogatory or inflammatory comments, doesn't it?" Marie's question was directed over her shoulder at Gabrielle.

"I'm not making derogatory or inflammatory comments about him. He can't stop me from reporting what I know any more than he can stop any other member of the press. And I can't believe, even with his far-reaching fingers, that he'd know about this series. Only June, me and a couple of people she works with even know I'm doing it."

"Elliott Tanner knows," Gabrielle pointed out.

"Elliott wouldn't do anything to hurt us," Marie said. "He's a good guy." The kettle's whistle sounded over her words.

"He's working for my father." Pulling out an antique dining chair from the table Marie and Gabi had purchased together at an auction one summer, Liam plopped down.

Marie put tea bags in the kettle. "You don't know that for sure."

Sitting down opposite him—keeping enough distance that they couldn't possibly bump into each other—Gabrielle said, "I think we do. I didn't say anything on Tuesday because it wasn't pertinent in the moment since we'd already pretty much figured out that Tanner showed up at your father's behest, but when I was at Connelly to meet with your father, I saw Elliott Tanner go into an office on the top floor."

"Did he see you?" Liam asked. "He didn't say anything to me about it."

"There's no way he saw me," she assured him, pulling close the cup of tea Marie placed in front of her.

Joining them, sitting at the head of the table

between the two of them, Marie asked, "Are you sure it was him?"

"I'm sure. The man he was with called him by name."

"Did you see who it was?"

"I saw him, but I'd have no way of knowing who he was, except that I saw the name on the door and Tanner called him by name, too. It was Williams."

Jeb Williams. His father's bodyguard.

The three of them looked at each other. "I think I know what's going on," Liam said.

HIS LIFE WAS never going to be the same.

"What's going on?" Marie placed her hand atop his. He felt her warmth. Her beauty—inside and out. But nothing beyond that. At all. Not even a little bit.

Gabi, on the other hand…

"I think my father's framing me," he said. "He's setting me up to take his fall." He'd never have thought so. Would have given his life on the knowledge that his father would never, ever do anything to seriously hurt him. But he'd have been just as certain that Walter would never be unfaithful to Liam's mother. That he'd never keep Liam's sibling's existence a secret. That he'd never out-and-out disown him. That he'd never gamble again…

"What!" Marie's horror was evident in her big brown eyes. Her blond hair, falling from its ponytail, could have been sexy. But it wasn't. At least not to him. "What makes you think such a thing? Oh, Liam, I know he's being cold right now, but—"

"—you found something." Gabi's quiet words reached him. It was as if she could read his thoughts. And he was beginning to realize that it had always been that way.

He told them about the Schlotsky account. The changed figures. His absolute certainty that nothing had happened while he'd been in the room.

"If push comes to shove, he's going to use that incident to prove that I've been crooked from the very beginning. He'll say that's why he never gave me any real responsibility. He brought me up to the top floor so he could keep his eye on me, but didn't ever give me an opportunity to do any damage. And yet I somehow managed to do it behind his back. I've been his safety net all along."

"So why would he cut you loose?" Marie asked.

Liam watched Gabi, who wasn't saying a word. Her expression gave him no clue as to her thoughts. He needed to know them. To know she'd be watching out for him, with him, letting him watch out for her for the rest of their lives.

In spite of the spouses they'd have someday.

"Because somehow he knew the FBI was looking at him. Just like he knew we'd signed the papers on this place two seconds after it was done. He's going to claim that he stumbled on evidence that led him to believe that I was into something bad. That he'd hoped that he could put an end to my criminal activities by getting rid of me. Firing me wasn't enough. Getting me away from the company wasn't enough. He had to completely disown me—cut me out of his will, which is a legal document that I'm sure he'll supply in court—to prevent me from cashing in on his reputation, trading on people's respect for him for my own nefarious gain. He'll say that he planned to cover my tracks and make up the damages before I was caught. Because I am, after all, his only son. He'll plead guilty to obstruction of justice."

It fit. He didn't want it to. Lord knew, he'd spent the better part of an hour pacing his own apartment—from one end to the other—trying to find the holes, any single tiny little pinprick hole, in his theory.

"What about Missy's offshore account? If your father is the one behind all of this, why not erase evidence of that account first?"

"Maybe he thought he had. Or he knew he only had a few minutes and went for the legally incriminating accounts first. Since he didn't appear put out by the fact that we went to Florida. His affair isn't illegal. I was a big part of the reason he was keeping them secret—you heard Missy say so. Obviously he doesn't care anymore if their existence is exposed."

"I'm not disagreeing with you, just playing devil's advocate here, but if he doesn't care if Missy and Tamara are exposed, why was he refusing to speak to me until I mentioned Florida?"

Liam's case grew stronger in his mind with every question Gabrielle posed. As did his sense of loss. "Because, while he doesn't intend to keep them secret, he doesn't want them hurt. He didn't think we'd bring Missy and Tamara into this or turn their existence into a big circus. He knows me. He knows I'd never hurt my little sister. Or use her, either."

"So why not call my bluff?"

Liam stared across at her. He had that answer, too. "Because he doesn't know you," he told her. His father had made no secret of his low opinion of Gabrielle.

In truth, Walter Connelly was the person who wasn't worthy of his son. Not that that was going to help him now. Or ever again…

Liam rubbed a hand down his face. "I don't know, maybe he just slipped up with Missy's account. They say that every criminal eventually makes a mistake. No one's perfect. Maybe that account was his. More likely, his first priority was keeping himself out of jail. Not protecting them. And the FBI got there before he could do both."

The look of fear on Gabi's face—there and gone in an instant—told him that he was making sense. His father was going to let him pay for his sins.

"He'll get a slap on the wrist, and I'll go to prison...." No one knew better than Liam how smart and capable and successful his father was.

And not just at investing other people's money.

How conniving he could be.

"You are *not* going to prison," Marie said.

Gabi remained silent. He wanted to lose himself in her kiss.

Even as he felt more nails sealing his coffin.

"I THINK YOU should fight the restraining order." Marie stood up to get them some more tea. She'd already put Gabrielle's cabbage rolls in the refrigerator. None of them were the least bit hungry.

Gabrielle shook her head, wishing she knew

what to do. Growing up in a rough neighborhood, she'd learned very early to watch for any danger in her path. How to keep herself safe.

And she was standing on a precipice that was giving way beneath her.

Liam needed her help. Her intensely personal need to help him was scaring her.

Marie had confidence in her. And yet she was worried about the effect Liam was having on Gabi. All three of them knew their friendship could be on the line.

And she had no idea what to do.

Funny, though. Now that the press was trying to frame Liam and Gabrielle in an illicit affair, Marie didn't seem to be as worried about it actually happening.

"My hearing is next Friday," Liam said, looking more tired than she could ever remember seeing him as he glanced at the document on the table and then over at her.

She'd been trying to figure out what was so elementally different about him that evening. And then it struck her.

Liam Connelly no longer believed he was invincible.

"I don't think we should make an appearance." She hated to have to tell him that.

"You think I'll lose."

"No. I think that you'll feed whatever fire is

burning here. It's wrong, Liam, what he's doing to you. But until we figure out how to beat him, until we can find proof that will stand up in court, until I can figure out how he's hoping to prove that you had anything at all to do with the Ponzi scheme, we need to not fan the flames. Let him think he's winning."

He nodded.

"What about Elliott?" Marie asked. "Should we let him in on what's going on?"

"No." Liam didn't hesitate. "He's working for the enemy, whether he knows it or not. He could be our ace, though. If we need something leaked to my father."

Gabrielle agreed with him.

And Marie stood with them.

One way or another, the three of them were going to get through this.

Together.

GABRIELLE WAS THE one who found the link between the Ponzi scheme and Liam. During his stint as a Connelly liaison—a complimentary term for delivery boy—he'd sent documents to every single investor who'd been scammed in the Grayson deal.

If he'd fudged numbers on one account—as Walter could prove with the Donaldson deal from years ago—then it wasn't a far reach to the conclusion that he'd repeated his pattern—his mode of operation. No actual documents with fudged numbers had turned up. But they could in time.

Or perhaps the forgery was to be found, this time, in the description of the land. Grayson development instead of swamp.

Before she told Liam what she'd found, Gabrielle made an appointment to meet with Kyle Donaldson away from Connelly Investments.

The fact that the man asked to meet her in a travel plaza off the highway between Denver and Boulder told Gabrielle that he had something to hide.

Or something to confide.

Either way, for safety's sake she told Marie where she was going that next Monday when she left work early to beat Elliott Tanner's mandated arrival and headed down the highway away from Denver. But she didn't tell anyone else. Marie didn't like what she was doing, but agreed to keep her secret.

She was halfway to her destination when she noticed the car that she'd seen shortly after leaving her office still on the road with her. And then noticed it again when she got off the highway for gas she didn't need. The nondescript black vehicle pulled into a fast food place across the street.

Changing her mind about the gas, she pulled away from the pump and sped by the black car on her return to the freeway. She already had Donaldson on the phone, changing their meeting plans to the following morning, when she recognized the driver of the car that was now immediately behind her.

Elliott Tanner.

THE NEXT MORNING, Gabrielle left for work earlier than normal to meet with a regular client an hour ahead of their original schedule. Her second Tuesday morning client had been moved up as well, so Kyle Donaldson could take the third slot.

Once Gabrielle was at work, she'd seemed to be left alone. She wasn't a threat to Elliott Tanner or anyone else who wanted to know what she was up to. She was dedicated to her job and while she was there, the expectation was that she'd be working. Doing her job well.

Liam was right about one thing—reputation mattered. It was how people judged you. And sometimes, you could use it to help them misjudge you.

DONALDSON SEEMED LIKE a nice enough guy when he came into her office. Held out his hand.

Gripped hers firmly. And took the seat that she waved him toward.

Gabrielle didn't care if the guy was likable or not.

She cared about what information he could give her.

Liam hadn't been out of his apartment since the night he'd been served with the restraining order. He'd finished his article. Was working on a second.

And had made travel arrangements for another trip to Florida. He was going to see Tamara, to make certain that she had a chance to get to know him, in case their time together was going to be short. But he'd promised not to leave town until Gabrielle had come up with a defense for him in the event that his father tried to hang him out to dry. He knew the inner workings of his father's company. And his mind. Gabrielle needed his help.

She wished she'd found the answers already. She wanted him out of the state. Away from the evil that seemed to be lurking just beyond their doors.

Liam was a good man. He didn't deserve what his father was doing to him.

Filled with a desperation she couldn't entirely contain, she faced Kyle Donaldson as though her life depended on the knowledge he could give her.

While she had the entire file of paperwork on the account that Liam had finalized in Donaldson's absence all those years ago, she didn't ask him about it.

"When you knew you were going to lose your home in foreclosure, even before that, when the housing market collapsed and you knew the home you'd purchased wasn't going to hold its value, why didn't you go to Walter Connelly and ask him for help?" she asked instead. "I understand the company had a one-time buyback program for its top executives."

She'd done her homework. And couldn't afford to be played for a fool. Donaldson's response would tell her something about him. And perhaps about Walter, too.

Liam was counting on her to get this right. And she had to succeed. More than with any other client. She was in love with the man. There was no getting around the fact anymore.

Just as she knew, with every fiber of her being, that she'd never be in a romantic relationship with him. He'd hurt her. And live with the guilt for the rest of his life.

Besides, she'd made a very clear personal decision over the past few days. She'd rather live with unrequited love than see her love for Liam turn to hate. As it would if she gave in to her feelings for him and it didn't work out.

She'd rather live with unrequited love than hurt Marie and lose the family the three of them had formed.

"I did go to the company." Donaldson brought her firmly back to the conversation at hand. She hadn't expected that response. "I applied for the buyback. I was told there were no funds left in the program."

Interesting. She made a note. So had whoever had been running the Ponzi scheme been short of cash before? And had this person been siphoning off from other viable Connelly accounts?

"I was also told that if I took the matter any further, I could expect my walking papers." He then proceeded to tell her about the Schlotsky deal. Gabrielle sat and listened to the entire story as though she'd never heard it before. Donaldson told it exactly as Liam had. "While I hadn't fudged those figures—I'd kept my own copy of the paperwork, even though that was against company policy, so I couldn't provide them or I'd be fired—I *had* been preoccupied and failing to keep my mind on my work. I'd completely forgotten the appointment with the Schlotsky brothers."

"So what does this have to do with the buyback request being turned down and you being warned not to take the matter any further?"

She only asked the question for confirmation of what she'd already surmised.

The tall, suited man with short gray hair shrugged, wearing an expression similar to the one Gabrielle had seen on Liam's face the other night at the table. An expression she didn't want to see on Liam's face ever again. It broke her heart.

Donaldson looked beaten.

As had Liam.

"I'd been forgiven for my lapse in the Schlotsky deal, but the paperwork was there, ready to support my dismissal, if I wanted to push things."

The man had spent the past several years living under a gauntlet.

"I just have one more question."

He nodded.

"Who made this threat?"

"Walter Connelly."

CHAPTER TWENTY

LIAM'S FIRST ARTICLE was due to hit the internet and—thanks to a small paying subsidiary sale— magazine stands simultaneously on the first of March. Which meant waiting another couple of weeks before he'd find out—possibly—his father's reaction to what he'd done. Some nights, late, he'd sit at his window, looking out over Denver, imagining that Walter would read the article and understand that Liam would always have his back. Understand that Liam had tried his best to please him while doing the healthy thing and carving out a life for himself. Understand that even now Liam was trying to help him.

Most times, he was resigned to the inevitable. He was a man without a father.

Gabrielle had called to tell him about her meeting with Donaldson earlier in the week. Walter Connelly had been blackmailing the man into silence for years. This was not a man who harbored sentimental feelings.

This was a man who was holding his own son captive. If the grand jury came back with an indictment on Walter, he was going to drop the bomb on Liam. Liam guessed he owed it to the old man that Walter hadn't already pointed his finger at him. But then he'd be admitting to his own guilt in obstructing justice, which could sway a grand jury not to go in his favor.

Better to hedge his bets. To see if he could walk away scot-free before settling for a lesser charge and hanging his son.

Gabi had called to tell him about Donaldson. And other than during his occasional trips downstairs for coffee, he hadn't seen either one of the girls. He and Gabi had talked about needing the family they'd formed.

About not jeopardizing that.

And yet the idea of her eventually marrying and having another man's children was bothering him more than the trouble with his father.

Liam had begun work on the second article. Had taken some walks, with Tanner tailing behind him, a couple of evenings. The man's presence was almost a comfort to him now—whether he was really watching out for him or spying for Walter. To Liam, in those moments, he was a sign that Walter still cared in some fashion.

As the week wore on, his crazy awareness of Gabrielle did not wear off. To the contrary, he found himself waking up with her on his mind. Or wanting to kiss her when he heard her voice on the phone. But he knew that the reaction was probably inevitable at the moment. Proximity. And the fact that she and Marie and the residents were pretty much his whole world right now.

He was free to go out. To do whatever he wanted to do. But that freedom wasn't worth the possible backlash of another swarm of press descending upon him to judge and twist his actions.

Not while he was possibly facing a trial that could lead to a very long jail sentence.

In his healthier moments, he was forgiving himself for some of his preoccupation with Gabrielle.

For the time being, she was his hope.

He was thinking about her at noon on Friday, imagining her in the plain office building several miles away, eating her lunch. Wondering if she'd packed a sandwich or last night's leftovers.

And started to hurt because he had no idea what last night's leftovers entailed. He hadn't been invited to dinner in days.

Liam sprang from his chair. He had to get a life. Move forward. At the computer, he pulled up flight timetables. He had to move his trip to Florida up. To one that left the next day.

Even if he had to fly right back on Monday to be there to help Gabi answer questions or read reports, then so be it. He had to get out of here.

But before he could click the save button and

authorize payment for the last-minute changes, there was a knock on his door. As though mocking his right to do what he needed to do.

Looking behind him, he was tempted to ignore the summons long enough to finish his purchase. To sit at the desk and type in payment information while whoever wanted his attention either waited or went away.

Grace's fallen expression came to mind. Marie's compassionate one. The straight face of the cop who'd handed him the restraining order.

Gabrielle. Needing him. Wanting him. Just stopping to say hello…

With a word Liam didn't mutter often, he pushed out of his chair with a bit more force than necessary and went to the door.

He was glad he had—and wished he hadn't—when he saw Gabi standing there in a long black coat covering most, but not all, of the beautiful long legs left exposed by her navy skirt and pumps to match. Her expression was dead serious.

"Get your coat. We need to go," she said.

He was wearing jeans. A maroon-and-blue pullover sweater he'd had since college. And an old pair of shoes. "Go where?"

Didn't she get that they couldn't be seen out together if they had half a hope of dispelling the rumors about them?

Her eyes, when he finally allowed himself to

focus on them, sent a shiver through him. She was upset. He grabbed his coat.

"What's up?"

"I had a call from Gwen Menard," she told him as they waited for the elevator.

"And?"

She watched the faded numbers as the old machine came down from the eighth floor. "They have some questions for you. I've already called Tanner. He's outside waiting to follow us down there."

He glanced at her, his keys jangling by his side. "You're taking me in for questioning?"

Gabi turned then, reached out a hand and let it drop. "Liam…" She broke off and he had the idea that she might be going to cry. He'd only ever seen Gabi cry once. The night she'd exposed her reporter mistake to him.

"Gwen said that if I bring you down now, we can avoid any kind of formal attempt to bring you in for questioning."

Every part of him stiffened. But he didn't panic. Or even get angry.

"Walter played his ace," he guessed. He couldn't think of the man as his father anymore.

Funny how what was foremost in his mind was the way Gabi's short black hair bounced when she shook her head. "They found the

Schlotsky account papers on one of the hard drives they confiscated. They had to be kept to correlate with the voucher that stipulated a second signing."

He knew that last part. Of course. He was the one who'd told her.

"And they brought Donaldson in for questioning."

He raised an eyebrow. She'd had his blanket permission to tell Gwen anything she discovered pertaining to the case that didn't incriminate him. The Donaldson thing—naming Walter as a blackmailer, but also making Liam look like a forger—could have gone either way.

The elevator doors slid open. He stepped on. So did she, a full foot away from him. They were the only two on board.

"You know they've been investigating all five of the top-floor executives named by your father. They found the original Schlotsky forms on Donaldson's computer. He told them what he told me."

"I'm sure Gwen ran straight to the grand jury with my father's blackmail attempt. Which will slam-dunk his indictment. At which point he hands me up on a platter."

There was no point in thinking otherwise. The way to deal with the situation was to face it head-on.

"Gabi…" He wanted to tell her he was innocent. To ask her to be his wife.

No…wait. What was he thinking? He was panicked. Losing his mind.

He wanted to kiss her and hope that he'd wake up in his bed with her beside him.

To know that he had her heart and that she had his, for the rest of their lives.

But he knew that when the case was over, when life returned to normal, the intensity of his feelings for her could change.

Would change.

Unless he was in jail…

"Don't, Liam. It's not worth the risk," she said. And he wasn't sure if she was talking about the case or not.

"Don't what?"

"Look at me like that. We'll get through this. And then we'll be normal again. You and me and Marie." She pointed to the space around them in the elevator. "Remember how we felt when we decided to buy this place? Like three peas in a pod that couldn't be broken?"

He did remember. Marie had been the one to voice the feeling, but they'd all experienced it.

Her calm calmed him.

"We'll get that back. As long as we don't do something irrevocable in the meantime."

She was right. His mind knew she was, whether his heart was capable of believing or not.

So he'd cooperate. Talk to Gwen Menard and anyone else who wanted to hear what he had to say. He'd keep his hands off Gabrielle.

But he wasn't going to kid himself. He was in deep trouble with this Connelly business. It would be his word against George's, who represented his father. Who'd covered for Liam in the Schlotsky deal. They had proof. He didn't. When Walter wanted them to, they'd find the correlation between every single one of the Grayson fraud deals and Liam as a communication liaison/delivery boy.

He drove to the FBI office. Gabi tried to keep up conversation. He hung on every word.

And when they were outside the glass door that would lead him to only God knew what, he couldn't ignore the tug of Gabrielle's hand on his. He stopped. Looked down at her looking up at him. She squeezed his hand.

"What are my chances of sleeping at home tonight?"

"Your chances are fine, Liam. They just want to talk to you."

Unfortunately, Liam didn't trust Menard to have been straight with Gabrielle.

Still, her words comforted him.

SITTING NEXT TO Liam at a brown Formica-topped table in the interview room, facing Gwen Menard and another agent, a computer expert named Jason Higley, Gabrielle focused on every word that was said, listening for double entendre, for entrapment, for anything that violated Liam's rights in any way. It was up to her to object to any and all of that kind of behavior. Though they continued to come up with questions, there was no new material on the table as far as Liam and Gabrielle were concerned. Nothing was exposed that they didn't already know.

Liam explained about his part in the Schlotsky dealings. Gabrielle already knew that Donaldson's story would have corroborated his. Not from Gwen, of course, but from her own interview with Donaldson. Whether or not Gwen knew about that interview remained to be seen. And could prejudice Gwen's faith in Liam's testimony.

She could have called Gwen, per their agreement, after speaking with Donaldson. She hadn't been certain that the call wouldn't also implicate Liam in some fashion due to the varying stories regarding those forged figures on the first documents.

They'd been there an hour and already she was exhausted.

But energized, too. Fifteen minutes into the

interview Liam's leg was touching hers. He was seeking comfort, she guessed.

And giving her comfort, too.

This thing between them…it might leave as soon as all of this was over. But in the meantime, it seemed to help.

And they needed all the help they could get.

IF THE FBI AGENT thought she was leading him into a place of relaxation—to then go in for the kill—she was mistaken. Liam answered her questions honestly because he had nothing to hide.

But everything to fear.

"Do you have any feeling as to my father's grand jury proceedings?" he asked when it seemed as though the agent had finally run out of steam. They'd been at it almost two hours.

"We have reason to believe an indictment will be forthcoming."

Which told him nothing. Political gobbledygook. They'd had reason to believe there'd be an indictment from the beginning or they wouldn't have taken the case to the grand jury to begin with.

"I have one last question," Menard said, both arms on the table as she leaned toward Liam.

Setting the stage, he thought. Getting intimate and friendly with him so he'd trust her. Funny, as attractive as she was, she didn't do a thing for him. For days he'd been checking himself, to see if other women attracted him.

There'd been some beauties walking below his window. One or two in the coffee shop. And... nothing. Not even the urge to say hello.

"Mr. Connelly?"

"Yes?"

"I said I have one more question."

"I heard you. I'm waiting for you to ask it."

And drawing strength from the touch of my attorney's thigh against mine.

"Your father requested an interview with me the other day. One without his counsel present."

He no longer had a father. "You said you had a question."

"He intimated that he was covering for someone. When I asked him to identify his alleged perpetrator, he refused to say another word, other than that he wanted to inform me that in the event of an indictment, he would be forced to expose this person. I think his point was to make me doubt that I have the right person."

"Or to do himself as much of a favor as he can in light of an upcoming obstruction of justice charge," Gabrielle said.

Liam didn't take his eyes away from his adversary. "Your question is?" Now he was being rude. And was sure he didn't care.

"Are you aware of anyone your father could be covering for?"

Liam willed his hurt into anger. And felt Gabrielle's leg press up against his more tightly. "No."

"And you can't shed any light on what he might be referring to?"

"In case you aren't remembering," Gabi broke in, "my client has been estranged from his father and is currently bound by a restraining order to stay away from him."

Gwen looked at both of them. Nodded. Gathered her papers into the manila folder she'd carried in.

"We're free to go, then?" Gabrielle asked.

"Yes." Menard stood. "But don't leave town," she told Liam. "We're going to have some more questions."

Don't leave town?

He wasn't under arrest. But his freedom had just been officially curtailed.

One step closer to jail.

GABRIELLE WAS FURIOUS. She barely spoke to Liam on the ride back to their apartment building.

She'd caught a glimpse of Elliott Tanner back at the FBI office. Had seen his eyebrow raised in question when they'd come out of the interview. But she'd ignored him.

For now she trusted no one with Liam's care but herself.

The danger of that thought didn't even bother her at the moment. She'd never been so angry in her life.

"What's got you all tied up in knots?"

Liam's sideways grin in her direction startled her so much she couldn't breathe. She took a moment. Watched the traffic as he pulled out. Found their place among all the other cars.

"Do you realize what your father's done? Or is getting ready to do?"

"Of course I do," he told her, not sure why she was asking. "It's what I've been telling you all along. The man is morally bankrupt."

"He's going to serve you up to them. His own son. I mean, that first night I met you, back in college, when I heard him pulling every manipulative stunt in the book to get you to move out of the dorm, I thought he was despicable, but I also thought he was doing it for the right reasons. Because he loved you so much and wanted what he thought was best for you."

"Don't feel bad. I thought so, too."

She was probably saying too much. Rubbing salt in a raw wound.

She was his lawyer. She had to defend him. And in order to do that, she had to understand. "How does anyone do that? Serve up their own son? Especially someone as incredible and kind and talented as you are?"

As soon as the words flew so passionately out of her mouth, Gabrielle knew she'd made a huge mistake.

She might just as well have told Liam Connelly that she was in love with him.

LIAM PULLED TO a stop at a yellow light and turned to look at Gabrielle.

She returned his stare as best she could.

What did they do now?

How did they pretend there was nothing going on between them? It was hard enough knowing that he'd never be the type of husband she needed, one who was all in with his wife for the rest of his life. He'd be faithful, she was sure of that. But his eye would wander. His mind. His desire for her would wane.

But the thought of losing his friendship...

He kept staring at her. Letting her see him, too. And she wanted nothing more than to give in to the powerful feelings between them.

And let the future take care of itself.

A horn honked behind him. The light had turned green.

Liam looked away.

She knew he'd let go of her.

And that it was for the best.

CHAPTER TWENTY-ONE

SHE DIDN'T CARE that it was a Friday night. Wouldn't have cared if it was in the middle of the night. Gabrielle rode the elevator up with Liam. She got off at her floor. Waited for the doors to close, for him to reach his floor, and then she fled.

Down the stairs.

And out the back door, climbing into her car and tearing out of the drive before a security guard could alert Elliott Tanner—if he'd been instructed to do so—that she was on the loose.

Driven by an anger so strong it was scaring her—and still not caring—she sped across town. Little things like gates and guards and security cameras, even the threat of jail, weren't going to stop her.

Or even concern her.

Liam had given her the only access code she needed. He'd told her, the day she'd sprung him from jail, how he'd managed to get on his father's property, only to find him not there. He'd related the obvious agitation of a housekeeper who'd helped raise him. Who loved him.

Related, too, that his arrest had come for trespassing at Connelly headquarters, with no mention of an additional charge at the home of Walter Connelly.

Betting on the fact that Walter didn't know Liam had visited his home that day, she was expecting the spare key to the gatehouse to be right where Liam had returned it after using it.

She parked far enough away to avoid security cameras. And kept to the brush as she half ran in the directions Liam had described when he'd told her about his breaking and entering escapade the last time he'd been to his boyhood home.

Almost as validation that she was doing the right thing, she found the gatehouse while it was still light outside. Found the key, too.

And made it to the front door just as Walter Connelly pulled up, driving himself, in a black Lincoln Town Car.

Apparently her luck had just run out.

LIAM HAD TO talk to Marie. Without Gabi present. Or knowing. And he wasn't comfortable with the idea.

He had no other choice.

Taking the stairs in case the elevator stopped

on the second floor and Gabi happened to have her door open, he showed up at the coffeehouse just after Marie had closed for the night. He helped clean up. Something he'd done a time or two before. She didn't ask him why he was there.

Or act as though anything was amiss.

They worked. She sent her employee home. Turned off the lights out front. And carried the cash drawer back to the office, where she'd count the day's income, make a deposit slip, put it in a bag that would lock automatically and drop it into the safe under a brick behind her desk.

Only a key at the bank would open the bag. Liam knew all the secrets.

"Talk to me," she said before she'd counted a cent.

He nodded toward the cash on her desk. "Count."

"You take the twenties." She pushed them in his direction.

He counted. So did she. Fifteen minutes later even that work was done. And he was still there.

"Gabi doesn't know I'm down here."

"Duh, Connelly. I wasn't born yesterday. You'd be upstairs, snagging whatever she's making for dinner if whatever you have to say was for both of us."

"You don't seem shocked."

"By what?"

"That I'm here to talk to you without Gabi knowing."

"I've got eyes."

"What does that mean?"

"There's something going on between the two of you. Gabi and I have already talked about it. It was only a matter of time before you came to me, too."

"This is serious, Marie."

Her smile fell away. "I know. I'm just trying to pretend I'm not scared to death."

"Listen."

She nodded, that compassion of hers—something he'd counted on more than she'd probably ever know—shining all over him.

"It's pretty much written on the wall that I'm going to jail."

She took a breath, as if she was going to object, but he held up his hand. Reminding her that she'd just agreed to listen. He needed to get this out.

"I'm feeling things for Gabi." He'd expected the announcement to sound cataclysmic. It didn't.

Marie hadn't even blinked yet.

"I realize that it's just because of all that's

going on, and her helping me, me needing to rely on her, but…"

"I don't…" Marie looked at him and fell silent. "But she's going to get hurt, Liam. We all know that."

He didn't know it anymore. But he couldn't tell her it wouldn't happen. Because he didn't feel as though he knew himself all that well. So much had changed. Outside of him. But inside, as well.

"Anyway, I love you both, you know that."

She nodded. And didn't say another word. He needed her to. He hadn't told anyone he loved them since he'd held his mother as she'd died.

"But Gabi… I'm falling in love with her."

In spite of how tightly Marie's lips were pursed, he could still see them tremble.

"She can't know," he said.

She nodded.

"With a possible arrest in my near future, I'm afraid I'm going to do something crazy."

He needed her to speak. She just sat there, tapping her hand on the desk.

"And then she'll get hurt."

Marie's hand stilled.

"I need her," Liam said. "I need you both, but her more at the moment because I need her representation." He wanted to think that his new feelings for Gabrielle, after all this time, at this exact time, were because of the case.

Marie wasn't moving at all. And then she said, "I think, if we're going to try to salvage something here, we need to be completely honest."

"I'm afraid I'm going to do something stupid. I can't walk away. And I'm going to do something stupid. If ever there were a time I needed you, Marie, it's now. It's not fair to you. I don't really even know what I'm asking, but please... don't let Gabi get hurt. Watch me like a hawk. And if you get worried, come to me. Let me know. I'll listen to you. I swear it..."

He sounded like an idiot. A flaming idiot.

"I think that what you're feeling has been a long time coming," she said. "Maybe the reason you've never been able to settle on another woman for any length of time was because, all along, in some place inside you, it was Gabi. I don't think it's the court case or needing Gabi as an attorney that's brought your feelings to life. I think it's moving into our world, leaving the persona of Liam Connelly behind, leaving appearance and responsibilities to the Connelly name behind, and just being yourself, Liam, that has done it."

He couldn't listen to that. Couldn't accept it...

"You know I'm right."

"No." He softened his tone. "No, I don't. But if you were, where would that leave us?"

"I don't know." Tears filled her eyes—something he was more used to seeing from her but was no less painful to him. "I've been worried for weeks," she told him. "But I'll tell you this. If this thing between you is as strong as it seems to be, there's not going to be anything you two will be able to do to fight it. Not forever. At some point, sometime, it will get the better of you."

"And then what?"

Marie shrugged. "Then we try to love each other through it, I guess."

It was a typical Marie answer. One he'd wanted.

But that night, it didn't give him much comfort.

SMILING AT A woman she'd never met but felt as though she'd known for years, Gabrielle took the cup of hot tea Greta handed her and set it on the small table between the armchair she was sitting in and the one next to it.

Both were in front of a massive cherry desk in an office larger than any she'd ever seen before. Funny—she'd known Liam all these years, felt as if he was more family to her than her own mother and brothers, but she'd never been in his house before.

"Thank you, Greta, that will be all." Walter Connelly dismissed the older woman as though she were a stranger to him.

He'd ordered Gabrielle off his property.

She'd refused to go.

He'd threatened her with a call to the police. She'd told him she'd welcome the opportunity to tell them everything she knew.

He'd shown her to a room with a couch and chairs but no books or television and made her wait there alone for half an hour.

And when he'd finally appeared and shown her to his office, he'd demanded that she wait for tea to be served. While he'd slowly sipped on a shot of something amber colored.

Not one second, of any of that time, had dissipated her anger one iota.

Or intimidated her, either.

The man was beneath her contempt. He just didn't seem to get that yet.

"Are you ready now?" she asked with utmost politeness as she left her tea to cool untouched beside her.

To her shock, Walter Connelly bowed his head to her. "Go on, if you must."

If she must? If she must? Oh, she must. He had no idea how much she must.

She'd been planning to sit calmly, her hands in her lap, but Gabrielle jumped up and planted her hands on the edge of the older man's desk.

"What in the hell are you doing? The FBI brought Liam in for questioning today. They told him not to leave town. As I'm sure you know. They actually think he could have done this. How could you throw your own son under the bus like that?" she spat.

His raised eyebrows didn't slow her down a bit.

"That's right, Mr. Connelly. I have no class. No training or tutoring or manners or whatever else you want to call the behavior that allows you to smile at a man while you stab him in the back."

The words were deeply satisfying. More so than she'd ever imagined they could be. They weren't what she'd come for.

"I just want to know why. What's Liam ever done to you? What's happened in your life to create this monster that would stab his own son in the back?"

Nope. Not what she'd come for, either. Well, except for wanting to know why. But the rest of it...

She took a deep breath. Sat down. Put her hands in her lap.

"Liam's a good son to you." She tried to get

a *sir* out but couldn't do it. "He majored in finance as you wanted him to. Joined the family business and worked hard at every job you've ever given him, no matter how menial. He's done his best to respect you. He's also become the type of man you taught him to be. One who is finally able to stand up for his right to have his own place in the world."

She loved him, this man she was describing to his father. Had probably always loved him. In some place deep inside herself where she knew her love would be safe. Some place that would allow her to love him from afar, without hope of ever having him for herself.

And then he'd gone into business with her and Marie. Given them a legal tie. He'd moved into their building.

He'd been in trouble and needed her in a way he'd never needed her before.

He'd touched that place deep inside her, reaching into it and exposing her feelings for him...

"And because he dared to want what he wanted..." She shook her head. The truth was, if Liam had ever wanted her, his father would have put a stop to it. Or sucked the life out of Liam until he finally gave in.

The man had yet to say a word. Or take another sip of his drink. She'd made another blunder. But it wasn't as if she could hurt Liam's chances with the man. They couldn't get any worse.

"I believed in you." She shook her head. "All these years, even that first night in the dorm room, when I overheard the despicable way you were manipulating Liam into going home with you, I thought your motives were good. All these years..." She shook her head again as she repeated herself. And then she looked him right in the eye.

"I've always thought you loved him."

Walter didn't blink. Just stared at her as though he was seeing right through her.

Gabrielle stood.

Turned her back on the man.

And left.

Standing at the window, looking down to the street below, Liam waited. Marie had talked him into coming upstairs with her to have dinner with her and Gabi.

She hadn't had to twist his arm as much as he figured she should have. Nor had she agreed to watch out for Gabi for him. She'd just told him they'd find a way to love each other through what came and then asked him to dinner.

That was what he called a good friend.

One he wasn't the least bit attracted to. Which

was how it should have been with Gabi, too. So they could all be together, family, forever.

They'd been laughing when they arrived upstairs. He couldn't even remember now what about. He just remembered her opening the door, calling out to Gabi and getting no answer.

Her frown concerned him, but he hadn't been truly alarmed until they'd both searched the whole place and seen no sign of her. Marie was fairly certain she'd never come home from work.

He'd been certain she had gotten off the elevator at her floor. He'd watched her do it. Watched her walk away from him with a pang in his gut.

While Marie was taking a second look around, he was on the phone with Tanner, who knew nothing about Gabi leaving their apartment.

His next call was to the police, to report a missing person. A report they couldn't take on an adult unless she'd been gone far more than a couple of hours.

Marie was the one who did the logical thing. She texted Gabi.

And had a text back almost immediately. Gabi was at a spa nearby. She was sorry she hadn't texted sooner.

She'd stopped in for a pedicure. Something she'd done in the past, when things upset her. A way she dealt with tension. Or figured out a tough case.

Odd that she hadn't let them know. Especially now, with Tanner and security guards looking out for them. Or maybe not. Maybe all of the 'watching over' was what was getting to her.

Gabi was a private person. Used to be anonymous. Liking it that way.

Obviously she'd needed to be left completely alone.

She'd text him when she got back. He felt certain of that.

Thing was, he waited all night.

And never heard from her.

AFTER THE PEDICURE Gabi had driven straight home. She'd had no place to run. She never had. She was who she was. Who she would always be. Not in a way that would ever stop her from bettering herself, or get in the way of her success, but in the way she was meant to be.

Who she was born to be.

A too-serious woman who had to do what she thought was right.

A woman who cared deeply. Who was loyal to death.

Who'd been in love with a man for more than ten years and had never let herself admit it.

She was scared to death of being hurt, so she worked herself to death.

The thought of Liam actually going to jail was almost more than she could bear. Living without his kisses was something she could endure. But a world without Liam at all? Knowing that there was no way there'd ever be a knock on her door in the middle of the night?

Her reaction to the reality that had hit her at the FBI office the day before had finally opened her eyes to the truth.

She couldn't stop herself from being in love with Liam Connelly.

No matter how much her head needed their little family to be just what it had always been, her heart needed something more.

Her resolve firmly in place Saturday morning—being honest with herself about the fact that she was in love with Liam—she was not clear yet on what that meant for her daily life, where the demands of professional ethics would collide with a woman's need to do all she could to protect the man she loved. Where friendship stopped and pain began.

Marie was down at the shop by the time she came out of her room. She wasn't ready to face her best friend. She'd escaped to a hot bath the night before, claiming too much stress. Marie hadn't said a word.

In the twelve years they'd known each other, that was a first.

She hadn't woken her that morning, either. Gabrielle had made it to the kitchen to think about eating, when her phone rang.

Not recognizing the number, she let it go to voice mail. And then listened to the message the second she was notified there was one.

She still had on sleep pants and a T-shirt. No way to present herself for a command from Walter Connelly: *"Ms. Miller. If I could impose on you to bring your client to the front of the Connelly building at ten o'clock this morning, I would be grateful."*

The request itself, coming from the man who hadn't so much as acknowledged her words the night before, was odd enough. The politeness with which it was offered made Gabrielle too nervous to think any more about eating.

She called Liam instead. Told him about the request and asked him how he wanted her to handle it.

When he said he wanted to be there and wanted her to be with him, she showered, dressed in a brown business suit Marie's mother had bought her for Christmas the year before and waited for her client to arrive at her door to escort her down to his car.

She didn't bother to tell him she thought it was a bad idea. He already knew that.

CHAPTER TWENTY-TWO

WHEN LIAM SAW all of the media representatives swarming the front steps, the curb and the curb across the street from Connelly Investments, he almost turned and left.

"What's he doing?" he asked Gabi. Dressed in a newer silk suit and shiny leather shoes, he stood back a full block and surveyed the situation.

A podium with a microphone was set up on the top of the steps leading into the ornate building. Cars, trucks and vans bearing various television and radio station logos and call letters took up every available parking space. Some were even parked on the lawn.

For a man who'd spent most of his life avoiding the circus of gratuitous publicity, Walter Connelly had certainly managed to make up for lost time.

"Where's his security?" Liam asked, drawn to the scene even while he wanted to turn his back and drive away.

"Based on that podium up there, I'm guessing his security is doing what he told them to do—allow the press to congregate."

She sounded so calm. "Did you come home last night?"

"Of course. Where else would I go?"

They were walking slowly toward the crowd. He intended to stay on the outskirts. And hope that he wasn't recognized. He wanted to loop his arm through hers. But didn't want to expose her to any more fodder for the gossip columnists.

Not that it really mattered at this point. The press would be far more interested in him going to jail.

"I'd suggest you don't get any closer." Liam heard the voice behind him and turned to find Elliott Tanner there.

"You knew about this?" he asked. He hadn't called.

"I called him," Gabrielle said. "I knew I couldn't stop you from coming, but I had to do what I could to make sure you were safe."

Didn't matter to Liam one way or the other. He was ready to take whatever the old man had to hand to him. Crucifixion would almost be a relief after all the hours of hanging out alone in his apartment waiting.

Even if he believed Marie, even if he dared

hope her cockamamie idea that he'd always been in love with Gabrielle were true, he had nothing to offer her as a man in jail who hadn't known his own mind until he was past thirty.

If what Marie believed about him was true, Liam had wasted ten years living in his father's shadow.

"What do you know about this?" he asked the bodyguard.

"Absolutely nothing."

Liam didn't believe him and turned back to face the crowd.

If the old man thought that he was going to teach Liam some insane lesson, show him who really had the power—because that's what Walter's life with Liam was really all about—he was going to be disappointed.

Let Walter hang him out to dry.

He almost wanted it to happen. So that he could finally fight back.

And somehow, someday, he'd win, too.

Because he was the man's son.

He'd been raised to stand up to adversity. To keep pushing forward until he tasted victory.

Gabi moved into his peripheral vision. A step in front of him.

And he was reminded that in the fight for his freedom, proving his innocence was not the biggest battle he had ahead of him.

THE FRONT DOORS of the impressive Connelly building opened and Walter Connelly, dressed in a suit and tie, came out alone. His attorney wasn't with him.

The crowd pressed forward. A couple of shouts rang out, questions, Gabrielle thought, but she couldn't make them out. Gabrielle stood next to Liam, her shoulder pressing up to his, with Elliott behind her. She tried to stay calm.

From her distance, she couldn't read the expression on the evil man's face. And feared that the day's debacle was a direct result of her visit to him the previous day. No one crossed Walter Connelly and got away with it. He was all-powerful. Or wanted the world to believe that, apparently.

He was actually going to throw his son to the wolves.

Before the grand jury had reached a decision.

He was going to show her and Liam and the world that he was right.

Walter moved straight for the podium. Surveyed his crowd.

"He's called a press conference to express his sorrow as he confesses that he feels he has no choice but to hand me over to the wolves," Liam said. "He's right now feeling supreme satisfaction that one phone call from him would garner this much attention."

Gabrielle didn't put it past the man.

And didn't trust herself to know any better.

And then she saw Tamara. And Missy. Standing in the shadows on the other side of the step, behind a pillar. Not far from Walter.

Tamara wiped her eyes as though she was crying. Liam didn't appear to have seen her. Gabrielle didn't have the heart to point them out to him.

"Ladies and gentlemen of the press, I come to you this morning a different man than you know me to be. A weak man. And, if you will, a frightened man. I come to you, not for myself, but because of myself. I come to you with one purpose. To hand you a story that every single one of you will run out and distribute. You have power, ladies and gentlemen. The power of the press. Today, more than ever before in history, this great country is influenced by your words. Brought together by your words. Called to action by your words."

Gabrielle didn't want to be impressed by the man's eloquence. It was clear by the stoic look on Liam's face that he wasn't.

He was staring blankly—his face pointed toward a place just beyond his father's left shoulder. She'd guess he was seeing none of the crowd. Of the cars or the vans or the trucks. Liam was doing what Liam did.

Going off to find the flowers in the mud.

Tears filled Gabrielle's eyes as she stood there beside him, watching him. Wondering at the life he'd led, a life that had taught him so well how to encase himself against the pain.

Wondering, too, if he'd ever know how much she loved him.

"I HAVE COME to you today because I don't have enough proof of what I'm about to tell you to be assured that justice will be done, and I want the truth known."

Liam heard the words and almost snorted. Had his father ever known the meaning of the word *truth*?

"I won't waste any more of your time," Walter said. "I have made some grave mistakes in my life. A couple of them are ones that I expect will interest you. Shortly after my son left for college, I realized I'd not been nearly as successful in my personal life as I had been professionally. Not comfortable with being home, I looked for something to fill my time. Something I'd once enjoyed. Something that had a way of taking my mind off everything else. I played cards."

His unsuccessful personal life—the innuendo to Missy and Tamara—was so Walter. Until the past month, even Liam wouldn't have known of what he was speaking.

"I knew better, having been down that road before. One game leads to another, and each one with higher stakes. When I won, I won big. When I lost, I used company money to cover my debts, drawing from a charitable fund I'd set up to offer a one-time buyback forgiveness to top executives who made a bad investment. I'd win, I'd fill the account. I'd lose, I'd drain it. And drain it. And drain it. It was only a matter of time before I was called to pay the piper. One of my top men applied for buyback funds that didn't exist. And instead of admitting what I'd done, I used a piece of dirt I had on him to blackmail him into silence."

The crowd was so quiet Liam could hear his own breath like a roar in his ears. In. Out. In. Out.

"The second thing…" Walter paused. All eyes were on him. From half a block away Liam could feel their pressure. "I'm even less proud of…"

Here it goes. He wasn't seeing the crowd anymore. Just the cement at his feet. The shine of metal off the cars on the road a few yards away. And, as he turned, the black of Gabi's hair. In. Out. In. Out. His breath roared.

He was going to be fine. He knew that now. No matter what, he'd be fine. He just needed to know that Gabi would be, too.

"About three months ago, I stumbled on some documents that troubled me. As I looked into the matter, I found evidence of fraudulent investments being made by a member of my staff. I won't bore you with the technical details, but while I very quickly figured out who was behind the criminal activity, I didn't have any way to prove it."

Liam waited. Almost eager now to have it done. Looking forward to taking the next steps. Energy filled him with every word his father spoke.

"I confronted the man..."

Liam's head shot up at the same time he felt Gabi's hand grab his arm. Holding on. As if he was holding her up. He turned to look at her. The shock on her face mirrored what he knew must be on his own.

His father had never confronted him. And then he remembered that Walter wasn't speaking the truth. He was spinning the tale that would lead to Liam's arrest.

His heart should be pounding with panic.

He wasn't feeling it, though.

Wasn't feeling anything at all.

"I was told at that time that my son, Liam..." Walter turned then, looking out over the crowd—as though searching for someone—and Liam's shoulders straightened. Had his father seen him? He didn't think so. And was glad. He didn't want the old man to have the satisfaction of knowing that he was witnessing this.

"I was told that Liam had been set up to take the fall if the Ponzi scheme came to light. I was shown a trail of paperwork that would be exposed as proof of Liam's involvement. For years patterns and situations had been contrived to leave Liam in the right place at the right time to make him look guilty."

Liam's lips started to tremble. He took a step forward and stopped, his gaze on only his father.

"In order to protect my son, I allowed this man, this trusted friend, to continue to use my company for his criminal activity, hoping that he'd do as he swore he would, which was shut down the scheme and repay every dime of the money he'd swindled before anyone knew what had happened. I'd like to believe he'd have done so if the FBI hadn't been ahead of him."

Walter coughed.

"I knew that what I'd agreed to was wrong, but I did it. And then immediately severed all ties with my family members, hoping that any fallout would be mine alone." Walter chuckled. A sickly kind of sound. "It's a testimony to the less than stellar man I've become that not one member of my family was shocked by my ability to shun them…"

Liam wanted to say that he'd been shocked. But he hadn't been. And knew the fault of that was not his own.

Knowing didn't stop him from caring that his old man was hurting from his sins. Beyond that he couldn't think.

Couldn't put it all together.

His father had been *protecting* him?

"However, it has recently been made known to me that my son has become a suspect in this investigation in spite of my attempt to protect him."

Gabi's fingers dug into his and Liam had an idea she knew something about his father's knowledge of Liam's interview with the FBI. But before he could follow up on the thought, his father continued.

"I see my son standing tall. Living with his integrity intact in spite of the wrongs being done to him. By me. And by you. And I am sickened again. Because I've stood by and let Liam—and the rest of my family—be hurt by these accusations rather than speak the truth, just to save my own backside. I was hedging my bets again. Betting that the grand jury would not indict me, that, as I'd been assured by my blackmailer, there wouldn't be enough evidence to get an indictment, and I could continue on with my life without admitting to the criminal activity I *have* done. All of this was carried out with the assurance that if I stayed quiet, Liam would be spared.

"Ladies and gentlemen of the press, my son is not a criminal. I am a fraudulent man in many ways, but I am not a thief. This morning I called Agent Gwen Menard of the FBI, confessed my part in this affair and told her that George Costas, my attorney, ran the Ponzi scheme. An event of which I was unaware until three months ago. I will plead guilty to whatever charges are forthcoming on my behalf. I will cooperate with the ensuing investigation and pray to God that there will be enough evidence forthcoming, that perhaps members of the public who have dealt with George will be forthcoming, and we will be able to put this to rest. That is all."

Walter turned from the podium. Didn't look right or left. Walked back into his building, appearing, for the first time in Liam's life, like an old man.

His vision was blurred as he moved forward, intending to go to him, and that's when he saw Missy and Tamara leave the shadows behind a pillar on the front steps and follow his father inside.

He didn't need Liam. He had his real family there.

"GO AFTER THEM." Gabi gave Liam a push.

"I'm not leaving you out here."

"Go, Liam. They're your family. He specifically asked you to be here. He wants you with him. It's where you belong." Her heart was breaking, but she knew the words were true. And had to be said.

He had what he'd always wanted. Proof that his father loved him. That when the chips were down his old man would be there with him.

He had his real family.

He didn't need her anymore.

"I'll see that she gets home," Elliott Tanner said from behind her. She'd forgotten that he was there.

When Liam nodded, but looked at her one last time, she smiled. Gestured toward the door. "Hurry," she said.

She knew, when he strode quickly away from her, that she'd done the right thing. He'd be back in his father's graces, such as they were. Back in his condo. In his job. In his life. Whatever feelings he'd had for Gabi would fade, as she'd always known they would. As he'd acknowledged they would.

In time, he'd probably come around again. Sit with her and Marie and confess his sins, such as they were. Maybe have some dinner. He'd help with the business of owning the Arapahoe.

And someday, maybe they'd even be best friends again.

But for now, Gabi had to walk way. To leave him behind. She had to find her own life, separate from him.

She had to love him enough to set him free.

IT WAS LATE at night before Liam made it back to the apartment building. Past midnight. He'd tried to get away earlier but couldn't leave Tamara. Or his father, either. It was going to take some time for him to feel like Missy was anything other than an adulterer in his mother's marriage, but even as he felt the anger, he knew his emotions were unfair.

A challenge he'd face at another time.

His father was resigned to doing some jail time. Liam was inclined to think that he'd be offered a deal—his full cooperation in exchange for no jail time. And a hefty fine—enough to pay back all of the investors who'd lost money due to George Costas.

In the meantime, the plan was to keep Connelly Investments open. With Liam having a more active role in the company. He was going to write. But he was his father's son.

While he'd never been given much of a chance to dabble with the investments, the thrill of carefully calculated risk, gambling, was in his blood.

He took the stairs two at a time, not wanting to announce his late arrival to the whole building with the old elevator clanking its way up the chamber.

Two security lights were out in the stairwell. He'd make sure they got changed in the morning.

Walter had asked him to move home. Or at the very least back into the condo. Liam had suggested, instead, that Tamara and Missy take it over. They could keep the Florida home as a vacation property.

He wasn't sure that was going to happen, either, though. Their home, their lives, were in Florida.

Regardless, for now, Liam was going to stay right where he was. Where he ended up in the future was not up to him.

There was no way to know if Gabi and Marie were still awake. The fact that they might be asleep wasn't going to stop him, in any event.

He knocked as loudly as he dared with other residents living down the hall.

And then knocked again, standing in front of the peephole so they'd be able to see it was him.

Another minute passed before the door opened and Liam's heart started to pound with a panic he'd never felt that morning standing outside on the sidewalk thinking that his father was going to crucify him. Thinking that he was going to jail.

This morning had been his father's time to face his own accountability.

Tonight was Liam's.

His own press conference.

His last confession.

Marie stood in the open doorway.

Alone.

"Where's Gabi?"

"She's in bed, Liam."

"Get her up." He tried to sound like his old self. To smile. And failed at both.

"No."

No?

He stood there, still in the suit he'd had on that morning, a faltering grin on his face, and didn't know what to do with himself.

"Go home, Liam."

Go home, Liam. Neither of the girls had ever said that to him before. Ever.

They should have. Years ago. Many times.

"But Gabi—"

"You need to leave her alone now. She'll be fine. She just needs some time."

This was it, then. His worst nightmare. This

whole thing with Gabi—it had already ruined their friendship.

And still, his need didn't dissipate. It intensified. "I can't, Marie."

He was being driven by something stronger than logic. Or even desire.

"Of course you can. I'm serious, Liam. You need to go."

He'd have liked to believe he'd have done as Marie asked if he hadn't heard the sniffle. He didn't think so, though.

"What was that?" he asked, looking toward the archway that led to the girls' living room.

"Nothing."

There were no lights on in there.

But...

He strode toward the room anyway.

"Liam, you can't go in there. You can't always just do what you want—"

Marie trailed behind him as he saw, by the light coming from the window, Gabi's silhouette, her head and arms hunched over her knees.

He moved toward the sight, his heart in his throat, but Marie blocked his way. She shook her head. Pointed toward the door.

"I have a confession to make," he said in a voice that didn't sound like his at all.

"Not tonight, Liam." Marie's teeth were

clenched as she bit out the words. "You're going to have to learn to take no for an answer."

Oh, Lord, he hoped not.

"I love you, Gabrielle," he blurted. "I am in love with you. It might blow our friendship, but not being honest will do that more quickly, and more permanently. I guess what I'm trying to say is that it's too late to prevent the risk. I am in love with you."

He turned to face Marie, not silenced by her frown. "I love you, too, though in a different way," he told her. "And I'm counting on both of you. We've always found a way to work through whatever problem any of us brought to the table," he told them. "Well, here it is. I am in love with Gabrielle. I can't seem to find any other woman even remotely attractive, which is a great thing. But there are all kinds of possibilities when I start to think about things that could go wrong between us someday. I don't deny that. I don't deny that I need our family together. Like we are right now. I need us. So what do we do?"

Neither woman said a word. Marie, openmouthed, stared at him. Gabi didn't raise her head.

Encouraged by the fact that Marie wasn't throwing him out, he said, "I watched Dad and Missy tonight. You need to see them together,

Gabi. It's like…he's…different with her. I look at them and see all the time they've lost just because he wouldn't tell me about her. About them. Because he didn't think his two worlds would meld. I don't want to be him. I don't want to make his mistakes. I don't want a lost life. If Marie is correct, and I'm certain she is, I've been in love with you since college, only I was too blinded by who I thought I was to see that. I've already been too much like him. I've wasted ten years. Assuming you're in love with me, too, I don't want to waste another minute."

As the words left his mouth, a huge weight lifted from his chest. One that he'd been carrying around far too long.

No one moved. No sniffles came from the couch. No words from Marie.

He understood. He'd broken the code of their friendship.

And even if there was no way Gabrielle would trust them enough to let herself love him back, he felt better. Not great. But better.

"So that's it." He glanced at Gabi's form for a long moment. Giving her time, if she needed it. To move. To say something.

To offer him some tea.

And then he turned to go.

"Wait."

She half choked the word. Her voice a couple

of octaves lower than normal. He had a feeling she'd been crying for a long time. And felt sick knowing it was because of him.

Because she'd known, as he had, that their friendship was being blown apart by the love between them no matter what either one of them wanted.

He stopped but didn't turn around.

"You can't just say you're in love with me and then leave. It's not right," she told him.

"That's true." Marie—in a bathrobe, he now noticed—nodded.

Swinging around, he watched as Gabi slowly unfolded from the couch and came to him. Stopped just in front of him. She was in her bathrobe, too, not that it mattered. Did she have any idea how beautiful she was with that hair sticking up all over her head?

"Come on, Liam, surely you don't need me to advise you on what to do next," she said, her face a mixture of consternation and something he didn't recognize. "I mean, when you came to confess your drinking or gambling when we were in college, you wanted me to tell you what you were doing was wrong, so I did. Because it was what you expected. But you didn't need to be told. You knew what you were doing was wrong before you ever came to our door."

Yeah. He had.

So why *had* he gone to them?

He'd gone to them, not for advice, but to know that someone cared about him enough to be there for him when he screwed up. He'd gone because he'd cared about them and needed to know that they cared about him, too.

Everyone needed that. "I'm not going to demand that you tell me how you feel about me, Gabi," he said now, words coming from deep inside of him. "I've spent the past twelve years taking from you two. It's time for me to give back. Long past time. So... I'm here. Night and day. I'm going back to work at Connelly and will continue writing as I have in the past—with the exception that I'm going to cover stories that matter to me, including the series about my father—but I'm going to be staying right here. Living here. Loving you both—you in a way I've never loved any woman—and fighting for our friendship."

"You aren't moving back to your condo?" That from Marie.

He shook his head. "Kind of surprising, isn't it? But this place...it feels more like a home to me than anyplace else I've ever lived."

Glancing down, he saw Gabi's eyes, like steel burning right into him. He'd gotten her all riled up and didn't know what to do with her.

Except grab her up and kiss her senseless for

the rest of their lives. Which would be more taking, when he'd just promised to give.

"What?" he asked her. "What do you want from me?"

It was a plea. Not an accusation.

"Forever, Liam. I want forever. Can you give me that?"

He understood then. Confessing wasn't enough. It had to be followed by action. Sometimes immediately.

He hadn't planned this part yet. Had figured it would be months—at least—down the road. If ever. And figured he'd be prowling around in the dark like a hungry bear while he waited for the time to be right...

"I'm probably going to be richer than sin and insist on having my shoes shined, but I promise that I will spend the rest of my life fixing the fill valves on your toilets."

He heard the words and panicked. Then grinned. "That didn't come out right," he said.

Marie was sniffling somewhere off to his right.

"I think it came out perfectly," Gabi said, still standing there looking up at him.

"I do, too," Marie chimed in.

"So, you'll marry me?"

"You haven't asked me yet. But don't worry, Liam, there's plenty of time for that." Gabi was smiling as she wrapped those lovely arms around him. "As your attorney I'd advise you to make it soon, though. Life is too short to waste."

"Way too short," Marie chimed in.

Feeling as though he was ready to climb a mountain in his bare feet, Liam gathered Gabi close, holding her in his arms for the very first time. It was better than anything he'd imagined it could be. "You still advising me, Gabi?"

Her nose crinkled as she pretended to think about that. "You said you never wanted to lose what we had…"

Liam laughed out loud, lowered his head and touched his forehead to Gabi's.

"Kiss her, already," Marie said. "Don't worry, I'm outta here."

Because his friendship with the girls dictated it, Liam did exactly as he was told. But he stopped as Marie moved past them toward her room.

Hooking her arm, he pulled her into their hug.

"We're going to be a family forever," he said, looking at both women. "I swear to you on everything I am, have ever been or ever will be, we're Threefold. Just one of us will be switching apartments as soon as I can make the arrangements." Marie was crying. But she nodded. And smiled, too, wrapping her arms around the two of them.

"I think we should do it quietly," Gabi said.

"Move rooms?"

"No, get married. We don't want to bring any more vengeance, or press, down on us."

"We could put something together by next weekend," Marie said. "Go down to the court-house. I'll be your witness. And figure out something for afterward. We should have some music. And flowers…"

There were still shadows in Marie's eyes. Some hard changes ahead for her as she adjusted to living alone. But the love in her heart came through loud and clear as she chattered.

Gabi listened. And nodded.

And Liam finally trusted that what he'd wanted all of his adult life had been there, waiting for him, all along.

Love.

A sense of belonging.

Home.

* * * * *

Look out for the next installment of
THE HISTORIC ARAPAHOE,
ONCE UPON A MARRIAGE,
coming in October 2015 from
Tara Taylor Quinn
and Harlequin Heartwarming!

LARGER-PRINT BOOKS!

GET 2 FREE LARGER-PRINT NOVELS PLUS 2 FREE MYSTERY GIFTS

Love Inspired®

Larger-print novels are now available...

LARGER-PRINT BOOKS!

GET 2 FREE
LARGER-PRINT NOVELS
PLUS 2 FREE
MYSTERY GIFTS

Love Inspired

SUSPENSE
RIVETING INSPIRATIONAL ROMANCE

Larger-print novels are now available...

LISLP15

YES! Please send me **The Montana Mavericks Collection** in Larger Print. This collection begins with 3 FREE books and 2 FREE gifts (gifts valued at approx. $20.00 retail) in the first shipment, along with the other first 4 books from the collection! If I do not cancel, I will receive 8 monthly shipments until I have the entire 51-book Montana Mavericks collection. I will receive 2 or 3 FREE books in each shipment and I will pay just $4.99 US/ $5.89 CDN for each of the other four books in each shipment, plus $2.99 for shipping and handling per shipment.*If I decide to keep the entire collection, I'll have paid for only 32 books, because 19 books are FREE! I understand that accepting the 3 free books and gifts places me under no obligation to buy anything. I can always return a shipment and cancel at any time. My free books and gifts are mine to keep no matter what I decide.

263 HCN 2404   463 HCN 2404

Name   (PLEASE PRINT)

Address   Apt. #

City   State/Prov.   Zip/Postal Code

Signature (if under 18, a parent or guardian must sign)

Mail to the **Reader Service:**
IN U.S.A.: P.O. Box 1867, Buffalo, NY 14240-1867
IN CANADA: P.O. Box 609, Fort Erie, Ontario L2A 5X3

* Terms and prices subject to change without notice. Prices do not include applicable taxes. Sales tax applicable in N.Y. Canadian residents will be charged applicable taxes. This offer is limited to one order per household. All orders subject to approval. Credit or debit balances in a customer's account(s) may be offset by any other outstanding balance owed by or to the customer. Please allow 4 to 6 weeks for delivery. Offer available while quantities last. Offer not available to Quebec residents.

Your Privacy—The Reader Service is committed to protecting your privacy. Our Privacy Policy is available online at www.ReaderService.com or upon request from the Reader Service.

We make a portion of our mailing list available to reputable third parties that offer products we believe may interest you. If you prefer that we not exchange your name with third parties, or if you wish to clarify or modify your communication preferences, please visit us at www.ReaderService.com/consumerschoice or write to us at Reader Service Preference Service, P.O. Box 9062, Buffalo, NY 14269. Include your complete name and address.

MMLPBPA15

LARGER-PRINT BOOKS!

GET 2 FREE LARGER-PRINT NOVELS PLUS 2 FREE GIFTS!

♥ HARLEQUIN®

super romance

More Story...More Romance